Book Title: When Life Begins

Published by Inzaar Publications, 2012
www.Inzaar.org

First published by Inzaar Publications, Pakistan.

Price In Pakistan: 300 Rs.

ISBN: 978-969-9807-02-2

To Order: Please contact Inzaar Publications at:
Email: abuyahya267@gmail.com
Phone number: (+92) 3323051201
Website: www.Inzaar.org

For details of other booksellers, please consult our website.

WHEN LIFE BEGINS

ABU YAHYA

An Unforgettable Tale
A Life-changing Story

TRANSLATED BY BASHIR NAZIR, ABU MASROOR, F
RASHID, ASMA KHAN ET AL.

Inzaar Publications
A not-for-profit organisation

Dedicated to the Grace and Mercy of
The Lord of the Day of Judgement

73010 Ilyas Press 10.11.2012 p5 (HK)

Contents

Translators' Preface

In the name of God, the Most Beneficent, the Most Merciful.

All praise belongs to God, Lord of all the Worlds. It is definitely a manifestation of his infinite mercy and beneficence that he bestowed upon his weak and humble servants the honour of working on this project to spread his message.

"When Life Begins", an English Translation of the revised edition of the original text in Urdu, is the fruit of efforts of a number of people who devoted their time, talent and efforts voluntarily. I have, therefore, appropriately titled this introduction as the "Translators' Preface" rather than "Translator's Preface". This subtle placement of an apostrophe makes it the result of teamwork rather than an individual effort. It also goes to highlight that sometimes even small, mundane and seemingly insignificant deviations lead to significant changes in the text and context. Hence, the translators have to be highly conscious and dedicated to the spirit of the original Text if they have to convey the spirit of the original text to the readers.

While regular translation demands such stringent discipline, the need for exactness becomes all the more important when translation involves statements and references from the Qur'an and sayings ascribed to the last Prophet, peace be upon him. It is for this reason that we have opted to keep the spirit of the original text alive, sometimes at the expense of diction and fluency. The reader may find some sentences as stilted and unidiomatic. To alleviate that to some extent, brackets have been used to clarify the meaning of a particular term or to insert the Arabic term for the English equivalent. In addition, a Glossary has been appended at the end of the booklet to define major

Islamic and Qur'anic terms and concepts for the benefit of those who are not familiar with them.

The Urdu Novel titled 'Jub Zindagi Shuroo Ho Gee' was published with the sole purpose of introducing the Islamic concept of Hereafter to Muslims and to invite them to live their worldly lives in accordance with the tenets of Islam so as to benefit from the rewards promised by God in the Hereafter. Little did anyone know that it would become a movement of such gigantic magnitude. The Urdu version soon achieved the coveted status of the most sold book in Urdu in recent times selling in excess of 80,000 copies in the first year of its publication. Concurrent with its popularity, demand for translation in English became stronger. As the initial chapters were translated and posted on the internet, the flood of emails requesting early completion provided impetus to the team of translators to work as fast as they could. Sacrificing other commitments, the translation team toiled for innumerable hours to make the target release date of the book in the Holy Month of Ramadan, 2012 a reality.

I must also admit that the translation project was a personally enriching, yet emotional journey for all of us. As we worked through various chapters, the powerful Urdu text evoked mountains of emotions such as guilt, regret, remorse for a life wasted, and shame on being presented to the All Mighty one day with the realisation that one would have nothing to offer but tears of regret and guilt for a life not spent as it should have been. One had to constantly, and with some effort, detach himself/herself, from that emotional state back to a rational frame of mind to concentrate on the task at hand.

The composition of the translating team is a testament to the huge inspiration and influence the original Text has had on its readers. I started the project on my own but as the translation was uploaded, offers of help started pouring in. About seven people actively helped to varying degrees in the translation work over the last year. These men and women came from diverse backgrounds with abodes over four continents and ages ranging from 14 years old to above 60. The fact that some of them have used pen names while others chose to remain completely anonymous is an indication of the altruistic motives of all the team members. I am humbly proud of leading a team of such dedicated, hardworking and willing volunteer translators, without whose untiring efforts, this translation project would not have been possible. May God All Mighty reward them for their efforts.

On behalf of the team, I would like to especially thank our families for their support, which was pivotal in the successful completion of this project. I am also thankful to those who proposed suggestions for improvement that were incorporated to enhance the quality of this work. Every effort has been made to be as precise and accurate as possible. As for any inadvertent errors in the translation that may have slipped by, I am solely responsible.

I am deeply grateful to Abu Yahya, the author of the original account in Urdu, for the enormous help and guidance extended to all of us in patiently explaining the concepts, statements, and moot points of his original text. In closing, I find nothing more appropriate to say other than what he had written in closing the preface to the Urdu version, that is:

Even if one person is saved from becoming the fuel for Hell, even if one person is added to the dwellers of Paradise, the efforts of our team will have borne fruit.

Bashir Nazir

Bashir_Nazir@Rocketmail.com

Completed on the night of 25th of Ramadan, 1432 Anno Hegirae corresponding to 13th of August 2012.

===============

Preface to the Revised Edition

A Book that became a Movement

By Abu Yahya

All praise, commendation and gratitude is only worthy of the One and only God, who bestowed upon us the ability to express due to his benevolence and compassion. May the Almighty shower eternal blessings on the personage who was given the gift of Qur'an and who then dedicated his life to show the people the way to Paradise, and to save them from Hell.

I can start the preface of my book, "When Life Begins" in two possible ways. The first is for me to praise the record-breaking popularity of my book. The alternative is, rather than singing my own praise, I should tell the readers about the favours and kindness of the Almighty God. The latter is the only befitting course for a humble servant of the Lord. I intend to follow this course.

When I wrote the book, I was quite scared. The reason was that in many places this humble servant had dared to write dialogues articulating the will of his Lord. I took some comfort from the fact that the Qur'an and sayings ascribed to the last Holy Prophet, peace be upon him, had guided me in my writing. However, there was one point in the book where I had transgressed my limits and made a certain claim, relying on my faith in the unlimited generosity of my Lord. It was the point where I had attributed a statement to the Lord that he would ensure that the book reached all the people who loved him and that he would convey its message to their hearts.

The least punishment for saying something beyond my standing would have been to prove me wrong in this very world. In that case, the book would have reached a few after its first publication and would have ended up in a pile somewhere, ready to serve as a meal for bookworms. However, my most compassionate Lord honoured the words of this humble servant in the most generous manner. The book was first published on the Internet and I can say without any exaggeration that it reached hundreds of thousands through that medium. As far as the printed book is concerned, more than 12 editions have already been published within a few months.

This incident is a living testimony to the fact that the creator and Lord of this Universe is a living and dynamic deity. He is aware of the minutest happening in the Universe. He is well aware of the sins that the criminals continue to commit blatantly and is also conscious of the hopes that his weak and feeble servants hold from him. Therefore, the most knowledgeable and kind Lord made humble writing of this servant a source of guidance for countless people. He is the one who put the thought of reading this book in the hearts of his servants as well as their subsequent mission to get others to read it too. Its effect is not confined to influencing people to motivate others to read the book, in fact; it is now a movement that has affected countless lives. It has ignited the love of God in innumerable hearts as well as a longing to meet him. Consequently, the faith of countless people has grown stronger and so many who were lacking in righteous deeds have mended their ways.

I received regular feedback from the readers after formal publication of the book. I had realised quite early that I would have to review some of its parts. Some friends had provided useful advice and suggestions. However, my other engagements and recurring printing of editions of the novel did not allow me the opportunity to work on the revision. I, therefore, decided to set aside some time specifically to make a few important changes and additions for the revised edition.

The changes and additions to the book are of two types. Firstly, I have made some amendments to the text and secondly, I have added an explanatory article at the end that answers some important - questions raised by the readers. There were plenty of questions to which I had routinely responded to via email. However, I have included some of the more important questions requiring further elaboration in this article. Thus new readers will now comprehend the book easily while the earlier readers will still enjoy a second reading of the book. Some of the readers may now also find answers to their questions in the article added to the book.

An important point to note regarding the changes is that conclusion of the book has been altered slightly. One reason for the change is that many readers felt that the intensity of belief that they experienced while reading the book decreased after reading the ending. For me, it was of paramount importance that the feeling of strong belief in the reality of this meeting with God should persist till the end. Second reason for the change is that I have decided to write a sequel at the insistence of various readers. In the context of the current ending of the novel, it would be a sequel but when both the parts are viewed together, it would in fact be its prequel. With the grace of God, the plot of the second part of the novel became obvious to me during the current month of Ramadan. Changes to the previous ending were also necessary to allow me to write second part of the book. However, I am unable to say at this point, as to when the second part would be completed. I request you to pray to the Almighty to make this task easy for me.

In the end, I would like to add a few words regarding the availability of the book. The availability of the book was also an issue until recently. Now it would be possible for the readers to easily order it from all over the world. In addition, we have also arranged a discounted rate for readers wishing to distribute the book to friends and relatives. You may contact us on the telephone number (+92) 332 305 1201 to order.

I pray to the Almighty to forgive our mistakes and accept this humble effort, Amen!

Abu Yahya

abuyahya267@gmail.com

On the Day of Arafa, 1432 Anno Hegirae, corresponding to 6th of November, 2011

===============

Preface

Some Clarifications, A few Apologies

By Abu Yahya

Voltaire (1694-1778) was amongst the most important personalities of the "Age of Enlightenment" that started in Europe. His writings and ideas laid the foundations of modern western thinking on Church & State. During his time, an earthquake struck the Portuguese city of Lisbon. A Tsunami and fire that raged through the city afterwards devastated it. A city where once millions lived was ruined. This tragedy sent shock waves throughout Europe. It had far reaching effects not only at political, economic, and social levels but it also affected the philosophy and prevalent ideas of the time. As was customary then, traditional religious leadership declared it a punishment from God. However, times were changing fast. Hence, there was a profound reaction. In the background of these events, Voltaire first wrote a poem titled, 'Poem on the Lisbon Disaster' and later, a novel, 'Candide'. The basic message he conveyed was that in the new world, there was no room for a perception of God as portrayed by Christianity, a God who punished the guilty and the innocent indiscriminately.

Initially, Voltaire's work faced criticism & restrictions but soon the ideas presented therein started to gain acceptance and he eventually became the predominant voice of his time. Slowly, the consequences of attributing incorrect ideas to the concept of God almost led people to denial of God's very existence. Thereafter, an era ushered in western societies during which, taking God's name was deemed idiotic. Akbar Allahabadi, an Indian poet of the British-occupied India, portrayed this scenario in the following verse:

The foes havereported me to the State

For taking God's name in this day and age

In the decades that followed, the concept of God regained acceptance in some shape and form; however, a concept of Hereafter that would evidence perfect justice of God and provide true explanation for the inequalities of this world never received general acceptance. Voltaire had a Christian background. The concepts about Hereafter in Christianity were vague and did not answer many sound questions that came to his logical mind. Hence, he became the founder of a movement for rejection of God and Hereafter that has dominated the world ever since.

Fortunately, Muslims possess a book like the Qur'an that unfolds the second and the last chapter of the story of human life, i.e. the Hereafter, without which it is not possible to understand the realities of this life and Universe correctly. In the Muslim societies of today, there is a conflict between religious extremism and unbridled open mindedness similar to the forward thinking era of Europe. The immense benevolence of God has given me this opportunity to present to the readers, through the medium of this novel, details of the second and the last chapter of the story of mankind before another Voltaire emerges from this conflict.

The reason for going into this detail is that the readers of Urdu literature are familiar with novels based on detective stories, romance, and historical or social aspects of the society. Traditionally, only novels in these genres are written and read. In reality, the scope of novel writing is much wider. Various components of a novel like its plot, development, characters, events, dialogues etc., rely on the particular genre of novel writing on which the novel is based. 'When Life Begins', is an unconventional novel as it does not fall under the genres mentioned above. However, despite being unconventional, it remains a work of fiction. Every novel is a work of fiction as it builds castles of imagination in an illusionary world. These castles may touch many heights of imagination, yet their foundations are firmly rooted in reality. My novel is a piece of fiction as far as the central character and the events surrounding it are concerned, however, the world of possibilities that this fiction introduces you to is the ultimate reality of the Universe. Unfortunately, this reality is currently concealed from the human mind and vision but the time is not far when this world will reveal itself to everyone as the ultimate truth.

For the readers, this novel would have been quite interesting even if the context were only confined to the aforementioned; however, the irony is that eventually, every reader of this novel as well as every inhabitant of the world is going to be a part of this work of fiction, destined to play the role of one of its characters. This irony has forced me to pick up the pen and venture into this field.

I aim to present to the reader a world of unseen and concealed possibilities, as a living reality in the form of fiction. It is a difficult and sensitive task as there is no physical depiction of this future world in front of us, nor can we allow our imaginations to run rampant. Fortunately, there is enough information in the teachings of our Holy Prophet Muhammad, peace be upon him, for us to form a mental picture of that world, and I have tried to portray it on the same basis. In such a work, due to the requirements of novel writing, it is necessary to write dialogues and construct imaginary scenes. Nevertheless, I have kept in mind the attributes of God mentioned in the Qur'an and the sayings ascribed to Prophet Muhammad, peace be upon him, at every step of this sensitive work. In spite of the care I have exercised, it remains a sensitive matter with possibilities for errors. I hope and pray for forgiveness of the Almighty for any such mistakes, seeking his mercy and beneficence.

At this point, I would like to share with the readers the fact that initially I did not intend to make this work public. I sat down to put some of my thoughts about the Day of Judgement on paper. However, within days it took the shape of the first eight chapters. After going through them, I decided that it was not appropriate for publication. However, I asked some friends for their opinion. Their feedback, in contrast, was to the contrary. Furthermore, the writing had an extraordinary impact on them. For most, it was a wakeup call and a life changing experience; they strenuously insisted that I should complete the novel and publish it.

In spite of the insistence of my friends, I could not persuade myself to complete the novel. When the pressure from the friends began to mount, I decided to perform a special prayer for guidance ("Istikhara"). This allowed me to give my undivided attention to the project and I completed the novel. Even then, I was still not ready for its publication. However, within a few days of its completion, I found that a potentially lethal disease had knocked on the door of my worldly existence. At that juncture, I decided firmly that God willing, I would publish it.

People regard me as a scholar and a writer. In fact, I possess neither the pen of a writer nor the brain of a scholar. My whole life's capital is a compassionate heart, and when this compassion grew in intensity, it took the form of the novel. This is my sole excuse for venturing into this delicate field. This excuse may become acceptable in the court of the Almighty if only I could assist in returning a few sheep lost from the herd back to the Guardian of this world. In today's world, people have neither the time nor the inclination to listen to the call of an unseen world; however, may be, this work of fiction would incline them to listen to the call of their Lord. May be, because of it, some servants may return to their Master. May be, some feet taking steps towards Hell would stop and turn back. May be, it would lead to the addition of one more resident to the Paradise.

If that were to happen, it would be my reward for this work.

Call for him, you may find his way
If not, life's journey is futile anyway

Abu Yahya

abuyahya267@gmail.com

===============

Chapter 1: Judgement Day

Earth had become devoid of all its creases. Rivers and mountains, ditches and hills, and oceans and forests, in essence, every depth and every height of this world had been demolished. As far as the eye could see, Earth was a level plane and on top was a fire spitting sky... however, the sky today was not blue, but it was a glowing red in colour. This redness was not due to the blazing flames of the sun but was an effect of the flames that periodically leapt upwards from the Hell towards the sky; they were like open-mouthed serpents trying to take the sun into their fiery embrace. This horrifying scene created by the leaping flames from Hell and the uproar from its blazing fires was making hearts tremble with fear.

These trembling hearts were the hearts of criminals. They were the hearts of the negligent, the arrogant, and the cruel; they were the hearts of murderers and the rebellious. They were the hearts of the world's pharaohs and tyrants. They were the hearts of those who considered themselves gods and icons of their time. They were the hearts of people who lived in the world bygone as if they were immortal, albeit, when they died, they became as if they had never lived on the face of Earth. They were the hearts of people who lived in God's Kingdom and ignored him. They were the hearts of people who ruled like gods over the creations of God. They were hearts devoid of love for fellow human beings and of remembrance of God.

Hence, today was the day when these negligent hearts were to become fuel for the raging fires of Hell and its unending punishments... punishments that were waiting to have their hunger relieved by stones, and by people with hearts of stone. It was a day of festivity for these punishments for; their eternal hunger was about to be quenched. Due to the intense fear of these punishments, these criminals of God were running amok in search of a sanctuary... but in this flat plane, there was nowhere to hide and no sanctuary to find. Everywhere there was calamity, disaster and hardships...and for these stone hearted criminals, a never-ending misfortune.

===============

No one knows how many years... or how many centuries have elapsed in this condition. This is the place of adjudication and the Day of Judgement... a new life has begun... a never-ending one. I too, stand in this place of Judgement, lost and speechless, staring with vacant eyes. In front of me, countless people run and fall in a chaotic manner. In the background, an echo of noises emanates from the roaring flames and is mixed with the shouts, cries, and wails of people. People taunt each other, hurl abuses, and blame each other; many are engaged in scuffles.

Around me, some are holding their heads, while others pour dirt on their faces. I see some people hiding their faces in shame; others are bearing disgrace. Some are banging their heads on stones; others over there are beating their chests. Some are blaming themselves while others are having a go at their mothers, fathers, wives, children, friends, or leaders, holding them responsible for their ruin. All of them have the same problem; the Day of Judgement has arrived, and they have not prepared for it.

Now! They may blame others or themselves, they may mourn or be patient, but now, nothing can be altered. Now! There is only a wait, a wait for the appearance of the Master of the Universe, following which the accountability will commence, and the destiny of every person shall be determined with justice.

Suddenly, a person near me shouted:

“Ah.... I was better off dead! Even the pit of the grave was better than this.”

I had been standing silent and speechless for a long time on this flat plane, completely unaware of the happenings around me, when the near-yelling voice of this person brought me back from the valleys of my thoughts, into the realm of reality. In an instant, everything became afresh in my mind, from start to end. My story, the story of the world and the story of life... all began to run in my mind like the reel of a film.

===============

I was at home at the onset of that dreadful day. It is not possible for me to explain the location of that home. For the casual observer, it was the dark pit of a grave; in fact, this was a door to the real world of the Hereafter... a door that could not be opened back into the world. I did not wish to open that door anyway. For, after passing through this door, I had now entered the world behind the veil... the world of Barzakh. It was a world that contained never-ending comforts for me. That day, my close, long-standing, and dear friend Saleh had come to visit me. Saleh was the angel who was assigned to my right side when I was alive. His closeness and presence was always a source of immense solace for me in my life after death and as usual, we were having a pleasant conversation that day. I asked him during that conversation:

"My friend, tell me something, why have you been assigned to me?"

Saleh replied in a serious manner, "You see, Abdullah, my companion and I were assigned to you when you were living in the world. He used to record your bad deeds and I, the good ones. You would not let me sit idle for even two minutes. Sometimes you would be reciting supplications for the Almighty, sometimes shedding tears in his remembrance and sometimes praying for fellow human beings; you would spend your time in ritual prayers, your money in God's way and your energy working for the welfare of people. In short, even when you were not doing such deeds, you would at least have a welcoming smile on your face for other people. Therefore, I was always busy in recording some activity of yours. You almost killed me because of overwork and exhaustion! However, you know we angels are not like you humans; we do not recompense bad deeds with bad ones! So, you see, despite these 'bad deeds' of yours, I am alongside you and looking after you".

I replied in an equally grim tone, "I 'wronged' the angel on my other side even more than I wronged you. He used to write down my sins but immediately afterwards, I would repent. The poor soul then used to erase all he had written and curse me, complaining that if I was going to make him erase it, why I made him write it in the first place. Eventually, he got so fed up that he prayed to the Almighty for my riddance. That's why, ever since I died, only you have kept my company."

Saleh burst into laughter on hearing this. Then he said:

"Don't worry, he will return at the time of accountability. According to the Law, both of us will have to present you in front of the Almighty."

As he uttered these words, his face showed a profoundly grim expression. He became quiet and bowed his head down, becoming immersed in deep silence. I had not seen him behave in this manner previously. As he raised his head up after a few moments, the ever-present freshness and smile had disappeared off his face, replaced by shadows of fear and sadness. He made an unsuccessful attempt to smile and said:

"Abdullah! Archangel Rafael has received his orders; the time for fulfilment of God's promise has arrived. The deadline given to the inhabitants of the world has passed. You will continue to enjoy the blessings of your Lord a bit longer, behind this curtain of Barzakh, but I have to depart now. I will meet you again when life begins again. When your eyes open, the Day of Judgement would have begun. I shall meet you again that day."

===============

The commotions of life were continuing as ever. The shopping malls had the usual activity and razzle-dazzle. There were various entertainment events going on in New York, Los Angeles, London, Shanghai, Delhi, Moscow, Karachi, and Lahore. Spectators were watching and applauding 20/20 cricket and World Cup football matches being played in the midst of floodlights that turned nights into days. People intoxicated with alcohol were busy drinking in pubs and bars while others watched strip tease in nightclubs. Actors were captivating appreciative fans in Hollywood and Bollywood movies. Movies, dramas, stage, television, belly dancing, and fashion shows had models and actresses dancing, gyrating, and parading their bodies while their financiers filled their pockets with money made from these enterprises... The owners of multi-national companies were the new conquerors of the new world; talented youth were happy to sell them their knowledge and skills, so that they could weave dreams for their future careers. The glitter and dazzle of media, the spiced up world of journalism and the upheavals of the world of politics with its never-fading treacheries and deceit were continuing unabated. Men and women were engaged in shopping in the bazaars of this world, surrounded by eye-catching shops and hailing shop owners. There were echoes of songs and music in lavish abodes of the prosperous, which were in sharp contrast to the silence of hunger and poverty rife in the shacks of the poor. People were singing songs of merriment in wedding celebrations but shadows of sorrow and despair shrouded funerals and hospitals. Religious leaders were safe guarding personal interests in the name of God, wealthy people, as ever, were oblivious to the trials and tribulations of the poor. Government servants were filling their pockets with tainted money from corruption and dishonest traders were filling their safes with income from adulteration and hoarding. Rulers were busy in exploiting their people while super powers continued to work on their schemes to maintain their subjugation of the world. In short, all were engrossed in their jobs and interests, as ever.

The dwellers of Earth were doing what they had done all along: tales of cruelty and disorder, stories of deceit and deception, race of greed and selfishness, attitudes of negligence and rebelliousness, obliviousness to God and Hereafter, political commotions, economic struggles, religious feuds, and inter-class tensions... everything was going on, as before. The prophets of God had already departed from the world centuries ago. Agricultural age changed to industrial age and then, industrial age transformed into the age of information; however, human attitudes did not change, nor did their sorrows. Human beings had the same old worries of work and livelihood, the same setbacks of love and romance, and the same predicaments of death and disease. At this time, as at any other time before, human beings were concerned about every worry under the sun except for the worry for the Hereafter; they had every fear except for the fear of God.

The sky witnessed the fact that the human race, which had spread injustice and chaos all over God's Earth, had now become an unbearable burden for the planet. Therefore, it was given repeated shocks, as reminders. The predictions of the final Prophet began to come true. The bare-footed, goat herders of Arabia managed to build the tallest skyscrapers, but the humanity did not take heed. The descendants of Noah's third son Japheth that is, the race of Gog and Magog, became the gatekeepers of the world. They started to attack the dwellers of Earth from the ultimate heights of greatness. Great Britain, Russia, America, and China... one after the other, took the throne of ruler of the world. All predictions of the divine scriptures came true, but humanity still did not come to its senses. Then followed tsunamis, floods and earthquakes, but the humanity remained in negligence. God created the information age, his non-Arab believers took the message of their Arabic Prophet and clarified the truth in its ultimate form in front of the whole humanity, so that, no reason was left to deny it. However, humanity still did not pay heed. Before the Day of Judgement arrived, the picture of the Day of Judgement was painted in its ultimate form to awaken the humanity but there was no change in the attitude of people. At last, the event that was bound to happen eventually did happen! Archangel Raphael heard the orders of his Lord and picked up the trumpet in his hand. Within moments, the end of the world was here.

The checkerboard of the Sun was folded back; stars began to lose their shine. Mountains as big as the Himalayas began to fly in the wind like balls of cotton wool... peaks turned into deserts. Seas gave rise to waves as tall as mountains and soon, the planes of this world became oceans. Earth emptied the bellies of its volcanoes onto its surface... rivers of fire started to flow through valleys. The planet off-loaded all its earthquakes... Earth was turned upside down. Cities became ruins while buildings turned to dust. Soon, habitations started to look like graveyards.

What worth did the frail human beings have in front of these upheavals? Only a while ago, people were busy making plans... for a new home, or a new shop and business venture... harbouring hopes for an upcoming wedding... busy searching for a new car or new clothes... planning for a bright future for their children... suddenly, those plans and schemes vanished from their minds. Mothers busy in feeding their babies ran for their lives, leaving the children behind. Pregnant women miscarried; the ones who were physically strong ran while trampling the weak whereas youngsters fled leaving the elderly behind.

Now, gold and silver lie on the side of roads, currency notes fly in the wind and precious goods lie scattered... but there is no one to take them, no one to gather them together. Home... business... relatives... relations and assets... all have been rendered irrelevant. Every soul is concerned only for itself. Today, man has forgotten everything and is only calling one God, but there is no response. Atheists and non-believers are also repeating God's name but no one can find a place of sanctity. The shadows of destruction are difficult to escape from; death is on the hunt everywhere. Hardships have surrounded people from all directions.

Finally, life surrendered, to death.

Life was over... but only because, life was about to begin, in earnest.

==============

I could hear the wind buzzing in my ears. A few raindrops landed on my face. I began to regain consciousness. I kept trying to get up for a long time, but my senses were not working fully. I remained in this state for a very protracted period. Then, I heard a familiar voice in my ears.

"Abdullah! Get up, quickly!" This was the voice of my long-standing, dear, and beloved friend Saleh. His voice worked like magic and I stood up quickly.

"Where am I?" was my instinctive first question.

He replied while tapping my shoulder, "You have forgotten, what I told you. The Day of Judgement has begun. Raphael is blowing the trumpet the second time. At the moment, its volume is quite low. Its sound is waking up only those people presently who were obedient to

God in the previous life…"

"What would happen to the remaining people?" I interrupted him.

"In a short while, Raphael will steadily up the volume so that, it will sound harsh. Then, this noise will transform into a loud bang. At that stage, the remaining people will also wake up but that awakening will be one of suffering and discomfort. We need to get out of here before that happens", he replied hurriedly.

I wondered to myself as I got up, "but where to go?"

However, Saleh immediately understood my concern from my facial expressions and replied whilst taking quick steps, "You are fortunate, Abdullah! We are heading towards Arsh – the Throne of the Almighty". Then, he provided some more details:

"At this stage, only the prophets, the Siddiqeen, the Shuhada, and the Salaiheen have emerged from their graves. God ordained the success of these people while they were still in the previous world. They are the ones who believed in God despite being unable to see him with their eyes. They found him despite being unable to touch him with their hands. They listened to his call without being able to hear his voice with their ears. They believed in his prophets, submitted to them, and supported them in an exemplary manner. Their loyalty was neither to their religious leaders, personalities, or sectarian elite nor to the prejudices of their ancestors. Their loyalty was only, and only to God and his prophets. They patiently sustained all kinds of sufferings, tolerated all kinds of scorns, and underwent all sorts of hardships, just for the sake of God. High morals and noble character was the only way of life to follow for them. All their lives, they were in love with their Creator and compassionate to his creations. Abdullah! Today is the day for recompense of these people and this is the beginning of their recompense."

As I listened to Saleh, my face displayed expressions of astonishment while his was gleaming with enjoyment.

"But, I was in Paradise and…"

Saleh interrupted me before I completed my sentence, and said light-heartedly:

"My dear friend that was the period of Barzakh, the world hidden behind a curtain, from your previous world. That was a life of dreams. The real life has begun only now. Only now will people receive the reward of Paradise. By the way, that life in the Barzakh was also a reality. Remember, our friendship started during that life?"

I shook my head and just stared at him. Some of this made sense to me but there was a lot more to comprehend. However, I decided that at that stage it would be more appropriate to leave myself at Saleh's disposal.

===============

My friendship with Saleh began when after my death or more appropriately, after I stepped out from the illusion of a finite world and entered the real world. People are usually very scared of death, but for me, death was a pleasant experience. The name of angel of death, Azrael (Izra'il) was a symbol of terror in the world, but he came to me in a very handsome façade. He separated my personality that is, my soul, from my body with utmost love and care. My body remained in the previous world while he transferred my true personality into this new world called the Barzakh. Barzakh actually refers to a veil or a curtain; a curtain appeared between the previous world and me as soon as the angel of death appeared. Because of this curtain, I lost all contact with that world. I did not know what happened to my family due to the grief of separation, although I had full confidence that because of the upbringing I provided them, they would be patient and content upon the will of our Lord.

I was in a new world now, with my true personality. This was the world of Barzakh. The angel of death Israel had handed me over into the care of Saleh in this world. Along with him, there were many good looking, well-dressed and well-spoken angels. All of them had bouquets of flowers in their hands, while on their lips they had salutations and prayers for long life. In this background of greetings and wishes for long life, together, all of them tried to reassure me that the days of trial were over; the days of the glorious success of Paradise had begun in earnest, they kept telling me. It was then, when Saleh gave me the glad tidings of my first reward at the start of my life in Barzakh. The reward was an audience with the Master of Earth and Skies! He also informed me that this honour was granted to only a select few. I cherished this news even more than the glad tidings of entering the paradise.

Hence, my journey began in the company of these angels. This was a new world. Over there, the meanings of distances, places, time, and space altered in such a manner that it is impossible to explain them in words. I was in a state of euphoria and trance on this journey, when suddenly, we were ordered to stop. It was announced that the angels of Earth had now reached their limit and must halt. Only Saleh was allowed to accompany me from there onwards. The journey into the unseen skies began. Soon, we stopped again. I was informed that Archangel Gabriel, the Trustworthy had specially come to welcome me. On seeing me, he said:

"Abdullah! You are meeting me for the first time, but I have met you many times previously."

As he lightly tapped on my shoulder, he spoke again:

"On the orders of my Master, I helped you many a times but you were not aware of it."

On hearing the word Master, my face became alight with excitement. The spiritual being of Archangel Gabriel sensed this even before I had a chance to put my feelings into words. He said:

"Come on, then! I shall take you to meet your Lord. Apart from prophets, the privilege of attending the court of the One and the only God is reserved for very few human beings. You are indeed, very fortunate!"

As we proceeded forward, a question came into my mind; I felt that it was appropriate to ask Archangel Gabriel [PBUH] about it. So I said:

"Are we going towards 'Sidrah tul-Muntaha', the limit which no creation can pass?"

"No..." He replied, and then clarified further:

"You are probably thinking about Mi'raj; that is the path of the prophets. The places where the prophets are presented for attendance are supreme. They are also allowed to witness places and events in the Universe that others are not allowed to see. Your path is totally different. The reason you have been called for is to grant you the honour of prostrating in the Court of the Almighty. Probably, it is because of you that Saleh has also been granted permission to come so far."

I looked back at Saleh; his face was glowing with joy. Gabriel PBUH continued his conversation:

"God is boundless. His abodes are countless. In your world, these abodes cannot even be imagined. Whatever knowledge you had on Earth was very little and limited. Now, after death, your eyes have truly opened. You can now see a world, whose enchantments know no bounds."

What I was observing was a testament to the truthfulness of Archangel Gabriel. I thought to myself, it is a great blessing of God that I did not die in a state of disobedience and rejection of the ultimate truth about him. Otherwise, I would have had to see an awful and horrifying scene on waking up after death.

Accompanied by Archangel Gabriel, we passed through various stages and approached the Bearers of God's Throne in the Empyrean *(Arsh). Here was a beautiful and subtle blend of Nur, colour and light, the description of which was beyond the realm of words. The heads of the bearers were bowed. Their faces displayed an air of fear as well as a light of serenity. Archangel Gabriel explained:

"Every command from the Court of the Almighty descends through these angels and every act of the creatures below is presented to the Almighty via them."

I was watching them with envy in this unique place of closeness to God. They also looked up at me and for an instance, a smile appeared on their lips. This gave me more courage. I took a few steps towards the empyrean. Every pore of my body began to sing praise for the One, whom, I had yearned to meet my entire life.

I do not know why but I began to tremble as I walked forward. The realisation of God's greatness overcame the intense desire of meeting him. At that instant, I felt so over whelmed by his grandeur that I started to retreat in fear. The Throne was still quite far but the realisation of the magnanimity of the Master of the Throne broke my will. I felt at that moment, that my being would breakdown into countless tiny fragments and disperse into the atmosphere. Perhaps, that is what would have happened, but at that instant, I heard the voice of Archangel Gabriel in my ears, saying:

"Bow down right here Abdullah! Only the noble prophets can go beyond this place."

Saleh and I both prostrated right there. Thus, I prostrated to the One I had prostrated to all my life without being able to see him, but today, this was after seeing him. Well, I did not really see him; I only saw the signs of his presence.

I do not remember how long and delightful was this act of prostration. The One who bestowed the Sun with a glittering sheet of light and the Moon with a cover of brightness, the One who provided fragrance to flowers and dressed the butterflies with colours, the One who gave sparkle to the stars and jingle to the blooms, the One who granted the skies their sublime crown and to the seas the dominion of vastness, the One who blessed the soil with fertility and adorned rivers with the beauty of flowing water, and the One who endowed man with the ability to communicate and the honour of receiving the revelation of the Qur'an... every moment spent in the feet of such a being was superior to any other honour. Even owning an empire comprised of the seven continents of the world could not have surpassed this experience. However, inevitably this moment had to end. I heard the delightful voice of the Bearers of the Throne chanting:

"'Hu Allah hu, la Illaha illa Hu', which meant, 'He is God, there is no deity worthy of worship except him."

This was in fact, an announcement that the Master of the Throne was about to speak. A voice proclaimed:

"I am God and there is no one worthy of worship but me."

The effect of this magical voice was more delightful than any melody I had ever heard before; it left my body in a state of absolute attentiveness. All my strength suddenly became focused in my ears and my sense of hearing. I wanted to hear more, but there was a pause. I realised that I was expected to say something. The first sentence that came to my trembling lips was:

"Master! This is the only truth I came to realise in my lifetime."

My voice was so faint that even my own ears could barely hear it. However, it reached the One who knows all, whether hidden or obvious; the One who even knows the secrets embedded deep inside hearts. He replied:

"Not everyone who knows this fact is able to reach here... do you know this, Abdullah? How come you reached here?"

This time, the magnanimous tone in the expression of my Lord had a tinge of affection about it.

"The reason is Abdullah, that you dedicated your life to informing other people about me. You spent your life warning them about the day they will meet me. You made my remembrance, and work for my causes a mission of your life... this is the reward for it."

At that moment, I just wanted to continue to listen to the words of the Master of Skies and Earth; this felt like the most intense desire I had ever experienced in my life. However, once again, the King of the Worlds became silent. I sensed that my Master was giving me another opportunity to speak. I said:

"Can I stay near you, over here?"

My Lord replied, "no one is far from me Abdullah, neither am I far from anyone. All my obedient servants who lived their lives in my remembrance are close to me, regardless of whether they are men or women. Anything else...?"

The last comment made me realise that the meeting was ending. I said:

"What are my orders, Master?"

"The time to obey orders has long gone", the Almighty replied. "Soon, it will be time for you to give orders as a king. For the time being, you should return. Life has not begun yet."

As I was leaving, I said:

"You would not forget me on the Day of Judgement, would you? I have heard a lot about the horrors of that day and your anger."

I could feel a beautiful smile spreading in the air. A sharp voice followed:

"You human beings are the ones prone to forgetfulness, Abdullah. The King of kings... your Lord, the One who provides for you, does not forget anything. As for my anger, it never over shadows my mercy. You remembered me your entire life with hope and fear. I will also remember you with forgiveness and mercy. However..."

There was a moment of a kingly pause... then he continued:

"... For your consolation, I am sending Saleh along with you. He will look after you."

This is the account of my first meeting with Saleh, and the real reason for the benefit of his company. I did not have a physical body during my life in Barzakh. Here, my feelings, emotions, experiences, and observations were akin to a dream. It was a non-physical life but one full of insight. I had full realisation of the blessings that awaited me in the Paradise. Saleh used to visit me regularly, whenever I wished for him to do so. Whenever he would come, he would inform me about all sorts of new things and answer all my questions. Slowly, our friendship became stronger. In our last meeting, he told me that life was about to begin. Hence, today, along with him, I was crossing the vast plane on the Day of Judgement, rapidly moving towards the Throne.

==============

As I was walking along with Saleh, I looked around; it was a never-ending plane, as far as the eyes could see. The atmosphere felt like it used to be just after dusk before sunrise, around the time of morning prayers; it was as if, daybreak was about to scatter all around. At that time, I could see only a handful of people in the field, albeit, all of them had the same destination. I wondered if anyone amongst those people was a prophet or a messenger. I looked towards Saleh; he knew what I wanted to know. He replied:

"All of them woke up earlier. We are in fact, going towards them."

"Will I get a chance to meet them?" I asked him eagerly, excited like a child.

He stopped walking and spoke gently:

"In fact, your life will now be spent amongst them. Abdullah! You have still not managed to grasp what is happening. The trial has now finished. There is no facade anymore. Life is now beginning in real and in this life, righteous people will live along with other righteous people forever, and the ones who are evil, shall live along with people who are evil."

The truth was that I had still not recovered from the shock of all that was happening around me. In fact, the entire introduction to this new world had already taken place in the Barzakh. That was a kind of non-physical world but now, here, on this Day of Judgement, everything was similar to the physical world in which I lived previously. My hands and feet, my feelings and the earth and the sky around me... everything was similar to what I was used to in the previous world. In that world, I had a home, a family, a neighbourhood, a region and a nation... suddenly there was an explosion in my head. I stopped immediately and grabbing Saleh with both my hands, asked him:

"Where is my family? My relatives, my friends, where are they? What will happen to them? Why can I not see them?"

Saleh answered while avoiding my gaze:

"Do not ask me such questions Abdullah whose answers I do not know. Every person is on his own today. No one can benefit anyone else. If their deeds are good, then remain confident that they will end up meeting you. No injustice shall be done to them. But, if their deeds are not good, then..."

Saleh left the sentence incomplete and became silent. On hearing his reply, my mood suddenly became sad. He put his hand on my shoulder and tried to elevate my spirit in these words:

"Have faith in God, Abdullah. You were a fighting soldier in God's army. For this reason, you have risen before others. Rest of the people are rising up now. Those people will also meet you, God-willing, in the right circumstances. For the moment, continue to move ahead."

My moral rose due to his reassurance and I started to walk briskly along with him.

================

Chapter 2: In the Shadow of the Throne

We were moving forward like delicate, yet brisk breeze. The walk was enjoyable rather than tiring. I am not sure how far we had travelled when Saleh said:

"In the shadow of the Divine Throne, we are about to enter the territory of the 'Guardians'. Look ahead! The crowd of angels is visible. Behind them is a tall door. That is the door to go inside."

On Saleh's prompting, I looked ahead and saw the angels and the door behind them. However, this door was peculiar as it stood without any supporting walls. It could well be that the walls were invisible since nothing was visible behind the door as if an invisible veil had obscured everything that was beyond.

On hearing his words, my steps became brisk and the distance began to reduce rapidly. The door was still far away but I could now see the angels clearly. They were very tall and looked stern. They had whips of fire in their hands, which made me uneasy. I grasped Saleh's hand firmly, and whilst trying to stop him, pleaded:

"You are perhaps heading in the wrong direction, Saleh. They appear to be angels of punishment."

"Keep moving", he replied without stopping.

Reluctantly, I had to follow him. However, I ensured that I walked two steps behind him so that in case we had to turn and run I would be ahead of him. Saleh had understood my feelings and he felt it was necessary to explain:

"Indeed, they are the angels of punishment..."

"And they are there to beat me up and cleanse me of my sins?" I interrupted him in mid-sentence.

He chuckled on hearing my words and replied:

"Remember, if you were to be beaten up, running away would not help. No one can match the pace and might of these angels. For your information, they are not standing here to beat you up. They are here only to discourage any criminal of God from coming this way."

As we approached them, they separated in two groups to make way for us. They also moved their whips behind them as a gesture of kindness. I hoped that they would smile or show expression of joy on seeing us, but despite my best efforts, I could not detect any such expression. Saleh commented:

"One of the reasons for their presence here is to make you appreciate the blessing of God that has saved you from angels like them."

Words of praise for the Lord flowed from my lips involuntarily.

Having passed through the angels, we approached the door and it opened automatically. As soon as that happened, I saw a picturesque view. The land beyond appeared to be especially blessed by the Divine Throne. I could feel pleasant cold winds seeping through my core while an aroma of enchanting fragrances enthralled me. As we entered through the door, I saw rows after rows of angels in front of us. They were attractive and their faces were adorned with beautiful smiles. They stood in reverential attentiveness with their hands held together in front. As we passed through them, they greeted us with prayers, salaam, and welcoming words. I could feel the warmth of their genuinely welcoming behaviour deep inside my soul; the fragrances emanating from their bodies were overwhelming my emotions.

When I entered that place, I felt the sensation of an extraordinary change within me. However, at that time all my attention was focused on the angels and the pleasant environment around. Hence, I did not pay much attention to it and attributed it to a change in the environment.

As we walked along, a thought came to my mind. I whispered in Saleh's ear:

"I can appreciate that these people are welcoming me because they regard me as a person who has succeeded but I do not know them personally. Are you acquainted with any of them?"

Saleh laughed on hearing this and replied:

"Abdullah, today every person will be recognised by what shows on his forehead. You may not be aware of it but your whole introduction is recorded there. Just watch what happens next."

A handsome angel, who stood at the end of the row and appeared to be their leader, came to me and greeted me, calling me by my name. I greeted him in reply. He then spoke in a soft and affectionate tone:

"Congratulations on ever-lasting success!"

I thanked him; he asked:

"Would you like to have a look in the mirror?"

I could not fathom whether he was serious or was trying to be humorous, as I could not find any reason to look in the mirror. He did not wait for my reply and signalled to an angel. The next moment, there was a full-length mirror in front of me. I looked at it and became sure that it was some sort of a practical joke as this was not a mirror. Rather, it looked like an extremely beautiful and life-like portrait of a handsome young man; in fact, he was more of a prince standing dressed in regal attire. However, it was painted so well that it looked like a real man standing in front of the mirror.

I looked at the angel and said smilingly:

"You have a good sense of humour but the painting is even better. You seem to be its painter, but who is the model?"

The angel replied soberly:

"The real painter is 'Al-Mussawir', the divine painter, God All Mighty. However, you are the model."

He signalled to Saleh who came and stood close to me. He then turned my face towards the portrait again. I could also see Saleh in the portrait along with the young man. Amazed, I looked back and forth many times at Saleh and the image in the mirror about which both were insisting that it was my own reflection.

"But definitely it is not me!" I said in an excited voice.

Saleh replied by reciting this verse:

"O the life of the whole world,

Is this someone like you, or you?"

"But how is it possible? I used to be an old man but even when I was young, I was nothing like this image!" I replied.

This time, the angel answered my question:

"You have moved from the world of impossibilities to the world of possibilities. You have come from the world of humans to the world of God. Today, no one would look like what he used to appear to other people in the previous world. Instead, today every person will look like how he used to appear to his Lord. In the eyes of your Lord, the appearances are determined not by flesh, but by a person's faith, values and deeds. Today, he has made you, as he perceived you while you were in the previous world.

By the way, this is also a temporary arrangement. Your final personality would only emerge when your standing in the Paradise is finally determined. For now, please move on as quite a few people are waiting for you."

===============

We were moving ahead. I was now able to fully appreciate the transformation that had taken place in me when I had entered the door to the shadows of the Divine Throne. My walk exuded confidence. It was perhaps the effect of seeing my reflection in that mirror that had made me believe that the Lord of Kaaba had blessed me with the ultimate success. The problems I had to deal with every day in my previous life now seemed to be long forgotten dreams. I had never imagined that the trials, tribulations, and deprivation of my previous life would bear such a wonderful fruit! I had often read abstracts about life in the Hereafter in the Qur'an and sayings ascribed to the Prophet Muhammed PBUH. However, there is a huge difference between what is described in words and what one can see, hear, and feel in person. Today, when I could see all these facts with my own eyes, it was a bit too much for me... I had realised even during my previous life that I would probably succeed in the Hereafter but I did not have the faintest clue that the success would be so spectacular.

"You have still not fully comprehended this Abdullah", said Saleh, who was, somehow able to read my thoughts. I became even more attentive on hearing this. He continued:

"The real life has not started as yet. You are still in the temporary stage of the Judgement Day. Real life will begin in the Paradise. Then, you will see the real payback from God. That would be the time to submit your gratitude. For the time being, look ahead and see where we stand."

His comments made me realise that I had become completely oblivious to my surroundings. I looked around. We stood in a sprawling, abundant, green plane. The sun was shining bright. Its light was bright, but not intense. The ground was covered in shade though I could not see any clouds in the sky. The earth was green in colour. Perhaps it was the effect of this greenery that the sky had acquired an emerald tinge to it rather than the usual shades of blue. There was a sky-high mountain in the middle of the plane. It was sky-high, literally, as it seemed from where we stood that its peak was touching the sky. There was a pleasing fragrance all around. It was a new scent for me but it utterly mesmerized my senses. I could hear songs in the background mixed with pleasant notes of melodies dispersed all around us in the air. It felt as if I was able to smell the fragrance and hear the melody directly in my mind without the help of my senses. This seamless blend of fragrance and harmony in perfect proportions resulted in a state of serenity and trance. I felt that my entire being was melting away.

I stood at a spot and closed my eyes to relish this sensation some more.

Seeing me in this state, Saleh said:

"The name of this mountain is 'Aaraf'. Let us go around it. I will give you more details about it as we go along."

I accompanied him in silence, mesmerized by the surroundings. We started our journey from the right side of the mountain. Having gone only a short distance, I saw a part of the mountain with a sign, 'The Nation of Adam'.

I asked Saleh, "Is Adam PBUH, over here?"

He replied, "No, all prophets are presently on the higher level of the mountain. You will see more of these signs displaying the names of nations of various prophets as we go further. All successful people like you, from every nation, will gather at these designated spots."

"So, will I have to go to the camp for the nation of Prophet Muhammad?" I asked eagerly.

Saleh shook his head to say no and then explained:

"Successful people will wait in these camps and at the end of the Day of Judgement, they will be taken to Paradise from here. You, on the other hand, have to go to the top of the mountain. Over there, the prophets and all those people from their respective nations who were witnesses to the truth, in support of their prophets, have assembled. They will witness judgement of the Almighty regarding human beings from there. They will also be called upon to give their testimony. Every unsuccessful person will be taken towards Hell from the Plane of Judgement whereas all the successful ones will be brought over to the camps of their prophets on the mountain. All nations will then be taken to Paradise from here, one after the other. One can also observe from the top every judgement that is passed. Paradise and the Hell are also visible from there."

We talked and passed by the spots designated for nations of various prophets. As only a few people were visible in these camps, I asked Saleh:

"It looks like everyone has not reached here yet."

He replied, "No, that is not the case. Actually, the number of successful people from the nations of other prophets is quite low. A large number of them belong to the Israelites and the highest number belongs to the nation of Prophet Muhammad [PBUH]. We have not yet reached the camps of these two nations, although at the moment, there are not many people present even there. Their numbers will increase soon. Come on, let's go up. A trip around this mountain would take too long."

===============

I have always enjoyed climbing heights. However, this was perhaps the strangest mountain I had come across. From the ground, it looked very tall and seemed to touch the sky. But, from the top, we could see the ground at the foot of the mountain as if it was only a little lower than where we were. The place that looked like the summit from the ground was in fact a plateau, which had various tall fortress-like structures built all over it. As they did not have any surrounding walls or doors, it was possible to see them from outside. I could see that there were servants walking around, other luxuries befitting royalty were also visible. Personalities of high stature, wearing crowns were seated on a regal throne. Around them, people sat on chairs and they also appeared to be of similar standing.

I asked Saleh about them; he replied:

"These buildings are temporary abodes of various prophets. People sitting around them are Shuhada and Siddiqeen of their nations. Siddiqeen are the people who supported their prophets during their lifetimes whereas Shuhada are the ones who spread the message onwards after they had passed away.

All of them are people who lived in the world for the sake of God and laid their lives in his cause. This success and prestige surrounding them today is a reward for their sacrifices."

"Can I meet the exalted prophets?" I asked.

"We do not have time to meet all, but we can certainly meet a few of them", he replied and then started to introduce me, one by one, to the great prophets of God. I was meeting the prophets who had always been symbols of greatness for me. I met Adam, Noah [(Nuh)], Hud, Saleh,

Isaac (Ishaq), Jacob (Yaqub), Joseph (Yusuf), Shoaib, Moses (Musa), Aaron (Harun), Jonah (Yunus), David (Da'ud), Solomon (Suleman), Zachariah (Zakriyah), John (Yahya), Jesus (Eesa) and foremost, the father of prophets, Prophet Abraham (Ibrahim), May God bless them all. All of them greeted me with a hug and a kiss on the forehead and congratulated me on my success.

After a brief conversation with these exalted personalities, we moved ahead. However, I could feel during my interaction with them that they were somewhat concerned and worried.

I asked Saleh about it.

He answered:

"You are not aware of it but all hell is breaking loose in the Plane of Judgement. Every prophet is concerned about the fate of the humanity. The wrath of God is so severe that no prophet wants his nation to face it. All prophets would like the Almighty to forgive everyone however, so far there is no chance of that happening. It is not possible to pray for it at this time and neither are they allowed to pray for such an outcome. People have suffered for centuries by now and so far there is no sign of the initiation of the accountability process."

Surprised, I said:

"For centuries! How come? It has only been a couple of hours since we came in."

He explained, "That is what you think, Abdullah. Today is only a few hours long for the successful people whereas for those outside, it is an extremely lengthy day, full of hardship and difficulties. Centuries have passed outside but you may find it difficult to comprehend it fully."

I could not visualise what he was saying but obviously, everything was possible in the world I was in now. I wondered how many more strange happenings were waiting to unfold in front of me.

==============

The companions of the Prophet including the Muhajireen (emigrants) and the Ansar (helpers) were sitting respectfully in a circle. There were also a large number of people belonging to the earlier and later periods of the nation of Prophet Muhammad PBUH. He sat in the middle with his head bowed. Everything looked normal apparently but I could sense that even here there was the same element of concern and unease that I had observed before with the other prophets.

"The Prophet of God is busy at the moment in praying to the Almighty God, the One and only. We better sit down and wait," Said Saleh as he headed towards the seats at the rear.

We sat on the seats in the rear. From there it was difficult to see what was happening at the front. I asked Saleh:

"When would the accountability start?"

"I don't know. No one knows!" He replied.

I became quiet on hearing his reply and sat back, resting my head on the chair. I do not know how much time had passed when I heard Saleh saying something to me:

"Wake up, Abdullah! Look, someone is here to meet you."

On hearing his voice, I opened my eyes and quickly stood up. I saw a highly respectable and distinguished personality standing in front of me. He had a smile on his face and I could feel affection in his eyes. Before Saleh could say anything, he introduced himself, speaking in a soft tone:

"Welcome Abdullah! I am Abu-Bakr. I am here to welcome you on behalf of the Prophet."

As he uttered these words, he extended his hands. Feeling quite excited, I gave him a hug. After the initial introduction, he took me aside, away from the other people and sat on a chair. I asked him as soon as we sat down:

"When would I be able to meet the Prophet, peace be upon him?"

"He is presently busy in praying and thanking the Almighty. You will be able to meet him later. Now, the most important news is that Almighty has accepted his prayer for commencement of the accountability. The moment when the Almighty accepted his plea, you had also prayed for something. Did you not want to go back to the Plane of Judgement to see what was happening there? Almighty has permitted you to do so. The accountability would start in a short while.

You can see what is happening to people until then. The Prophet has sent me to you with this message."

I was happy to hear this. The messenger of the Prophet also smiled when he saw my happiness. He continued after a pause:

"The atmosphere is severe outside. Saleh would be with you but it would be better if you have this drink before you go. It will protect you from the afflictions outside."

He then offered me a glittering golden glass. I took it in both hands and started to drink.

A strange thing happened as soon as the glass touched my lips. Although I was not thirsty at all nor was I experiencing any sort of discomfort or restlessness, yet the satisfaction I got from the first sip was such that it surpassed the gratification a person would have experienced on having the first sip of water after centuries of thirst. As soon as the first mouthful went down my throat, I realised for the first time what was the real meaning of words like delight, fulfilment, serenity, sweetness, and freshness; this experience was so unique that I do not think any human would have ever had this experience before. I experienced an intense feeling of satisfaction and exhilaration through each vein in my body as each drop passed from my tongue to my throat, from the throat to my chest and from the chest to my stomach. I wanted to finish the whole drink in one gulp but the immense respect of the esteemed personality sitting in front stopped me from doing so. I asked in a subdued voice:

"What is it?"

He replied, "It is the first introduction to your new life and the new world. This is a drink from Kauthar. After drinking it heat and thirst of the Plane of Judgement will not bother you."

I immediately realised why this drink had such an extraordinary effect on me. It was water from the pond of Kauthar in the Paradise and undoubtedly, it had all the characteristics I had heard about in my life. From that point onwards, I also had a better understanding of the comforts of Paradise. In the previous world, the delight from food and drink was because of two things; firstly, it required a person to be hungry and secondly, the item being eaten had to be tasty. In the

Paradise, everything would be extremely delicious even in the absence of thirst and hunger; it would still provide the same satisfaction and pleasure that only a very hungry and thirsty person used to get in the previous world. I came to understand now that in the Paradise, there would no hunger or thirst. However, one would be able to eat as much as one wanted without experiencing any discomfort or satiety.

===============

Chapter 3: The Plane of Judgement

Both of us were walking rapidly again. As soon as we left the limits of the Throne, we encountered an extremely hot and humid atmosphere. It felt as if the distance between the Sun and Earth had reduced from 90 million miles to a mere mile! There was no breeze. Everyone was drenched in sweat. There was no sign of water anywhere. I was under the influence of the drink from Kauthar; otherwise, it would have been impossible for me to spend even a second in this atmosphere. However, I could see countless extremely weary people loitering around in the same suffocating atmosphere. Their faces displayed horror, their eyes were full of fear, and their hair was covered in dust. Their bodies were soaked in sweat. Dirt was all over them; their feet had blisters with pus oozing out of them. I had never seen such a horrible scene of despair and fear in my life before! There was chaos and disarray wherever one looked. Everyone seemed to be concerned only with his or her own self. I was searching for familiar faces. The first face I recognised was that of my teacher, Farhan Ahmed. He saw me from a distance and immediately turned away, trying to avoid eye contact. I said to Saleh:

"Stop him Saleh! He is my teacher. I want to talk to him."

He stopped me from moving towards him instead, and spoke in a remorseful voice:

"Abdullah, do not add to the humiliation of your teacher. If someone appears to you suffering here today, it means that Justice has been done to him and he has been found lacking in deeds, as per the scales of divine justice. That is why he is in such a state."

I spoke in anguish:

"But Saleh, I learnt all about belief in God, focusing on the Hereafter and ethical values from him."

"You may have..." Saleh replied carelessly, and continued:

"However, his knowledge failed to become a part of his personality. God does not pass a judgement based on a person's knowledge. The fundamental factors that determine the decision are one's deeds, character, and personality. The role of knowledge is really to help lay the foundations of one's personality on sound footing. If the personality has not developed on the right foundations, the knowledge in fact becomes harmful for the person. As a Persian poet once said:

When knowledge is only skin-deep, it is like a poisonous snake
Only when it sinks deep in the heart, does it become a true friend

The same thing happened to your teacher, Abdullah. He was a good writer. He spoke well too. However, his character and personality were not in accordance with what he preached. Therefore, in a way he was also nurturing snakes. These snakes of knowledge have bit him hard today. When you see people here, you will not find them as per their appearance and words in the previous life. Instead, they will be a true image of what they really were in the life bygone.

Remember! God does not judge people based on their words and external appearance. He only looks at their deeds and personality. Particularly, people with knowledge would face a much tougher standard of accountability today. Many lapses that would be acceptable from ordinary people on account of their lack of knowledge would not be accepted coming from scholars."

"But he sacrificed a lot..." I said, in his defence.

"True, but he got his compensation for that while he was still alive", Saleh replied. He continued further:

"Errors in knowledge may be overlooked today. However, failings of personality and deeds will result in the same state as your teacher is in.

Anyway, the day has only begun. Let us see what else happens before it ends".

I stood in a state of shock for a long time. I was an orphan with no one to look after me. My teacher meant everything to me. He was my mentor; he helped me in my education, arranged my marriage, and gave me a purpose in life. He was dearer to me than a real father would have been; hence, I was shocked to find him in this state. Because of that, I became quite oblivious to my surroundings.

Around me, countless people were walking, running, and struggling along. Loud echoes of the roaring flames were mixed together with the shouts, cries, and wails of people. People were busy taunting each other, hurling abuses at each other, and blaming each other. Many were engaged in full-blown scuffles and fights.

Around me, a few persons held their heads in their hands, while others threw dust on their faces. I could see people hiding their faces in shame; others were being disgraced. Some were banging their heads on stones; others were beating their chests in anguish. Some were blaming themselves while others were having a go at their mothers, fathers, wives, children, friends, or leaders, holding them responsible for their ruin.

All of them had the same problem; the Day of Judgement had arrived, and they had not prepared for it. Now they could blame others or themselves, they could mourn or be patient, but it was not possible to change anything. All that was left to do was to wait, wait for the arrival of the Master of the Universe, following which the accountability was to begin, and the destiny of every person was be determined with absolute justice.

I kept standing aloof from all that was happening around me for God knows how long. Suddenly, a person nearby cried out:

"Ah... I was better off dead! Even the pit of the grave was better than this."

His lament made me aware of my surroundings again. In an instant, all memories from the start to the end were refreshed in my mind again.

I turned back and looked at Saleh. He was staring at me with a blank expression on his face. He said:

"Abdullah! You chose to come to the Plane of Judgement leaving your allocated station behind, in order to observe what was happening here. It is inevitable that you would come across more scenes like that. As such, you need to be mentally prepared. To save you from further shocks, I have to inform you that right now, one of your daughters, Leila and your son Jamshaid are also present on this Plane of Judgement; both are in trouble."

Saleh's words shook me to the core. I started to feel dizzy and sat down on the ground, holding my head in my hands. Saleh also sat down quietly next to me.

Tears were running down my cheeks. However, no one around me took any notice. No one cared about what was happening to others. Why was a person sitting on the ground? Why was someone standing? Why was someone lying down? Why was somebody crying? Who was yelling and wailing? Nobody cared! Today, every person was concerned about his or her own self only. No one had the time or the inclination to stop by and enquire after me. People passed by us indifferently.

After a while, I asked Saleh, "What is going to happen now?"

"Obviously, the accountability will start. Only then would we know something for sure", He replied definitively, and then explained further:

"Those people who had made this day their foremost priority in the previous world and led their lives preparing for it, have woken up today in the fortunate position of having been declared successful beforehand. They include those who fulfilled the requirements of true faith and morality as well as those who strived hard in the way of their Lord. They had reaped only goodness in their lives. They fulfilled the rights of their fellow human beings and met obligations of their Creator. Therefore, for them, death itself was a harbinger of relief from the trials of the previous world. They have received divine protection since the start of this Day of Judgement."

"But all human beings committed sins in their lives. Did they not"? I asked.

"True! They all sinned. However, their good deeds made up for their minor sins. The tears of repentance they shed immediately after committing any significant sins washed those sins away. Today, all those people are under the shadow of the Throne. They will only face brief ceremonial accountability before their eternal success is declared.

In contrast, those people who committed major sins that practically invalidate one's faith, like rejection of the truth, assigning partners to God, hypocrisy, murder, fornication, rape, apostasy, dishonesty in trusts belonging to orphans, repeatedly ignoring the limits set by God and all other sins of similar nature, will be sentenced to Hell." Saleh explained the Law in detail.

"But there are always human beings who fall in between the two extremes; what will happen to them?" I asked.

Saleh replied, "You are right. There are people who have faith in their hearts as well as some good deeds to their credit. However, they committed many sins and did not repent. Such people will have to bear the harshness of the Day of Judgement as a payback for their misdeeds; only then, they may have a chance of forgiveness.

All those people stuck on the Plane of Judgement today are those who are either major criminals destined for Hell or those who had faith but also committed many sins. So, the tribulations they undergo today are directly related to the number of sins they committed as well as the gravity of their sins. The ones with fewer sins will be relieved right at the start of the accountability. However, as I mentioned before, the time that has elapsed so far is equal to hundreds of years of your previous life. Even if these people are pardoned at the very beginning of the questioning, the centuries spent on the Plane of Judgement are enough to eliminate any lingering after-effects of the misdeeds committed in those fifty years of life. Whereas, people with a lot of sins to answer for, may have to bear the hardships, sufferings and toils of this extremely harsh environment for thousands or hundreds of thousands of years to come."

Saleh's explanation made me realise that sins that seemed so trivial in the previous world have caused so much misery today. Alas! If only, people had not considered their sins as trivial, if only, they had developed a regular habit to repent! If only, they had realised the seriousness of ills like backbiting, spitefulness, wasting money, pomp and show, slander etc. If they had appreciated the significance of the rights of God and other people, if they had stayed away from disobedience to God and had instead followed the way of the Holy prophets, they would have managed to avoid the present situation where the short-lived gratification of each sin had turned into an agony spanning centuries.

I asked Saleh:

"Does anyone know at this time if he or she will be pardoned or not, and if so, how?"

Saleh replied:

"This is the real predicament. No one knows what future holds for him or if there is any hope for salvation. Only God knows. This is the reason the last Prophet of God as well as other prophets and messengers were praying for the commencement of accountability. If this happens, at least the ones with true faith in their hearts would be separated from those destined to Hell and therefore get salvation, after going through the process of accountability. As you know, no one is able to say even a single word to help someone else, nor is there any possibility of it. The good news is that the last Prophet's prayer has been accepted; if you recall, his representative Abu-Bakr, the Truthful, conveyed that news to you in person."

"But, why can I see no sign of start of accountability?" I asked Saleh with surprise. He replied:

"The Almighty has accepted his request but as far as its execution is concerned, he will do so as per his own larger plan and wisdom. It is possible that all the people who rose from their graves may not have reached here yet."

I replied, "What do you mean? Have they not managed to get here despite a lapse of so many centuries?"

He replied, "How do you think they will get here? Do you think they will use aeroplanes, trains, buses, and cars to commute? Today, everyone is rushing here on foot. The sound of Archangel Rafael's trumpet had forced people to head in this direction. The Almighty has filled the oceans with earth and flattened the mountains to allow people to get here easily. Even then, it will take them some time as they are coming on foot. The only exception is the righteous people, who were accompanied by angels who brought them here straight away. Anyway, let's see what is happening to the people gathered here until the accountability begins. If I remember correctly, this was the reason you came here, right"?

Saleh held my hand and started to walk ahead without waiting for my response. People's faces were glowing red due to intense heat. Dirt and rubbish was flying all around. Worried people were roaming around, alone and in groups. My eyes were searching for a familiar face but could find none.

Suddenly, a girl appeared out of nowhere and before I could have a look at her face, she fell down at my feet and started to sob uncontrollably. I looked towards Saleh with great concern.

He said to the girl in a flat voice:

"Get up!"

Saleh's tone caused a chill to run up my spine.

The girl also pulled herself up, looking quite scared. I now looked at her face. It had darkened due to fear, apprehension, and grief. There was dirt over her hair and face. Her lips were parched due to thirst and her horror-stricken eyes had shadows of fear and terror in them.

Suddenly, an unbearable wave of anguish passed through me. The first time I saw that face I had involuntarily praised its beauty. It had a glowing fair complexion, an eye-catching profile, attractive features, rose-petal lips, a blue hue to the eyes, and jet-black hair. God had bestowed her with such natural beauty that it did not require any make-up or adornments.

However, today that face looked completely different. Beauty of the years gone by was now buried deep under layers of grief and sorrows of the Judgement Day. The person standing in front of me as a picture of utter lament, horror, and remorse was in fact Huma, my daughter-in-law and the wife of my eldest son Jamshaid.

"Please save me, Papa! I am in a lot of distress. This environment will kill me! I did not face any hardship in my life but now it seems to me that I will not see any relief ever again. For God's sake, have mercy on me! You are very close to God; please save me..." Huma started to weep bitterly.

"Where is Jamshaid?" I asked in a sunken voice.

"He is around. He has also been looking for you. This is such a large place with so many people that it is impossible to find anyone. He is also in a bad state. He was very angry with me. As soon as he met me, he slapped me and held me responsible for his doom. I am a bad person, Papa. I destroyed myself as well as my family. Please forgive me and save me. I am petrified of God's retribution; I cannot bear it."

Huma was pleading with tears running down her cheeks. Fatherly emotions started to rise in my chest; after all, she was my daughter-in-law. Before I could say anything, Saleh spoke again, with the same emotionless tone:

"You should have thought of that in the previous world, Madam! You have come to your senses now, however, do you remember what were you like in the world? May be you don't remember, so let me remind you..."

Saleh signalled and suddenly a scene appeared in front of us. It was Jamshaid and Huma's bedroom. I felt as if everything around me had disappeared and I was standing in the room along with them, able to see and hear everything.

==============

"Jamshaid, I cannot live in this country anymore! We should move to a Western country," said Huma as she sat at the dressing table, brushing her short cut hair.

Jamshaid was lying on the bed, watching TV. He did not reply.

"Did you hear what I said Jamshaid?"

"Yes, I heard you. My whole family lives here. How can I leave them behind?"

"Just like you left them and moved in with me?"

"That was different. At least I go and see them once a week now. Secondly, we go on foreign trips every year anyway. So, what's the point in moving abroad?"

"No, kids are growing up fast. I would like to raise them abroad."

"But I want my kids to enjoy the benefit of my parents company. I didn't get any share of their nobility; at least I would want my children to be like them."

"But, I want the kids to stay away from your parents, Jamshaid! Even if one of them is influenced by them, his life will be ruined."

The phone rang. Jamshaid picked it up. Some words were said at the other end. Jamshaid put the phone down after saying okay and said to Huma, "Your dad is calling us down". He then replied:

"Why are you so negative about my parents? They accepted you as their daughter-in-law just for the sake of my happiness, despite the fact that they did not approve of your ways. Even when you forced us to move out of our ancestral home, they did not feel bad about it."

"Hold on, that's not the case!" Huma snapped.

"Your parents may not have liked my ways but you were madly in love with me, which forced them to give their blessings to our marriage. You have enjoyed a much better life over here since you left them. You are a business partner of my Dad. You deal in millions. Your decision to marry me has proved to be a win-win deal for you, Jamshaid! You have not suffered any ill-effects because of your decision to leave them."

"Whenever I hear you talk like this, it reminds me of what my father used to say. He always said that the true verdict about profit and loss shall be passed on the Day of Judgement."

"Come on Jamshaid, stop this useless religious talk. Such ideas irritate me! There is no such thing as Judgement Day. This world's system has been running like this for millions of years. If you are smart, powerful, and wealthy, you are the winner! All others are losers and idiots. Moreover, you know this Judgement Day talk is nothing but rubbish.

By the way, for your kind information, my Dad has this assurance from his Peer that he will have him spared on the Day of Judgement. My dad gives a lot of money to him."

"Yes obviously, the way we earn money by illegal profiteering, violation of the Law and other means prohibited in our religion, we have to make it clean somehow! I know all about it. Your Dad and Chaudhary Mukhtar are business partners in various ventures; they make money through dishonest means."

"Really? If you are so concerned about ill-gotten wealth and dishonesty, why don't you quit?"

"I can leave the business but I can't leave you. I am well aware that if I am employed elsewhere, I would not be able to afford your expenditures or maintain your current standard of living. Alas, my love for you has left me stranded in the middle of nowhere! In fact, I belong to a family where all that matters is whether money is earned by religiously lawful means or not."

"That's why they are living such a miserable middle class life! You are lucky that you moved out to live with me at my parents home; otherwise, just like your brothers, you would have owned only a motorbike or a mere 800 cc car, and would have died after living a pathetic life in a flat somewhere."

"We all have to die one day whether we live a lavish life or one of deprivation. Who knows what will happen to us in the Hereafter?"

"Don't worry, nothing will happen to us! We will enjoy a life of luxury over there too. Even your God will not be able to do anything against the wishes of my dad's Peer!"

"Don't utter these blasphemous words, Huma! Moreover, why would he be my God anymore? If I haven't remained loyal to him, why would he remain on my side?"

As Jamshaid uttered these words, his voice choked and his eyes became wet. However, Huma did not see the tears running down his face as all of her attention was focused on the mirror. She got up after she had finished her make-up and said to Jamshaid:

"Okay, let's stop this pointless discussion! Let's go downstairs. Dad is waiting for us."

===============

Saleh signalled again and the scene came to a stop. As it disappeared, any faint hope Huma might have had disappeared with it. Saleh spoke again in the same brutal and deadly tone:

"Did you see that? Every single word that came out of your mouth has been recorded. So go Madam, go and find your dad's Peer who had the power to have you spared, the one in front of whom even God could not..."

Saleh left the sentence incomplete but the anger that exuded from his voice while he repeated Huma's words shook me with its intensity. Huma turned pale with fear. Before Saleh could say anything else, she ran away, screaming.

After seeing Jamshaid in that scene, my condition had again become unstable. Obviously, like Huma, he would have also been wandering in this plane suffering all the hardships. I wondered what I would do if Jamshaid appeared in front of me in this state. I was still thinking about it when Saleh patted me on the back and said:

"Come on Abdullah, let's go."

I do not know what was in his touch but as soon as he touched me, the level of anxiety that had overtaken me was suddenly reduced. I started to walk with him quite relaxed and fresh. Around us, it was the same commotion of worried and horrified people. We had gone ahead only a little more when I saw Mr. Chaudhary Mukhtar. He had probably seen me and was heading in my direction. Mr. Mukhtar was the business partner of Jamshaid's father-in-law. He was my acquaintance only in that capacity. As he came closer, he tried to embrace me but Saleh stopped him with the movement of his hand and said:

"Keep your distance and speak."

Saleh's tone was so harsh that he seemed like a stranger to me. Despite this insult, Mr. Mukhtar's enthusiasm did not fade. He said:

"I was certain Mr. Abdullah that you would come looking for me. Do you remember that I had a mosque constructed and you used to pray in that mosque? In addition, I also used to help the poor."

"I remember Mr. Mukhtar", I replied in a low voice.

"Then please put in a word for me. I have been roaming around in misery for a long time. Whoever you see over here is only concerned with himself. No one talks properly, nor gives any advice."

As he said this, he involuntarily looked at Saleh. I also turned my head to look at him. Saleh looked at me for an instance, and then started to talk while staring at Mr. Mukhtar's face:

"You certainly had a mosque built but it was not for the sake of God, rather you wanted a good name for yourself. When one donates money for the sake of God, one's head is bowed, hands are fastened, and the voice and the heart are full of humility and fear of God. However, you were not like that when you made donations. You wanted to be recognised by others as a pious person. Therefore, you had your wish granted during your life. Now, you will have to explain how you earned all that money.

Moreover, it was not often that you spent money on a good cause. Would you like to tell us how you spent millions in order to get close to a famous movie star? You are guilty of fornication. You indulged in it not once, but repeatedly. You fornicated with many different women. You had illicit relations with famous actresses and fashion models. Even if we leave aside how you spent your money, the way you earned the money included various prohibited and forbidden means. You were involved in adulteration. You hoarded stuff illegally. You sold goods at exorbitant rates. The fundamental principles of your business were to underpay utility charges, commit fraud, and deprive employees of their rights. At the peak of your career, you formed a media group. On one of the TV channels belonging to your group, you used to show religious programmes to keep the public happy, whereas on another one, you used to promote immoral attitudes and vulgarity in the society, all in the name of art and entertainment."

Saleh was speaking non-stop and words were flowing out of his mouth like arrows heading straight for their target. It was not possible for Mr. Mukhtar to respond to these but he had nowhere to run. He kept listening, with his head bowed in shame. The harshness in Saleh's voice produced expressions of hopelessness on Mr. Mukhtar's face. However, Saleh did not stop and continued further:

"Look back, Mr. Mukhtar! Your mistress is standing behind you."

Mr. Mukhtar turned around quickly. I also looked around to see who was standing behind him. In front of us was standing an old woman who had a face like a witch and an extremely strong stench emanating from her body. Saleh touched me again which caused the smell to disappear but I could see that Mr. Mukhtar could still smell her. The ugly woman moved forward towards Mr. Mukhtar calling him by his first name. Mr. Mukhtar slowly started to retreat, backing away from the woman and then without any warning, he started to run away from us. That woman or witch, whatever she was, also started to run after him.

"Who was that woman?" I asked Saleh after they had disappeared from sight.

"She used to be his mistress. She was famous in her times as an actress, dancer, and model. Her name is Champa", as Saleh introduced her, I was shocked. I said:

"Champa? But she used to be very pretty; she was well known for her beauty."

"Yes, not only did people talk about her, she was also a role model for them. See how that ideal personality looks like now! That woman used to promote vulgarity in the society with her explosive and revealing dances. God has decided that she will be imposed as a punishment in Hell on those very people on whose hearts she used to rule", said Saleh laughingly.

I remembered that lewdness and immorality had spread to its highest level during my time. Television allowed these actresses to reach the living rooms of all homes. The societies of that time had elevated such women who spread vulgarity and nudity, to the highest levels of respect and importance. For the owners of TV channels and film studios, these women were the cheapest and the easiest way of making huge profits. They filled their coffers with money by promoting their filthy dances, enticing moves and revealing garments. Young men were madly in love with them and wanted to marry women who looked and acted like them. Women used to style their clothes and makeup after them. It was because of them that, girls of good moral character but ordinary looks lost their true value in the society. So many of these virtuous women grew old, all alone, unable to find suitable husbands. Many left this world in silence, hiding the scars of society's lack of appreciation within their bosoms, deep under the cover of their nobility.

My face showed signs of anguish. Saleh recognised them straight away. He held my hand and started to walk in a direction. We stopped after a little while and he said to me:

"God has made some arrangements to alleviate your suffering. However, before I show you that, it may be better if you see this scene from the world bygone."

As he said these words, a scene started to run in front of my eyes like a movie. I felt that I was a part of the scene and was able to understand it without any explanation.

===============

Rays of morning sun were entering the room in spite of the curtains on the windows. It was time to go to college but on this cold winter morning, Shaistah did not feel well enough to leave her warm bed and get ready. It was her habit to do some study after the morning prayers and before she got ready for college. Today, she had gone back to bed after offering the prayers. She had not felt well since last night.

"No! I have to go to the college, otherwise my students will lag behind in their studies..., and I need to make breakfast for Mum and Dad as well", she thought. She then gathered all her strength, got up from the bed, and quietly walked over to her parents' room situated next to hers. She opened the door slowly and looked inside; they were in a deep slumber. She smiled with satisfaction.

Shaistah had devoted her whole life to her family. She was only a child when her father was disabled. She was the eldest amongst three sisters. Somehow, her mother managed to get all of them educated, earning a paltry income sewing clothes. After completing her education, she started to teach in a school and later joined the faculty at a private college.

It was a time for dreaming and making big plans. Shaistah was not too pretty, but youth is beauty in itself! For Shaistah, however, youth was a harbinger of new responsibilities, leaving no room for dreams and desires. She was now responsible for the household expenditures, her father's medical treatment, house-rent, and education of her two younger siblings. Both of her sisters were better looking, so, as they reached the right age, most marriage proposals were in their favour.

Shaistah did not create any hurdles in the way of her sisters' happiness. She readily arranged their weddings and got them settled in their new homes. Her youth began to fade away in the process and now she found herself alone, with the sole responsibility of looking after her aging parents.

During these difficult times, Shaistah kept her faith only in God. She loved God immensely. This love was so intense that none of the hardships in her life managed to breed any resentment in her. Shaistah was regular in prayers and fasting since childhood but she became familiar with the true sweetness of God's love only after reading books of her spiritual teacher, Abdullah. It was now the sole aim of her life to transfer the true essence of God's love and submission into the young hearts of her pupils.

Shaistah was an excellent teacher and her students respected her immensely. It was for this reason that they listened to her attentively and conversely, she always taught them with utmost enthusiasm.

For some reason, however, Shaistah felt sad today. It might have been because of not feeling too well but she felt depressed. After breakfast, she stood in front of the mirror to get ready for college.

She looked hard at her face. She could see signs of youth fading away. A painful smile appeared on her face as she mumbled to herself:

"Shaistah, you lost! You did not get anything but loneliness."

She closed her eyes, perhaps as a sign of acceptance of her defeat.

However, at that very moment, she heard the words of her teacher Abdullah echoing in her ears:

"The one, who makes a deal with God, never suffers a loss."

She opened her eyes with a smile.

She said to herself in a sustained voice:

"Let's see... we will see what happens. Not much time is left anyway!"

===============

The scene disappeared; I looked at Saleh and said:

"I don't know this girl."

Saleh replied, "You will get to know her soon. By the way, whatever you wrote went a long way."

He started walking. After some time we reached a place where some stern-faced angels stood. They looked similar to the angels we had seen under the Throne, whose job was to stop ordinary people from moving ahead. On seeing Saleh, they allowed us to pass through.

After a short distance, we came across a door. Saleh opened the door and entered it with me following behind. I realised straight away that the door was a gateway back to the other world, as on the other side, there was a completely different environment in contrast to the exhausting atmosphere in the Plane of Judgement. I said spontaneously:

"Saleh, are we going back to the tents of the prophets?"

He replied smilingly:

"Yes... the remedy for your grief can only be found over here."

We walked ahead and reached a magnificent tent. There was a man with a glowing face standing at the door. He had an air of high respectability about him. He was a complete stranger to me. On reaching closer, Saleh introduced me to him:

"This is Abdullah. He is a follower of the last Prophet of God, Muhammad PBUH, from the later part of that age. Abdullah, this is Nuhoor, a very close companion of Prophet Jeremiah PBUH. Nuhoor, you wanted to meet him, didn't you?"

It was not only an introduction to a companion of a great prophet but it also explained to me why I was there.

I extended my hand for a handshake. However, Nuhoor instead hugged me enthusiastically. I said to him after the embrace:

"I have not had the honour of meeting Prophet Jeremiah yet, but to meet you is no less of an honour. The life of Prophet Jeremiah and the circumstances surrounding him were always a great source of guidance for me. I am very keen to meet him."

As I said these words, the life story of this great prophet of the Israelites was running in my mind. In the sixth century B.C., the Israelites were in a state of severe moral decline. Due to their moral decay, they were suffering the divine punishment of political domination by Nebuchadnezzar, the King of Babylon, which was a superpower of that time. Their leaders, however, did not address their moral weaknesses and focused instead on regaining political supremacy. Prophet Jeremiah highlighted the flaws in their morals and faith, and encouraged them to work on the correction of their flaws instead of confronting a superpower. However, his people did not listen to him; instead, they hanged him upside down in a well and thereafter started an uprising against Nebuchadnezzar. As a result, Nebuchadnezzar descended on them like divine punishment, and devastated Jerusalem. He killed six hundred thousand Jews and took an equal number along with him as slaves.

As I was thinking about this, Nuhoor replied:

"You will also meet him soon God-wiling, but at the moment, I want to introduce you to someone else".

As he said this, he turned towards the tent and said to someone:

"Will you come out for a second, please? See who has come to meet you."

As soon as he said that, a girl came out from the tent and stood beside Nuhoor. Her attire resembled that of a princess and she looked like a fairy.

She bowed her head and greeted me respectfully. She then said to me:

"I am Shaistah. You do not know me but you are a teacher to me and due to this association, I am your spiritual child. I was once surrounded by dark shadows trying to lead me astray but I found the light of God's true religion through your writings. You are the one who first introduced me to God. I discovered the true nature of a human being's relationship with God because of your work. Look at me now! God has bestowed a great honour on me. I am to be married to a companion of a great prophet."

Saleh had shown me the scenes from Shaistah's life only a few moments ago, but the radical change in her form astonished me. The happiness I felt due to my encounter with her was difficult to put in words. I said to Shaistah:

"I heartily congratulate both of you. I hope you will invite me to your wedding!"

"Yes, definitely; that's why I called you so I could show Nuhoor that his in-laws are not ordinary people". She replied smilingly.

"In that case you selected the wrong person", I replied quickly. I then turned towards Nuhoor and said to him:

"However, Shaistah's statement is absolutely correct. Your in-laws are not ordinary people, and how could they be? Shaistah belongs to the nation of Prophet Muhammad PBUH. This relationship to the last Prophet makes her family very important."

Saleh interjected at this moment and said:

"Let's leave the decision about status and position for later. Now, I have to take Abdullah back. So, please excuse us."

We left after saying goodbye to Nuhoor and Shaistah. Saleh said to me on the way back:

"Did this take care of your sorrow?"

I had just witnessed the immense blessings of God on his servants, which had left me speechless. I therefore, kept quiet.

Saleh continued:

"This girl managed to attain such a high position because of her patience. God tested Shaistah through tough circumstances and a plain appearance. In spite of all the hardships, she remained steadfast and grateful to God; she remained devoted to him. You have seen today that those people who were not recompensed in the previous world have become entitled of a very high reward on account of their steadfastness."

I stopped walking. I looked up at the sky, saw the Master of the sky in a new light, and then bowed my head in gratitude and appreciation.

===============

Chapter 4: Naimah

As we walked along, we came close to the door that led to the Plane of Judgement. I inquired from Saleh, "Do we have to go back to the Plane of Judgement now?"

"Why? Has your interest to go there waned?" he asked in a surprised tone.

"No, it's not so. I thought that since I am already here I might meet my family as well. When we came here at the beginning, you took me up directly. By now my family members would have reached the camp for the last Prophet's nation."

"You humans are used to conveying your emotions wrapped in the garb of civility. Why do you not say clearly that you want to go to your wife? Why do you keep using the term "family members'?" Saleh commented chuckling, which made me blush. Then he smiled and said:

"Don't be embarrassed, my friend. Let's go to her. This servant has been appointed to fulfil all your desires."

The meanings and connotations of time, paths, and places had completely changed in this world. That is why the moment Saleh uttered these words, we found ourselves near the mountain that had camps of all the prophets and their nations.

"Perhaps I told you when we came here the first time that the name of this mountain is Aaráf. Remember? You went on its summit. And look, there is the camp of the nation of the last Prophet."

The area at the foot of the mountain, where we were, was quite wide, and had the capacity to accommodate a lot of people. Yet, it was jam-packed. Such a large gathering was nowhere else around the mountain.

I said to Saleh:

"It looks like all the Muslims have arrived."

"No. In fact very few are here. The nation of the last Prophet is very large. That is why the number of people from this nation who were righteous and close to God, is also very large. Otherwise most of the Muslims are still running around worriedly in the Plane of Judgement."

"Will the Muslims from my era be here too?"

"Unfortunately, there are very few of your contemporaries here. The majority are from the time closer to the demise of the last Prophet. Very few people from the last eras of humanity were able to reach here. Most of the Muslims of your era were either materialistic or sectarian. Both types are currently enjoying a tour of the Plane of Judgement! That is why you will find very few of your acquaintances here. You can meet the ones you know after entering paradise at the 'Grand Gathering at the Court'. For the time being, we are only going to meet your 'family' to give a treat to your eyes and then return immediately. The accountability may start any moment!"

"What is 'Grand Gathering at the Court?" I asked.

"After the accountability and judgement when all the people destined for Paradise have entered it, they will have a gathering in the Court of the Almighty. That gathering is known as the 'Grand Gathering at the Court'. In that court, people of Paradise will be awarded their formal titles and entitlements. It will also be an opportunity for the people to meet their Lord, as well as an occasion to honour the people who have been declared close to the Almighty."

I wanted to ask more questions but we had reached quite close to the camp.

It was a huge tent city. In this city, camps were set up according to the different periods of time. Owners of some of the tents could be seen talking to one another aside their tents. I could see many of my companions and friends who had supported me wholeheartedly in spreading the word of God. I felt such joy in my heart on seeing them that words would fail to describe. They were the ones who never let their youth, careers, families, or wishes overwhelm them. They kept all those facets of life within limits and dedicated the rest of their time, abilities, wealth, and passion in the service of God. As a reward for these sacrifices, they had achieved everlasting success before others, as promised in the world.

We saw many distinguished personalities of the Islamic history, and greeted people as we walked by. All of them invited us to dine with them in their camps but Saleh politely declined with gratitude. However, I did promise to meet them all later on.

On the way, Saleh said:

"Each and every one of these exalted persons is worthy of spending time with. It is good that you have arranged to meet them later. It won't be so easy to even make an appointment with some of them later on."

He stopped for a second and looking at me compassionately, said:

"The fact is that even getting an appointment with you won't be that easy Abdullah! You cannot comprehend it yet but you are going to be a person of high stature in this new world. But the truth is that you were always a person of high stature as per the standards of the Lord of the worlds."

As Saleh said this, he embraced me. Then he whispered in my ear, "Abdullah! It's an honour for me to accompany you."

I looked towards the sky and gently answered him, "The real honour is to worship God; to invite his people towards his worship. It's an honour for me that God bestowed the honour of doing this service to someone like me who is as worthless as a tiny grain of sand."

As I said this, my eyes started to fill with tears of gratitude.

"Yes, you are right, Abdullah. The Almighty allows a grain of sand the privilege of reflecting the glorious sunrise. If you shined like the sun, it was by his grace. But this honour is only reserved for his sincere servants who dedicate their lives to his worship; the rebellious, the instigators of evil and the neglectful people are never given this privilege."

We started walking again and came close to a beautiful and delicately woven tent. I could feel my heart beating faster. Saleh turned towards me and asked:

"Is your wife called Naimah?"

I nodded in affirmative. Saleh pointed towards the tent with his finger and said:

"That is her tent."

"Does she know that I'm here?" I asked with a pounding heart.

Saleh answered, "No." Then he gestured towards the tent and said, "This is your destination."

I slowly ambled towards the tent and, after saying Salam, sought permission to enter. My heart started pounding fiercely when I heard the voice coming from the tent:

"Who are you?"

"Abdullah."

As soon as I uttered these words, the curtain was pulled up and darkness fell in the entire world. If there was any light in the world, it was emanating solely from the face in front of me. Time, era, centuries, and moments, everything stopped. I just stood there, silently staring at her. The name Naimah means radiance. But that radiance could be so beautiful, I only realised it at that moment.

The last time when we were together, our association of a lifetime had matured into a comfortable companionship of old age. It was a time in our lives when love did not depend on beauty and youth. Nevertheless, Naimah had sacrificed all the wishes and desires of her youth for my sake. She was by my side even when I chose the thorny way over an easy life. She supported me through life's difficult moments and ups and downs to the best of her abilities, until death did us apart.

But today, as the transient curtain of death had pulled back, facing me was pearly white moon light, sparkle of the stars, shine of the sun, fragrance of the flowers, delicateness of the buds, freshness of the dew, splendour of the morning light, and beauty of the dusk twilight, all of them emanating from her face.

I was trying to analyse a companionship of years in a few moments in my thoughts. Naimah's eyes were wet as tears ran down her cheeks.

I extended my hand to wipe the tears away and taking her hands in mine, said:

"Didn't I tell you, with a little wait and perseverance, we'll win this war?"

"When did I not believe you? Now my faith has turned into reality. It feels like you went out of our home for a little while and then came back. We persevered for a short while and now we have won a great war."

"We had to win, Naimah. God never loses; and neither do people who fight for his cause. They may stay behind in the world, but they'll always be ahead of everyone else in the Hereafter."

"What happens now?" Naimah closed her eyes as she asked as if she was imagining the surroundings of Paradise, a life that was about to begin.

"We spent our mortal life in spreading the message of God. Now, he will compensate us with ever-lasting life in Paradise."

Saying so, I closed my eyes as well. I could recall every moment of my life that was full of hardship and struggle. I had dedicated the best years of my youth and adult life in the service of the religion as ordained by God. I had even devoted the diminishing strength of my middle age in his way. I was an extra-ordinarily talented and intelligent person. If I had made success in this life my goal, I would have easily achieved the pinnacle of accomplishments here. However, I had decided that if I had to make a career, an estate, a high status, and a name for myself, I would only do so for the life in Hereafter.

All my life, I had not only battled with myself over the desires of life, but I had also battled against prejudices and emotions. I never let myself be dirtied by sectarianism, personality-worship, or prejudices. I always tried to understand the religion of God with honesty and with intellect and then followed it sincerely and honestly. I spread his religion in the entire world and ignored the rebukes. God blessed me with the love and friendship of Naimah that gave me the fortitude to fight in every situation. Now, we had won our war against Satan. The struggle was over now and it was time to celebrate.

We were in that state when Saleh coughed to make us conscious of his presence. He said:

"You can have an extended meeting later. We have to go right now."

I returned to the present on hearing his words. I introduced Saleh to Naimah:

"He is Saleh," and then added with a laugh, "He is not inclined to leave me alone at any time".

Naimah looked at Saleh and said, "I have met Saleh before. He was the one who brought me here and informed me about you. Otherwise, I would have been very worried".

I turned towards Saleh and said, "When did you leave me to bring Naimah here?"

"You probably don't remember. When you were up on the summit and quietly praying to the Lord to allow you to proceed to the Plane of Judgement, I left you. Abdullah, it is your weakness as well as your strength that when you are with your Lord, you are completely oblivious to your surroundings."

"I was not in my senses a few moments ago either but you didn't care to leave me in that state!" I said, turning towards Saleh.

"Well, if I had left you two together, then our next meeting would have been after the Day of Judgement! You know, you humans are quite ungrateful, and forgetful too. Have you forgotten where you were supposed to go?"

"Ok, Naimah! We need to go. You should stay here and I'll be back shortly."

"But what about our children?" Asked Naimah.

"They're fine. Why don't you go and look for them? They will be around somewhere close by. Otherwise, I will bring them myself in a short while. Right now, I need to return to the Plane of Judgement immediately. We will be able to meet and sit together all our lives afterwards."

After Naimah's last question, I could not afford to stay there any longer, otherwise I would have had to tell her about two of our children who had not managed to make it up to here; and that would have been very agonising for her.

Naimah nodded, looking a bit puzzled.

================

On our way back, I said to Saleh:

"In this life, many families will experience quite a lot of break-ups. Some people will lose their wives and vice versa."

"Obviously, It will happen" he replied. "People had a chance to excel only in the past life which is over now. Here, if someone is left behind, nothing can be done about it. However, no one will be alone over here. No one will wait for the ones left behind. New relationships will be formed. People will find new partners. There will be new marriages."

"I don't think we will have the same kind of family system here as we had in our past life", I commented.

"You are correct. Actually, the institution of family was established in the previous world because of some basic flaws in human nature. The basic purpose of a family was to take care of minors and the elders. Men were made heads of household to give strength and stability to the family. To keep the family intact, women were made weaker than men in certain areas whereas, on the other hand, men were made dependent on women due to some of their inherent weaknesses. Women were not only a blessing for men; they were also a necessity for them. The system of the world could not have run in the absence of this arrangement. But their paths would separate now. Women will remain a source of pleasure and happiness for men but women themselves will no longer be dependent on men. For obvious reasons, their worth and importance will increase and so would their sense of importance!"

"So it would be more beneficial to be a woman in this world. A woman would be able to get a man's attention whenever she would desire. However, a man will have no control over her although he would still need her."

"Yes, you are right."

"So we men will be worse off."

"Yes", he replied.

"This is a serious problem; is there any solution to it"? I asked.

"In Paradise, there is a solution for every problem. The solution to this problem is Hoors, the Maidens of Paradise."

"But the women will be jealous of them."

"No, it will not be so. When it comes to beauty and status, the Maidens of Paradise can never compete with the women of Paradise, so the issue of jealousy will never arise. On account of their deeds, the women of Paradise will enjoy a very high status and will be more beautiful than the Maidens. They would not care about other activities and interests of their husbands. Also, bear in mind that the Paradise is the world of the Almighty and not of humans. Do you know the difference between these two worlds?"

I just looked at him with a blank expression. He answered his question himself:

"In the world of humans, one feels jealous of one's adversary in love. In this world, the adversary also becomes a beloved!"

"It looks like a convincing argument but I guess only the women of the Paradise can pass judgement on it."

"Paradise is a place for the purified. By the grace of God, their purity will not allow any negative feelings to find a place in their hearts." Instead of responding to my question directly, Saleh stated the point in principle and then continued to explain further:

"Actually you are still under the effects of the past world of humans. That was a world for trial. Therefore, negative emotions were also placed in the hearts along with the positive ones. Those negative thoughts emanated from within the human personality. Every pious man and woman was responsible for controlling those negative emotions, despite the adverse circumstances. You can understand this by the example of human secretions like sweat, faeces, urine, blood etc. which originated from within the human body but you were instructed to keep your body clean from them through ablution or taking a bath. Similarly, the negative emotions were also a filth emanating from within you. You were supposed to wash away those negative emotions like anger, hatred, falsehood, jealousy, arrogance, malice, cruelty etc., with the help of patience and resolve. Pious men and women had to bear this hardship throughout their lives. But today they will be liberated from all such hardships."

"What do you mean?" I asked.

"I mean that neither will their bodies produce any unclean secretions nor will they experience any negative thoughts or emotions. Paradise is a beautiful abode for beautiful people to live in. It has no room for ugly emotions."

"But I think the point to learn from this whole discussion is that the Maidens of Paradise are inferior to the women of Paradise and are just good enough to make do! That is why the women will not be jealous of them."

I added laughingly, "Poor Muslims were crazy for the Maidens and experienced all sorts of taunts from other people for nothing!"

Saleh responded to my joke in a serious tone and said:

"You are wrong in both cases. The fact is that men will no longer be an asset valuable enough for women to feel jealous about in Paradise. As far as the Maidens are concerned, do not insult them by calling them 'inferior' and 'just good enough to make do'! Although they are not like the women of Paradise, you still cannot consider them inferior in any aspect."

"Ok. What do they look like?"

"Where do I begin? They are the ultimate examples of femininity and the last word on physical beauty. Their unparalleled beauty and elegant appearance does not require any make up, garlands, pearl necklaces or other adornments. The most beautiful ingredients from all parts of the Universe are used for their creation. When one combines the colours of flowers, the delicacy of wind, drift of the rivers, steadiness of the earth, sparkle of the stars, scent of the blooms, light of the moon, rays of the sun, evenness of the sky, height of the peaks and depth of the valleys, only then, a Maiden of the Paradise is created.

Their splendour meets the ultimate scale of beauty. They are tall and fair with a golden complexion. Their skin is flawless from top to bottom. Their eyes are large and dark but they change their colour to match any dress. Their eyebrows are smooth and eyelashes long. They keep their gaze lowered but when they look up, that look goes through the heart like an arrow. Their faces are worthy of reading like a book, foreheads are wide, cheeks have a reddish hue, noses are straight, lips are delicate as rose petals, their teeth shine like pearls, and when they speak, their words have the sweetness of honey. Their hair is shiny, soft as silk, and dark in contrast to their fair colour, and extends to their calves. Their voices are sweet and melody to the ears, their words are like showers of pearls and their smiles can brighten up a day. Their bodies smell of the fragrance of modesty while their breaths have a beautiful aroma. The velvet dresses on their perfumed bodies and the shinning jewellery that adorns them give the appearance of the full moon playing hide and seek with the clouds."

"Have you ever seen them?" I asked.

"No. No one has ever seen them; like others, I have only heard about them and I am narrating what I have heard to you."

He then continued his discourse but turned to poetry to describe their beauty further:

I have heard when she speaks; words take the shape of flowers

If that were so, then come, let us go and try to talk to her

I have heard at night the moon stares ather throughout

That stars descend from their heights to have a peek at her

I have heard in the day butterflies tease her on her form

And at night fire flies stop and gaze at her

I have heard hereyes are like those of a gazelle,enough to kill with a look

And that deer of the whole forest come to steal a peek at her

I have heard her black eyes are enough to bring the world to its end

Thus, the kohl sellers heave a sigh at their loss looking at her

I have heard since she has started wearing ornaments

The mood of the jewels has changed to great pride

I have heard that the shape of her body is such

That the flowers shorten their petals to peek from behind

When she stops, all movements revolve around her

And when she walks, time stops to have a look at her

Even if these are all fables, all figments of imagination

Even if she is a dream,let's see if we can turn it into reality

As Saleh kept on speaking tirelessly, I started at his face in silence. When he had finished reciting the poetry, I said:

"Your words seem to be an exaggeration, a story, or a dream. Yet, I must say that even if it is a dream, it is a beautiful dream!"

"This dream has not ended yet. The physical make up of a Maiden of Paradise is like a winding brook that begins its journey as snow in the thick, dark clouds in the sky. Staying on mountaintops, it takes the shape of waterfalls and streams that run down the mountain slopes, resting a while when it reaches the planes. After caressing the dizzying heights, it flows downwards, going over mounds, and reaches the valleys where it finally submits itself to the sea of goodness, piety, and God-mindedness – the person who had led his life with steadfastness and consciousness of God. This happens because this brook does not allow itself to be polluted by any filth or impurity throughout its entire course. It keeps every unrelated gaze away from its sight and touch. It covers a distance of thousands of miles whilst maintaining its chastity; for the same reason, it does not accept anyone less than a person who is pure and unblemished. And at last, its existence, a blend of youth's rising and falling waves, merges in its own sea forever."

"I cannot decide whether I should praise the Maidens or the power of your expression", I commented.

"Praise should be solely for God. However, please remember that I am an Angel. The emotions I have just expressed are those of a human, not mine. Whatever I have learnt about human emotions and words, most of it has been due to your company. So, if you wish, you can praise yourself". Saleh replied.

"No. Praise and glory should solely be for God. But tell me something, will they be humans?"

"Yes they are also humans. Similarly, Ghilmán, the boy servants of the residents of Paradise are also humans. These boys will not grow up and will always remain boys."

"Why will they remain boys? Servants are considered to be better if they are of mature age and hence, more knowledgeable?" I immediately raised an objection.

"No, that is not the case. Despite being young, they would be extremely good judge of peoples' moods and needs. During functions in the Paradise, whenever a glass would need to be refilled, they would just have to look into the eyes of the person holding it to decide how much more of the drink is desired. So, their intelligence and understanding would be beyond comparison. However, they would retain the form of boys so that they are active and agile, capable of performing any task in the blink of an eye. Their attire, appearance, and looks would be such that they would look like precious pearls scattered around in the gathering. Another reason for them being kept as boys eternally is to avoid the need of any conjugal necessities. However, in contrast, the Maidens of Paradise would be completely mature girls who would become wives of the residents of Paradise."

"Will the Maidens and the Ghilmán be especially created for the residents of the Paradise?" I asked Saleh.

He replied, "There is a long story behind it."

"We are not short of time. Go on, tell this story too!" I said.

"Listen! Today is not the first time human beings are being presented to God for judgement."

"What do you mean? Was there a Day of Judgement even earlier?"

"No, there was no Day of Judgement earlier. However, all human beings have been created once before."

"Are you referring to the Covenant of Alast?"

"When you enter Paradise, you can ask the Almighty as to when that event took place. All I know is that it happened once. In fact, the trial that human beings were put through this time was preceded by another such incident. The foremost event that took place was an occasion when God offered an opportunity to all of his living creations to enjoy his company eternally in the Paradise. But to be able to do so, they first had to spend some time in the world without being able to see him. All they were supposed to do was to obey his orders, worship him, and submit to him without seeing him. Governance of the world was to be temporarily handed over in trust to the beings who accepted this challenge. The beings who accepted the challenge had to show that despite being the empowered rulers they were ready to obey him without seeing him. Those who used this authority and free will correctly were to be rewarded with the eternal company of God in the Paradise whereas those who failed this test were to face punishment in the Hell."

"What happened then?" I asked.

"Well, all living beings got scared and stepped back. The reason was that the Paradise was beautiful but the Hell was equally terrifying! You just saw hardships of the Judgement Day with your own eyes. Who in his right mind would present himself for such a trial?"

"And probably, we the emotional humans opted for this test." I said.

"Yes, that is exactly what happened. But, the decision to go through the test from God was taken by the collective soul of the entire humanity. Thus, it was a pre-requisite for God's ultimate standard of justice to create every single human being and ask directly about the extent of the test he or she was willing to undergo.

Abdullah! This happened because your Lord is not unfair to anyone, not even in the smallest way. That is why he first created all human beings and then unveiled his complete scheme of the test to them. Obviously, majority of the human beings were already prepared to take this test. Thus, they agreed to it being fully aware of its implications.

However, for those humans who refused to take such a risk, the Almighty decided that they would take up the role of those children who die before reaching maturity. The same children will then become Ghilmán and Hoors.''

''Did the rest of the humanity agree to such a tough trial?''

''God showed his ultimate benevolence even in this matter. As you are aware, not everyone was tested in the same manner in the world. Each individual chose his or her trial that day. Those who had a lot of resolve chose the times of the prophets for their test. Their test was to believe in and support the prophets during those eras of widespread ignorance. The prime condition for their success was that they had to stand firm even in the face of worst opposition, to remain steadfast despite all kinds of challenges and to pass on the message of their prophets to other people. That is why there was a huge reward for them in the Hereafter; however, in case they denied and rejected the prophets, they had to face a severe punishment as they had the benefit of direct guidance by the prophets. Examples of such people include Abu-Bakr, may God be pleased with him, on one hand, and people like Abu-Lahab on the other hand, who was one of the worst enemies of the truth.

The second, and lower, level of the test was whereby people chose to become part of the nations of the prophets after the prophets had passed away. Their test was to protect themselves from going astray, sectarianism, deviations, and ignorance of later times while holding steadfast to the divine law. They were also expected to promote good deeds and to help stop people from bad deeds. Those responsibilities were assigned to them as they had the teachings of the prophets to turn to for guidance, and because they were born as Muslims. Therefore, they did not have to pass through difficult trials to recognise the right path. It also meant that they had more guidance available to them compared to other people; hence, they had greater opportunities to reap rewards. But in case of negligence, their accountability was to be very tough as well.''

''Other Muslims and I belonged to this group, did we not?''

''Yes, you are right. The third group comprised of people who selected an even easier test. They were born in circumstances where they did not have access to any direct guidance from the prophets. Their test was based on the innate divine guidance present in the nature of every human being, that is, a test based on belief in Oneness of God and universal moral values. Unlike other Muslims, they were not subject to the tough trials of following the divine law nor of the companionship of prophets through arduous times. Obviously, their accountability is also going to be quite lenient; accordingly their risk of facing dire punishments is also low and the opportunity to reap great rewards for them is also less."

"What about the prophets?"

"They were the ones who decided to take the toughest test. That is why they received direct guidance from God and the criterion for their accountability was extremely strict too. You are well aware of what happened to Prophet Jonah. He had not committed a sin; he had only reached an incorrect conclusion and acted upon it without divine approval. As a consequence, the Almighty locked him up in the belly of a fish."

Saleh summarised his lengthy conversation in these short words:

"The real principle at work for all of the groups is the same. Those who received more guidance will face stricter accountability and consequently, will reap either greater reward or worse punishment. Those who received lesser guidance will face lighter accountability and therefore lesser rewards or punishment. However, the decision about which of the three groups each human being belonged to was taken by human beings themselves and was not decided by the Almighty."

"That implies that if I received more guidance in the world, it was at my own request."

"Yes, you are absolutely right! That is why you have managed to attain such a high level of success today. If you had not appreciated that guidance, you would have been a candidate for equally severe punishment."

"Oh dear, I can't believe that I took such a huge risk!"

"That was the rule of your world - No risk No gain!"

I truly realised at that moment, the significance of what I had achieved as well as the magnitude of the danger I had managed to avoid. Spontaneously, I fell down on the ground in prostration. I kept thanking my Lord for a long time for helping me pass this test. Then, Saleh tapped me on my back and said:

"Get up, Abdullah!"

I got up and holding Saleh with both of my hands, said:

"Saleh, I will never die now! I will never experience illness, old age, fear, grief, sadness, and hopelessness in my life. I feel like jumping, dancing, laughing, and screaming to tell the whole world that I have succeeded! I want to proclaim the beginning of my rule today! I want to announce that today is the day when my life begins!"

Saleh just kept looking at me silently with a smile on his face. When I became quite, he said:

"Indeed, life will begin; but before that, we need to go back to the Plane of Judgement. We have to witness many events. God has given you a unique opportunity. Come on. Let's go back to the Plane of Judgement."

===============

Chapter 5: Two Friends

Once again, we stood in the Plane of Judgement. Naimah's question about our children was still ringing in my ears.

I said to Saleh, "I want to see my kids; the ones who are here".

"It means that you are now mentally prepared to meet them in their sad state."

"Yes, I am ready. I could not find the courage earlier. Even the shock of seeing my teacher in this place was too much for me. After I saw my daughter-in-law Huma as well, I was at the end of my wits. But I realise now that it is time to face the bitter truth."

"Well, we are still in the Day of Judgement. It is only after entering the Paradise that you would be completely relieved of every shock, fear, and grief". Saleh rationalised the sadness written all over me.

"Yes, Holy Qur'an has described Paradise similarly. It described it as a place where there would be no regret from the past and no fear for the future", I referred to a verse from the Qur'an.

In reply, Saleh explained another important concept:

"Yes. Paradise is like that. When accountability starts, Paradise and Hell would be brought closer so that people can see them simultaneously. When the Almighty makes a decision about granting Paradise or Hell to a person, that person will also be informed about what he or she did not get. That is, people would be told in clear terms about the torments they have been saved from or the potential blessings they have been deprived of in this world."

"What do you mean?" I sought further details.

"When it is announced that a person will go to Paradise, he will also be shown the likely place in Hell where he could have landed, and he was saved only by the grace of God. Similarly, when a person is assigned to Hell, he will also be shown what choice location was reserved for him in Paradise that he had lost due to his misdeeds.

"That would be a huge torture even by itself!" I exclaimed.

"Yes, it will be the first and the foremost happiness for the people of Paradise to know what they have been saved from, whereas the first torment for the people of Hell will be to know that they have been deprived of such great blessings and high stature forever. You may remember I had explained earlier that when all the souls chose their tests, the ones who opted for high positions in the Paradise had also risked equally worse positions in Hell in case of failure. Hence, today the joy of attaining an exalted position in the Paradise will be accompanied by the good news of having been saved from the worst parts of Hell; similarly, the heart-sinking news of a life in Hell would be worsened by the equally depressing regret of having failed to achieve a high rank in the Paradise."

"Oh my God!" the words escaped my lips involuntarily.

Engrossed in the discussion, we moved ahead at a leisurely pace. The condition of the Plane of Judgement was the same as earlier, or had perhaps become worse. I could see and hear the same sighs, cries, wails, distress, remorse, and penitence as before. People portrayed the same misery and despair as I had seen earlier. A question was etched on every face – 'What now'. However, the answer was nowhere to be found. There was torment on every face and no relief was in sight. I could not stop wondering what my son and daughter would be going through at this time.

Two girls were sitting on hard, rocky earth in the same Plane of Judgement, totally helpless. Their eyes were visibly swollen as they had been crying their hearts out. Their bodies looked exhausted, faces were distraught and eyes lifeless. Sorrow was all over their faces and could be seen even from a distance. One who looked more miserable said to the other:

"Leila, I can't believe that what is happening is real. Humans can rise after death like this; a new life can begin after the life in the world. It is so unbelievable. Oh, how I wish it were a nightmare. I wish I would open my eyes and find myself lying on my soft bed in my air-conditioned bedroom! Then I would go to college and tell you that I had such a horrible dream... I wish it were a dream! I wish it was a dream!"

She started to weep bitterly. Leila said to her:

"It does not matter anymore whether you believe or not, Aasmah. It is the reality and not a dream. In fact, what we had witnessed in the previous world was somewhat like a dream. We have only woken up now in the true sense of the word. But what's the point of realising it now?"

Both of them were quiet for some time. Finally, Leila said wistfully to Aasmah:

"If only, I had not befriended you! If only, I had not followed your ways!"

"Yes... and if only I had followed your ways! Both of us would not have been in this state. I wonder what would happen next". Aasmah said, in a remorseful tone.

After a brief silence, Aasmah added:

"Leila, tell me, how long did we live in the world?"

"I don't know... may be a day... or ten days; or perhaps only an afternoon. It used to feel as if that life would never end. Now it seems like a dream."

"I can't even recall any part of that dream."

As Aasmah said so, she was lost in her thoughts of the life gone by. Maybe she was trying to flip through the pages of her past to try to find a good deed that could comfort her today. However, she could not recall any such act. Each memory that she recalled seemed like a charge sheet of her misdemeanours.

"Don't I look awesome today?" Asked Aasmah, as she gracefully twirled her body round and took a couple of steps to stand in front of Leila like a model. Leila sat on a bench in the shade of a tree in her college, sipping juice. Her dear friend Aasmah stood facing her, showing off her new dress. Leila did not respond. Aasmah asked again:

"Come on. Tell me, how do I look?"

"You have not left much to imagination despite wearing clothes!" Leila finally responded casually, taking another sip of juice.

"What...?"

"What else! No doubt, the print of the fabric looks superb but it reveals your body more than it hides. I know you like sleeveless blouses but even your shoulders are fully exposed in this dress."

"Well, well... madam! You have no right to criticise me as I only wore this Eastern dress due to your squabbling. Otherwise, as you know, I only like jeans and T-shirts."

"Come on Aasmah. That is also only partially true; the fact is that you only like to wear fitting jeans and body-hugging sleeveless shirts."

"Do you expect me to come to college wearing a Burqa?" Aasmah replied sarcastically.

"Aasmah, we study in a co-education institution. It is our responsibility to be careful about how we dress". Leila made a sage point.

"I am sorry, but I don't agree. In my opinion, it is actually the responsibility of the guys to guard their gaze. Why do the clerics not ask them to do so?"

"Of course it is their responsibility, but don't we also have some responsibility?"

Aasmah immediately responded in a combative tone:

"Does that mean we are not even allowed to dress the way we like? Are we not allowed to look beautiful?"

"Of course you are allowed to wear what you like and look beautiful, but as long as it is within the limits of modesty."

“Come on, please stop. Don’t talk like Madam Shaistah. She always lectures on modesty and now you are doing the same. Listen, do not to follow her example otherwise you will end up like her. You will also fail to find a suitable match and will be left all alone due to your modesty!”

“Aasmah, it is quite bad of you to say so! You should not make fun of such a nice and honourable teacher. By the way, it is not her fault if she could not get married; rather, moral decline of our society is to be blamed for it.”

“Ok, forget it! You know what? Supermodel actress Champa has just launched a new design that I am wearing today. The person who designed it holds international repute. You know what, this suite cost me a lot! Although you refused to attend the exhibition with me, it was so much fun. A fashion show was also held at the end. Champa wore the same design at the show that I am wearing today. Why don’t you make one for yourself too?”

“So that after I wear it my parents can kick me out of my home!”

“Don’t worry. You are always welcome to stay with me! Your family is quite orthodox. I like your mother, Naimah Auntie, but she is always admonishing. Moreover, uncle Abdullah... it seems like he will only rest after he has spread Islam in the whole world! The rest of your brothers and sisters are also the same except your brother Jamshaid, who is cool. That is probably why he lives on his own.”

“Actually, Papa thinks that he is the one who has gone far from him due to his deeds. Mama is of the opinion that I have also been spoiled due to his bad influence.”

“I don’t see anything wrong with you. You seem quite virtuous to me.”

“What? I am virtuous... Come on! It is due to the habits formed in childhood that I pray regularly and fast once a year during Ramadan. Other than that, I do the same stuff as you do, because of your influence.”

“But look how much fun you have with me. One hardly lives for 50 or 60 years. We might as well enjoy it to the fullest!”

"No doubt it is fun being with you. However, Papa says that in the Hereafter where one day will be equal to thousands of years, it would be extremely difficult to account for even one day! He says that all the joys of these 50 years will vanish in thin air if that happens. My sisters, mother and brother Anwar, all of them, try to lead virtuous lives because of his influence."

"Don't talk about them, Leila. They lead a boring life, not a virtuous life! Even thinking about such a boring life sends a chill down my spine! That is why I seldom visit your home these days. All they talk about is Paradise! The only discussion in your household is about the Hereafter and virtuous deeds. 'Say your prayers regularly, try to fast, keep your head and bosom covered', etc. I don't like all this rubbish."

Expressions of displeasure appeared on Leila's face on hearing this. She replied:

"Don't talk about my family like that. They have never said anything of the sort to you. They do all these things themselves and only give me sincere advice. They have never tried to admonish you. Only once did my dad say to you that 'since you are Leila's friend, try to be a friend who ends up as a friend in the Paradise as well. I hope that both of you will never indulge in deeds that bring you displeasure of the Almighty. It would be a shame if you two were to end up cursing your friendship on the Day of Judgement!'"

"I am sorry, Leila. I think you took offence to what I said. But do you realise that you have also repeated your father's sermon to me just now. All they think about is the Day of Judgement!"

Leila looked even more infuriated when she heard Aasmah's comments. Aasmah immediately sensed it and said:

"I am sorry dear, please don't mind! I promise I will not utter a single word about your dad again. Let's go to the canteen, I am really hungry."

===============

The heat in the Plane of Judgement was unbearable. I was trying to figure out whether people were suffering more due to thirst or because of fear of being thrown in the raging fires of Hell. I was engrossed in these thoughts when I heard Saleh's voice:

"Abdullah get ready, I am taking you to meet your daughter."

Unconsciously, I bit my lower lip. As we moved forward, we saw two girls sitting on rough and rocky ground. I recognised both of them from a distance. One of them was Leila, my youngest and most beloved daughter. The other was Aasmah, Leila's best friend.

The weather was extremely hot. Sweat was pouring from bodies like water. Hunger had already disappeared because of anxiety, but the thirst had made everybody miserable. Both of them were also exhausted due to thirst. Aasmah's condition was dire and due to the intensity of thirst, she was licking the sweat dripping from her arms. Obviously, how could that quench her thirst? If anything, it made it even worse. On the other hand, Leila was sitting with her head on her knees.

Aasmah was the only offspring of a very wealthy family. God had endowed her with everything... beauty, wealth, and status. Parents had their loving daughter schooled at the best educational institutions. Right from childhood, she was not exposed even slightly to Urdu. Arabic and recitation of Qur'an with its meanings were out of question. The influence of English medium schools was so profound that she could speak English perhaps better than native speakers could. But in such schools, English was not taught as a language. It was learnt in an atmosphere subservient to a supposedly superior foreign culture. Thus with the language, Western culture had also entered her life along with its accoutrements. In this culture, others were greeted with a 'hello' or a 'hi' instead of 'Salam'. Jeans and shirts were the preferred dress and Western music and films were considered essential pre-requisites of life. However, Aasmah had a long and wealthy legacy and did not belong to a family of upstarts. Consequently, a degree of refinement, etiquettes, and respect for elders was still a part of her personality, although it was only skin-deep. For this reason, I had tolerated their friendship in the hope that Leila's company may have a positive influence on Aasmah.

Their friendship began while they were at college. I do not know what was common in their attitude and chemistry that despite coming from such diverse backgrounds, this college camaraderie transformed into a life-long friendship. However, unfortunately in this friendship Aasmah was influenced by Leila to a much lesser degree and Leila accepted Aasmah's influence a lot more.

No doubt, Leila was my daughter, but regrettably, she could not adopt my philosophy of life. More than me, she was influenced by Jamshaid, my elder son who like her, was also wandering somewhere in the Plane of Judgement. On one hand, she was spoiled by her elder brother and on the other by her friendship with Aasmah. Aasmah was an only child and consequently, had been overly pampered by her parents all her life. The result was that today she had to receive her share of heartache. Most children of my era went astray due to the excessive love and spoiling of their parents.

Children have been dear to parents through all ages. In my time, however, a unique phenomenon developed. Parents became infatuated with the love of their children to such an extent that they became their puppets. Perhaps this was the effect of having fewer children. In olden days, every household had eight to ten children. Therefore, parents could not pay more than a certain degree of attention to each child. But in my time, most households had only two or three children, and the parents devoted their lives to providing them with every blessing in the world. They met their undue demands and put up with their tantrums. They also avoided inculcating discipline in them. They not only tried to meet their legitimate desires, but also those that were un-due. They spent their wealth on their children's education. For the sake of a better future, they sent them to the West. Tragically, those children never returned to their motherland and settled in the developed countries, leaving their old parents alone. Even if that did not happen, the role of parents in this new way of life was quite limited. However, despite all of the changes, the parents were happy and took great pleasure in seeing their children thoroughly Westernized.

In the opinion of parents of my time, it was more important for their children to learn to speak English in a foreign accent than to know the fundamentals of their religion. It was more important for them to get their children educated in pricey educational institutions than to teach them about faith and moral values. The children learnt the lessons of self-interest and selfishness from their parents instead of possessing true love of God, love for his people, a desire to serve humanity, and work for its betterment. They spent their time watching television where they received daily lessons in materialism and uninhibited fulfilment of desires rather than benefiting from the company of the family elders and learning about modesty, morals, and etiquettes. The world and success in this world was presented to these children as the most important goal instead of eternal success.

The concepts of God, religion and Hereafter were relegated to mere formality and rituals. The ultimate standard of being religious was to arrange for a Moulvi to teach the child Qur'an in Arabic, and that too without translation. As far as the meanings of Holy Book were concerned, the Moulvi would not know them, neither would the parents, and hence the child would never know them either. If they had understood Qur'an by reading its translation in their mother tongue, they would have found that Qur'an was devoid of talk of worldly materialistic goals just as much as their lives were devoid of the talk of the Hereafter.

The reason for this may or may not have been understood clearly by many people in the previous world but was crystal-clear to everyone today. Time spent in the previous world was in fact not the real life. That time was merely an examination or an afternoon spent by a traveller in a roadside cafe. Real Life was about to begin now, a never-ending harsh reality that was staring everyone in the face today.

As we reached closer, Aasmah saw me. She nudged Leila. Leila raised her head and looked up. Her gaze met mine. When I saw the helplessness, horror, and grief in her eyes, my heart felt like being torn apart. She got up, ran towards me, and embraced me tightly while crying loudly. She was inconsolable, and the only words coming out of her mouth were, 'Papa, Papa"! I kept myself composed with great difficulty. I felt that if she continued to cry perhaps the self-control holding my emotions would fail. I said to her as I stroked her hair:

"Stop crying, my child. Did I not repeatedly try to make you learn to live for this day? Did I not say that the world is nothing but a façade?"

"Yes, you were right, but I failed to see the reality". While saying so her sobs became even louder.

She was clinging to me. In my mind, running like a movie, I could see her life story from birth, childhood, adolescence, and adulthood to various other stages. Sometimes, she appeared like a doll lying on the bed whose crying would make me concerned. Sometimes, dressed in a frock she looked like a fairy that could take my breath away with every little movement of hers. At times, she appeared like an innocent flower bud standing there in her school uniform, carrying her school bag. I could see her dressed in college uniform, looking like a flower in bloom; and then, I could see her in her wedding dress. She, my flesh and blood, was crying in my arms in extreme distress, looking like a picture of utter hopelessness and fear.

I felt as if someone had driven a cold chisel through my heart. I held her by her arms and moved her away from me. I then stood up, holding my head in my hands. Leila spoke in a sobbing voice:

"I have found no one here from amongst my family. My husband and my children are not around, nor is there anyone from your side of the family except brother Jamshaid. He is in a dire state, Papa! He has been desperately looking for you. You are his only hope."

I looked at Leila and said:

"That stupid boy had pinned his hopes on wrong things in the previous world and even now he is pinning his hopes on the wrong person. In the world, he had rested all his hopes in his business, wife, and children. He is now facing the consequences of doing so. Now he is pinning his hopes on me although I cannot do anything."

In the meantime, Aasmah also came close. After hearing me, she said:

"Uncle, the only hope I had was in you. Now, even you have given up on me."

"Aasmah, do you recall what I had said when you came to our house with Leila for the first time?"

"Papa, I remember what you said to Aasmah". Leila answered instead of Aasmah. She continued:

"You said to her, 'You are a friend of my daughter. Be a friend who would be with her in Paradise as well. I hope that both of you do not annoy God and consequently, end up in a difficult place together. If that happens, both of you may end up blaming your friendship for your misery, on the Day of Judgement.'"

After saying so, Leila started to cry again. Aasmah also began to sob.

I turned round and looked towards Saleh who had been standing there quietly through this dialogue. I was hoping in my heart that he might say something that would raise their hopes. When he saw me looking at him, he said:

"Abdullah, obviously, everybody's fate is entirely in the hands of God. Every action of a human being, even as tiny as a grain of barley, will be present in his or her Book of Deeds. Every action will be scrutinised today. Motives, triggers, instigators, circumstances, actions, and their consequences, all will be analysed in minute detail. Angels, physical environs, organs and limbs, in short, everything will be a witness. It will become absolutely clear that every good or bad deed is worthy of some reward or punishment. The reward of a good deed would range from ten to seven hundred times whereas the reward for actions done with steadfastness and in support of the religion of God will be innumerable. In contrast, bad deeds will be penalised only as much as the effect of the deed itself. However, if unrepentant sins like polytheism, murder, and fornication are included in a person's deeds, they will destroy that person. Furthermore, sins like usurping the rights of orphans, taking undue share from inheritance, slander, and other similar crimes are so heinous that they would negate all good deeds and may take that person straight to Hell.

These are the basic principles of reward and punishment. Based on these, the Almighty will take just decisions. Rest assured no one would be treated unfairly even as much as a grain of barley. As far as your children are concerned, the only hope is what I have already mentioned to you. Except for people like you, who have already been declared successful as they took precedence in embracing or supporting the truth, rest of the people with true faith in their hearts would face accountability and would then be spared, eventually. You know your children better than I do. So you would have a better idea of the likelihood of their success."

"I am more concerned about my son", I replied.

This reply encompassed all my assessments, hopes, and fears. I further added:

"He was very fond of posh cars, big houses, and getting rich. If someone is hooked on these things, he can end up with any ill fate. Such people often lose the ability to differentiate between right and wrong as well as permissible and un-permissible means of earning one's livelihood. Even if they manage to avoid the illegitimate sources of income, they often fall prey to afflictions like extravagance, negligence, pomp and show, miserliness, arrogance, and lack of awareness of rights of other people etc. All these habits can take them to that tough spot of accountability in the Court of the Almighty from where, it is very difficult to escape unscathed."

Unexpectedly, Aasmah replied in response to my statement:

"Leila used to say all this to me after listening to you. She also gave me some of your books to read but I could not understand them, as I did not know how to read Urdu. It is my ill fortune that I wasted my entire life in negligence, love of the world, following latest fashions, pomp and show, extravagance, and arrogance. I was obsessed about looking beautiful. I wasted millions on jewellery, clothes, and cosmetics but I never spent anything on the poor. If I ever did anything for them, I considered it a big favour to them although God had endowed us with a lot of wealth and prosperity. Not only this, when I was angry, I used to take it out on my subordinates and servants. I was of the opinion that modest clothes were actually a symbol of poverty. Bad habits like backbiting, badmouthing, and spitefulness did not bother me and I considered them as trivial. I did not know that these trivial misdeeds would come back to haunt me in this manner today. I just did not know..."

As Aasmah said this, she broke down in tears again. Leila commented in a very sad tone:

"We met Aasmah's parents. They were in bad shape! I wonder what will happen to them." Then she looked at me and said:

"Papa, what will happen to me?" As Leila said this, tears began to roll down her cheeks.

"You just have to wait, my baby. It looks like it will not be long before the accountability begins. I have pinned my hopes on God's mercy. Considering that you have endured so much hardship today, he will forgive those sins that you committed just because you took them to be trivial."

"Alas, Papa! I wish I had followed your advice! You repeatedly tried to make me understand that Faith does not mean reciting a statement only. It means making God the prime focus of one's life. You used to say that God does not need rituals of our worship; he wants to see our hearts laden with true faith. I remember you saying that he does not care for a few half-hearted prostrations, rather he desires a servant who is truly dedicated to him. Faith was a part of my life but I did not allow it to engulf my personality. I did pray to God at your insistence but his remembrance did not become the focus of my life. I used to fast during the month of Ramadan but I could not nurture true piety in my heart. I had to do all what was ordained by God for only fifty or sixty years in the world, but over here centuries have passed roaming around helplessly in this heat and hardship."

On hearing Leila, Aasmah put her hand on her shoulder and said whilst sobbing, "At least, you are better than I am. In my life, I did not even pray or fast. Moral depravities, showing off, extravagant spending, arrogance, violation of other peoples' rights, etc. are all in addition to them. What will happen to me? I can see no other outcome for me apart from Hell!"

Aasmah started to weep bitterly. It looked like my heart would give up. I did not have any strength left in me to stay with them any longer. Saleh appreciated my state and said to them:

"Abdullah has to leave now. Both of you should wait for the decision of the Almighty. It would not be long before the accountability starts."

After saying so, he moved ahead, taking me along, holding my hand. I wanted to say a few words of consolation to Leila but when I turned back, I was shocked to see that the scene had changed completely. We were now standing somewhere else.

"I had to take you out of there rather quickly Abdullah, or else you would have been hurt even more. Would you like to meet your son now"? Saleh asked.

"No, I do not have the strength to face anymore of this at the moment." I replied in a definite tone. My heart had now sunk deep in a sea of sorrow. I wished dearly that I could somehow return toEarth and dedicate my life to a better upbringing of Leila. I appreciated that it was not possible. Another thought came to my mind like a poisonous snake. I asked Saleh:

"Saleh, am I also responsible for Leila's plight? Do you think I am answerable?"

"No, it is not the case. Look! Even the offspring of a prophet like Noah, Peace be upon him, ended up in trouble. However, it was not Noah's fault. The main obligation of a human being is to pass the correct message onto others. The decision of accepting orrejecting the message lies with the individuals themselves. Leila made her own decisions. As such, you are not responsible for her plight."

I felt as if a burden had been lifted off my shoulders. However, the very next moment I realised something very frightening in my heart. What would happen if I ended up in the dock because of my daughter? I realised that I would have no qualms in letting my dear daughter be thrown in Hell in order to save my life. It was so because the punishment of this day was so severe that no relation or association was of any consequence when compared to it.

===============

Chapter 6: Whose Kingdom is it Today?

The environment of Plane of Judgement was harsh and stressful. In addition to the callous surroundings, people were also going through mental anguish of uncertainty about their future. They were experiencing severe stress, bitterness, and anger. This bitterness was not only directed at their own selves, but also at their leaders who had led them astray. Consequently, whenever the followers found such leaders, they beat them up mercilessly. It worked as a prelude to the actual punishment.

The Plane of Judgement was littered with such scenes. People were beating up other people and venting their anger on them: Followers on their leaders, youngsters on their elders, and disciples on the clerics. But it was of no benefit now! Nevertheless such scenes were in a way a source of amusement for those worried and wretched souls.

We kept moving ahead amidst these scenes. On the way, I said to Saleh:

"I am concerned that in the previous world we used to get distraught due to shortages of electricity and intense heat even though it was for a short period. Such a long time has elapsed over here and people have not had any respite so far. I do not experience the hardships of this environment due to your companionship. But the people who are here are being dealt very badly."

"Mind your words, Abdullah. They are not being treated badly. Justice is being done to them. No doubt, they are being dealt with severely. It is for this very reason that all other creations had refused to assume the burden of decision making and power in the world so as to avoid this very stringent test of reward and punishment today."

"If ordinary people have to face such severe hardships, I cannot visualise what would be happening to those who had power and decision making status on behalf of the people."

I was thinking about the corrupt rulers and dishonest public servants when I made this comment.

"Do you want to see what is happening to them?" Saleh asked.

I nodded. Saleh spoke as he started to move in a different direction:

"Until now, we were in an area for holding people who have yet to undergo accountability. The case of the people you have referred to is similar to those who were foremost in submission to the truth; the latter are currently standing beneath the Throne, surrounded by the rewards of God, and will not face any accountability apart from the mere formality of the announcement of their success. Likewise but conversely, Hell has been decided due to their bad deeds for some unfortunate souls. We are heading in their direction now."

As we progressed, the intensity and severity of the heat continued to increase rapidly. I realised it when I noticed an increase in the quantity of sweat dripping from the people. Sweat was not coming out in drops. It was streaming down. However, the ground was scorching hot and as soon as the drops of sweat touched it, they evaporated. Due to thirst, the lips of these people were protruding out.

They were gasping as if a camel parched with excessive thirst, but to find any water here was out of question!

Terror was predominant on their faces, more so than the signs of distress. The reason for the terror also became apparent soon.

Suddenly, there was a commotion in the crowd. People started running helter-skelter. When the crowd dispersed, I saw two angels running after a person. They were similar to those we had come across while going to the Throne earlier. One had a whip of fire and the other's whip had nails on it.

Their target was trying his best to save himself. But the angels would not leave his side. It soon became apparent that the angels were deliberately trying to tire him out. They would come near him and whip him once and say, “O ruler, get up and take a walk in your country”. As soon as the whip hit him, he would fall down, scream and cry in pain, get up and start running again. The angels would also repeat their act.

It did not take me long to recognise the person. Saleh also introduced him:

“He was the head of state of your country.”

In a short while, the head of state had been run down again after being beaten by whips of fire and nails. Thereafter, the angels started tying him with a long chain glowing like red ambers from being heated up in fire. The head of state was helplessly moaning and pleading for mercy, but it seemed that these angels did not know the meaning of the word. They kept doing their job mercilessly. When his entire body had been chained, other angels arrived.

The first team said to them:

“We have captured the head of state. You now need to go and round up all his supporters, lackeys, courtiers, and friends who were party to this ill-fated man’s cruelty and corruption.”

Consequently, there was a similar chaos again in the crowd, with people running, fighting and being beaten up.

In a short while, a large group had been assembled that included ministers, advisers, bureaucrats, relatives, rural landlords, industrialists, and all types of un-savoury characters. The angels grabbed them by their hair and started dragging them with their faces on the ground. When they passed by us we could smell their skins burning.

As I started to feel sick from it, Saleh immediately put his hand on my back which made the sickening odour disappear, allowing me to breathe fresh air again. They dragged them on and took them further away to the left. I kept staring at the patches of blood and lines drawn out on the ground by their bodies that were left behind.

==============

After seeing this horrific scene, a sigh escaped my lips involuntarily. I thought:

"Where is their authority now? Where are the days of luxury and extravagance? Where are those magnificent palaces, those corridors of power, lavish clothes, wasteful foreign trips, spectacular cars, grandeur, pride, and majesty? Ah! They chose a horrendous and perpetual misery for such trivial and temporary gratifications."

Saleh said:

"They were all cruel, corrupt, and extravagant; the decision about their ill-fates had already been taken in the previous world. However, it is not their real punishment. The real punishment will be meted out to them in Hell. The angels are taking them in that vicinity. From there, they will be taken for accountability where they will hear the verdict of eternal disgrace and punishment. Thereafter, they will be taken back to the same spot to our left, from where, one after the other, they will be thrown in Hell in groups."

On hearing about accountability, I instinctively thought about the time and asked Saleh:

"Saleh, our Prophet's prayer was accepted a long time ago. But why has the accountability not commenced so far?"

"To you it looks like a long time as you are in the Plane of Judgement and here the time passes very slowly. However, under the Throne only a very short time has elapsed. Do you want to know why it has taken even this much time?"

"You had told me that it is because of the people who are to be pardoned on the basis of hardships they are undergoing here. It will be used as an excuse for their reprieve."

"Yes, that is one of the reasons. But the second reason is to make people realise that over here, total and absolute authority is in the hands of God. The point is, Abdullah, human beings did not appreciate their forgiving and merciful Master. Today, that Master is making those people realise that human beings are entirely dependent on him and at the same time, they are worthless for him.

The first manifestation of his power and grandeur was the Dooms Day when the world of the people was destroyed and everything they possessed was ruined. The entire might of human beings was not able to save them from that horrifying incident. The second occasion is today, the Day of Resurrection, when everyone has truly understood that there is no worth or value of anybody in God's presence. The third occasion will commence shortly, that is, the Accountability, when God will take the control of Skies and Earth directly in his own hands."

"Was it not so up till now?"

"No, it has not been like this so far. Until now, as is apparent, angels have run the system of this Universe as per the commands of the Almighty. Soon he will take control of all affairs of the Universe directly in his own hands so that all creatures including the Jinn, human beings, and angels realise that all authority and power are solely in God's hands. Presently, the entire Universe that was spread across an unlimited distance over the skies is being pulled back. You are aware that in the previous world, this Universe was spreading further by the second. Now at God's command, distances are shrinking and the multiple galaxies, stars and planets spread all over the Universe are being made to come close again."

"Why is it so?" I asked, surprised.

"God Almighty will distribute them as rewards amongst the inhabitants of Paradise. Thereafter, those who have been rewarded will establish their dominions and authority there. This act of consolidation of the Universe is what the glorious Qur'an had referred to as wrapping up of the skies around God's right hand."

Having said so, Saleh looked towards the sky. I also followed.

The Sun was still burning bright. I noticed for the first time that the Moon was also present close to the Sun but it had lost its glow and was slowly moving towards the Sun.

On seeing this, Saleh said:

"Today, the earth, and skies have transformed into something totally different. The earth has swollen and become huge and its size has increased tremendously."

"I remember that the diameter of planet Earth was twenty five thousand kilometres."

"But now there has been a manifold increase in it. In addition, it has become more beautiful and picturesque than ever before. Archangel Raphael had blown the trumpet twice. On the first sound, everything was destroyed, but on the second sound, human beings had risen again. Between these two sounds, on God's command, planet Earth became larger and the angels created magnificent homes, palaces, and gardens on it for the residents of Paradise. In addition, they created the best facilities for relaxation and amusement, as well as a new world whose beauty is simply beyond your imagination. Every dweller of Paradise will be given a home on this Earth, along with large plots of land to use as they may wish. In the centre of Earth will be volcanoes with scorching lava and brooks of boiling water; this will be the abode of the dwellers of Hell."

I tried to summarise what he had just stated:

"I was already aware of what you have explained by reading verses of the glorious Qur'an. As per Qur'an, the owners of Earth would be pious servants of God. It states that the surface of Earth would be transformed into Paradise, which would become the abode of the people of Paradise. In the centre of Earth would be the dwellers of Hell. The stars and galaxies would be distributed amongst the dwellers of Paradise as gifts and dominions. By the way, what will be in them?"

"These details will be revealed in the Grand Gathering at the Court. Do you remember that we had talked about the Grand Gathering at the Court earlier?"

"Yes, you had said that after accountability and judgement, all people destined for Paradise would be presented in the Court of the Almighty; that meeting is known as the Grand Gathering at the Court. During this, the dwellers of Paradise will be awarded their formal titles and entitlements. This will also be an opportunity for the people to meet their Lord as well as an occasion to honour people considered to be worthy of being close to the Almighty."

"Yes. That day, rewards will be given and tasks will also be assigned."

I noticed that the lightless Moon had now merged into the Sun. On seeing this, Saleh said:

"The signs manifest in the sky are changing. Merger of the Moon into the Sun is one of them. This implies that all skies have been now been folded. Any moment now, Almighty Lord of the Universe will become apparent to everyone and the much-awaited Court of Accountability will commence. At that time, you and the entire world will find out who is this most esteemed and supreme entity called the God Almighty."

Saleh's sentence had not even finished when there was a loud bang. Everyone was shaken up. As the noise came from the sky, everyone's gaze turned upwards.

Saleh and I also looked up like everybody else. An astonishing scene appeared right away.

There was a large breach in the sky. A little while later it ruptured and shattered into small fragments like the clouds. The breeches took the shape of multiple gates formed in the sky.

From every opening, huge armies of angels began to descend to the earth. They were so many that any sort of counting or estimate was futile. There were various groups of angels and every group had their own appearance and dress that was unique. The angels began to descend in the centre of the Plane of Judgement where they encircled a vast elevated area.

==============

The angles were descending from the sky and arranging themselves in numerous circles, all of them standing with their hands held together respectfully. Their number was multiplying with every passing moment. Meanwhile, the clamour of people had ended as well. Everyone seemed spellbound, looking in the direction of the angels with awe-stricken eyes. All one could hear now was the sound of a few whispers. The reason was that everyone was asking the person standing next to him about what was going on.

I had an idea of what was happening but I still sought a clarification from Saleh. As expected, he replied:

"The accountability is about to commence. Court of the One and only is being set up. This is the first stage. The angels are descending and will continue to do so for a long time. Then, at the end, the Bearers of the Throne will arrive. When you saw them last, they were four in number. Now, four more will join them and thus eight angels will come down along with the Throne of the Almighty."

"The Throne of the Almighty..." I muttered to myself. Saleh explained a bit more:

"I am sure you can understand that God does not sit on a throne. He is above and beyond such human concepts. In fact, the Throne is only a point of contact for his creations. It is just like Kaaba in Mecca in the previous world, which was called the Qiblah. It served as a pointer. As you know, that Kaaba was called the Home of God but that did not mean that God lived in it. However, when people faced towards it while praying, it served as a point of contact and focus of attention for them. In the same way, people will be able to have a dialogue with the Almighty today via the Throne."

I asked:

"So, people will be able to actually listen to God?"

"Yes, just like Moses heard God through a tree in the valley of Mount Sinai. Abdullah, I want to tell you one more important thing."

I was already quite attentive yet became all ears when he said it.

"As soon as the Bearers of the Throne descend, the Throne will light up with the reflection of God's pure light called Nur. It will then spread all over the world and the whole world will light up with God's Nur, indicating that from then onwards, everything will happen under the direct control of Almighty. There was a verse in the Qur'an that stated that on this day, God would take the entire world in his fist; this is the true meaning of that verse.

The very first order of the day would be for everybody to prostrate in front of the Almighty. Abdullah! That order will create a shocking scene. You will see that all the angels will prostate. All prophets,

Siddiqeen, Shuhada, and pious persons present in the shadow of the Throne on the right hand side will bow down."

I could not help but ask:

"What about the people present here on this side of the Plane of Judgement?"

"This is the important and shocking event I had alluded to. Any person who had rejected the truth, a hypocrite, one who was defiant to God or a criminal in his eyes will not be able to prostrate in front of him. Such people will try their utmost to bow down but their necks and spines will go rigid like wooden boards making it impossible for them to bend; in addition, the earth will also resist their movement in its direction."

"What about the others?" I asked.

Saleh continued:

"Those having a mixed bag of deeds but with fewer sins will manage to bow down and prostrate, and due to this they will be called for accountability right away. For the rest, the stronger the faith and better the deeds, the more they will be able to bow. Some people will be able to bow down to the level of the knees, some less than that and others will only be able to bend their necks for prostration. In essence, the less one bows, the greater his misery would be."

I nodded, as I understood the concept and said:

"So it means that when that happens, people will get an idea about their fate."

"No, although I am saying so, they would not be aware of it. However, they will feel extremely embarrassed for not being able to prostrate or will be a bit contented if they manage to bow down.

But people will truly come to understand who is God. They will discover the entity they had chosen to ignore during their lives. They will know the King of all kings, the One who rules over all emperors. They will recognise the only One who deserves to be worshipped. They will appreciate the One who controls this Universe, the One who is the source of all that is good. They will know the One who can make or break anyone's destiny with a slight gesture; the One who can question anyone about any deed but no one can question him about anything. They will fully understand that only for him is all praise, every word of gratitude, and every act of worship whether performed stood up, kneeled over or in prostration. They will know who is the One who deserves to be the focus of all offerings, all expressions of humility, all acts of love, all supplications, and all chants of 'God is great'... God is great! God is great! God is great.."

As Saleh spoke the last few words, his body began to tremble, and he fell on the ground in prostration as he continued to utter the words, 'God is great".

At the same time, I noticed a peculiar light spreading all over. The whole atmosphere was lit up with that special light. Meanwhile, all the angels started to chant loudly the praise of the Lord, supplications of admiration and thanks, and cries of 'God is great'.

I realised that the atmosphere was now lit with the reflection of God's Nur from the Throne. But I kept standing there, looking down. I did not dare to look up towards the Throne.

After a short while, I heard the familiar but authoritative voice of Archangel Gabriel, the Trustworthy:

"Whose Kingdom is it today?"

All the angels shouted back:

"Lillahul Wahidul Qahar' – 'it belongs to the everdominant One and only God"

Gabriel, the Trustworthy kept asking this question repeatedly and the angels kept repeating the same reply loudly. This created such an awe-inspiring scene that the hearts started to tremble.

Finally, a loud voice said:

"Where are the servants of The Most Merciful? Where are the slaves of The Lord of the Worlds? Where are the ones who consider God to be their Lord, their King, and their Sustainer? Wherever they are, they must bow down in front of the Lord and Master of the whole Universe."

As soon as I heard that, without making any effort to look up, I straightaway went down in prostration next to Saleh on the ground.

==============

The Plane of Judgment suddenly became very quiet. There was pin drop silence. The safety I felt while in prostration was unmatched by any previous prostration in my life. I do not know what others were saying in this state, but I was repeatedly begging for forgiveness and mercy.

I do not know for how long there was complete silence. Suddenly a voice called out:

"He is God. There is no God but him."

I knew that this announcement from the bearer of the throne meant to inform that the Master of the throne would speak out next.

"I am God and there is no one worthy of worship but me."

They were the same words that I had first heard while in prostration close to the Throne, however the voice was completely different. The gravity, severity, and harshness of the voice were such that the bravest of the people present would have trembled on hearing it. For a moment, there was a pause, accentuated by the profound silence all around. Then a voice harsher and louder than even a thunderbolt said:

"I am The King. Where are the defiant? Where are the arrogant? Where are the kings of Earth?"

These words hit the ears of the people like a thunderclap. No one was in a position to answer this question. If anything, people started to weep and cry. My body started to tremble because of the sternness, firmness, and ferociousness of the voice. I suddenly recalled every single occasion in my life when I considered myself as powerful, mighty and in charge, even if only within the confines of my home. I wished that the earth would split open and I would hide in it. I wished I could somehow escape the wrath of God. In a state of utter helplessness, I cried out:

"If only my mother had never given birth to me!"

My heart and mind could not take this any longer. I lost consciousness and collapsed on the floor.

===============

Chapter 7: Testimony of Prophet Jesus PBUH

As I opened my eyes, I found myself lying on a soft and comfortable bed. Naimah was by my side, looking concerned. As soon as she realised that I was awake, her face lit up.

She asked:

"Are you alright?"

"Where am I?" I asked.

"You are with me in my tent. Saleh brought you here unconscious."

"Where is he?"

"He's outside. I'll call him in."

Saleh stepped inside, saying salaam even before Naimah had finished her sentence. He had a smile depicting satisfaction on his face. I sat upright upon seeing him and asked him:

"What happened?"

"You fainted, my friend."

"By God, it was the first time I saw that facet of my Lord. All my expectations about him proved to be wrong. He is more magnificent than I could ever imagine. I regret every moment of my life that I had spent in anything other than appreciating his magnificence."

Saleh replied, "This is due to the difference between being and not being in his presence. God was behind a veil in the world. It was the first time today that God addressed humanity without the veil. You were fortunate to have discovered his greatness while he was still hidden from you and you humbly submitted to him. That is why you are enjoying his special blessings today."

"But why did he faint?" Naimah asked, interrupting our conversation.

"Actually we were standing left of the Throne along with the criminals. The Almighty started his address in a state of wrath, and since his wrath was especially directed towards the people on the left, its effect was most profound there. But God is never overwhelmed by his attributes; that is why, even in his anger, he was aware that one of his beloved servants was present on the left side. He therefore, caused Abdullah to become unconscious. If he had not done that, Abdullah would have had to face the wrath and fury, which the people of the left side were experiencing at that time."

When I heard this, tears of gratitude started to trickle down from my eyes. I got up from the bed and bowed in prostration. These words involuntarily came out of my mouth:

"My Lord! When have you ever ignored me? From my mother's womb until today, none of your engagements has caused you to ignore me. And I? I have never valued your gracious existence. I have never thanked you enough for your blessings. I have never worshipped you the way you deserve to be worshipped. You are free of any flaw. You are exalted. All praise is for you and only you deserve to be thanked. Forgive me and take me under the shadow of your blessings. I will be killed if you do not forgive me. I will be ruined."

I continued to recite this prayer for a long time. Naimah stroked my back gently with her hand and said:

"Please get up. You have spent your entire life according to the will of God. I know you well."

I got up quietly and said to Naimah, "You do not comprehend the extent of the blessings and greatness of God, Naimah. Otherwise you would have never said that."

"Abdullah is right, Naimah" said Saleh. "Even the greatest deed of man is nothing as compared to the smallest blessing by God. If God had taken away the power of speech from Abdullah, he could not have spoken a single word. If he had taken his hands away, he could not have written a single line. All blessings and capabilities were due to God. Man is insignificant. To God belongs everything."

"You are right. I had not looked at it in this light." Naimah nodded in agreement.

"Where do we go from here?" I asked Saleh.

"Accountability has started. You have to go there. But before that, there is some good news."

"What's that?"

"When the accountability started, God decided to question the nation of the last Prophet first. And you know what, your daughter Leila got salvation in the process."

"Is that so"? I shouted in shock and excitement.

"Yes, Saleh is correct", said Naimah. "I have already met her. She is in the other tent along with her brothers and sisters. They are waiting for you."

"What about Jamshaid?" I asked Saleh.

A solemn silence answered my question.

"Then I would like to go back to the Plane of Judgement. Perhaps there may be a way out for him."

"Alright, let's go." Saleh replied and holding my hand, he led me out of the tent.

===============

After we came out of the tent, I asked Saleh:

"What can I do for Jamshaid?"

"You were not able to do anything for Leila, how would you do anything for Jamshaid? Would you dare to tell God what he should do?"

"May God forgive me! I did not mean that." I replied instantly, but having heard Saleh's reply, my enthusiasm to save Jamshaid had cooled down. After a pause, I asked Saleh:

"Tell me what happened in the Plane of Judgement after I had passed out?"

"Even when you were in your senses you did not fully comprehend what was going on there. If you want to know the real story, ask one of the criminals. As each group of angels descended, the criminals became more and more frightened. And when the orders were given to bow down in front of the Almighty, everyone did so except for those wretched people who kept standing with their chests bulging out in arrogance in front of God."

"Was this because their backs had become stiff like boards?"

"Yes, that was their punishment. After that, when God Almighty declared that he was the King, and where were all the others who claimed to be kings beside him, those criminals still remained standing with their chests bulging out in arrogance.

I wish you could have seen the condition of those criminals at that time! Their hearts were sinking; they felt suffocated. Their eyes were wide open with fear and horror. They felt utterly helpless and unable to stop themselves from standing upright in total arrogance in presence of the Master of the whole Universe."

"What happened then?"

"Obviously, the accountability was to take place on an individual basis. However, at that point, it was made obvious to the criminals what their fate was going to be. This was done by completely opening the gates of Hell. Consequently, the atmosphere on the left side became horrifying.

It looked like Hell was boiling with anticipation and excitement, and was ready to burst with rage when it saw the criminals. Its loud uproar and shrieks could be heard from a distance. Its flames were leaping out.

They were so gigantic that the sparks coming out of them were as big as huge palaces. The dancing flames and sparks created such a scene as if yellow camels were dancing in the sky. Don't ask me about the condition of those people when they saw that scene. They realised that the hardships they had faced in the Plane of Judgement were nothing as compared to what they had just seen."

"How did the accountability commence?"

"Adam [PBUH], father of mankind and the first Prophet, was asked to testify first of all. He stated, 'I present myself to you, O the only one worthy of praise. I am present and ready to serve you with all my energy; all goodness is in your hands.'

Almighty said, 'Separate the dwellers of Hell from amongst your children, Adam'.

'How many should I separate?' He inquired.

'Nine hundred and ninety nine out of every thousand', The Almighty replied. Abdullah, you cannot imagine the mayhem that followed when people heard that."

"But why did the Almighty decide to send such a large number of people to Hell?" I inquired.

"It was not a judgement. It was only to demonstrate that out of all the people present in the Plane of Judgement, only one out of a thousand deserved to go to Paradise. In fact, the humanity as a whole has miserably failed the test of faith and morality, Abdullah. Therefore, purely based on Almighty's justice, such large number of people deserves to go to Hell on merit.

You may remember, the last Prophet had said that if one were to divide God's compassion into a hundred parts, only one part had been manifested in the world while the remaining ninety-nine parts had been reserved for the Day of Judgement. Thus, he displayed his mercy and instead of deciding the fate of those people first who were destined for the Hell, he decided to start accountability of those first who had the most chance of success and deliverance."

"You mean people who were generally good?"

“Yes, those people from every nation were called first whose accountability and success was only a formality. This process started with the nation of the last Prophet. Other nations will also have their turn soon as from amongst the entire population of humans, successful people are only one per cent.

He will pass judgement on the fate of the rest of the humanity later on. The advantage of this would be that if hardships in the Plane of Judgement could recompense for sins of some, then that could happen.”

Saleh paused for a moment and then said with regret:

“However, I do not hold much hope for the rest of the people.”

“Why?” I asked.

“It is due to Shirk. God is very sensitive about polytheism. You are aware that it is one of the foremost issues that plagued the humanity throughout its entire history. It will be the main reason for the doom of most people today. It is so as there is little hope that this sin will be forgiven. Yes, if someone's circumstances and environment could be accepted as an excuse, perhaps then. Otherwise anyone who has knowingly indulged in Shirk does not have even the slightest hope of being forgiven today.”

“Even if he is a Muslim”? I asked.

“Yes” Saleh replied.

“Shirk was a flame from the fire of Hell. Today, it will definitely burn every person who knowingly ascribed partners to God, whether it was in his being, in his attributes or in his obligations and powers. If someone worshipped a deity other than God, or prayed to that deity or prostrated in front of it, considering it to be a partner of God and having a share in any of his attributes and powers, he would get burnt by that flame today.”

“God is great! There is no god but the one God!” I said spontaneously.

===============

"I have not understood something." I said to Saleh as we walked along.

"What is it?"

"From the first to the last Muslim, they must be in hundreds of millions and even billions; how did, then, Leila's turn come up right at the beginning?"

"Do you think that the God Almighty looks at identity cards of people to decide who is a Muslim and who is not?"

"What do you mean?"

"I mean that the vast majority of Muslims did not prefer to identify themselves as Muslims. For most people, their identity happened to be their sect, leaders or creed. Thus, today when the accountability of the nation of the last Prophet began, initially only those people were called who truly believed in the Oneness of God, associated themselves only with the ways of the last Prophet, avoided sectarianism, and kept their religion away from innovations and deviations. They were the people who ignored their biases and associations when it came to matters relating to the truth. They accepted the truth whole-heartedly whenever it became apparent to them. Among them were the pious who stood in the shadow of the Throne today as well as those whose good deeds were mixed with bad. However, the most merciful God over-looked their bad deeds and forgave them due to their pious actions. Such people were small in number though, that is why Leila's turn came so soon. At least in this respect she did well. All of her limitations in her deeds were ignored because of the hardships she had suffered in the Plane of Judgement. In addition, your compassionate Lord elevated her status so she could be with you, although her deeds were not like yours."

"But, my accountability has not even started yet."

"Your presence here signifies that your fate has already been decided. However, it has not been declared yet. Don't worry. The declaration will only be made at the end of the day when the accountability is finished."

"Why?" I inquired, and Saleh clarified:

"Remember, I told you that there are four types of people whose deliverance is decided at the time of their death? That is, the prophets, the Siddiqeen who supported their prophets during their lifetimes, the Shuhada who were witnesses to the truth after the prophets had passed away, and the Salaiheen who were pious people of all times."

I nodded in affirmative. Saleh continued:

"The prophets and Shuhada are the people whose real accomplishment is that they became witnesses to the truth in front of other people in the previous world, in addition to passing the message of Oneness of God and the Hereafter. Today, they will present details of how they performed their role of bearing witness to the truth to the Almighty so that, others do not have an excuse to say that they were not aware of the truthful and the righteous way. This is because these prophets and Shuhada had clearly explained the truth in the previous world.

Therefore, the rest of the people will be held accountable on the basis of their testimony and their eternal future will be decided accordingly. These decisions will continue to take place until all human beings have been dealt with; in the end, Shuhada like you will be called and their success will be announced to the whole world. Only after all this has been done, will the people be moved towards the Paradise or Hell."

"It means that people will not go to Paradise or Hell immediately."

"Yes, they will not go immediately. Instead, as each person has his accountability completed, he will be asked to stand to the right with respect and in comfort if he is successful, and if unsuccessful, he will be moved to the left hand to stand in disgrace and punishment. When everyone's accountability has taken place, people will be taken in groups towards the Paradise or Hell."

"Who will be the first to enter the Paradise?"

"The last Prophet will request for the doors of the Paradise to be opened; then, the residents of the Paradise will enter amidst a spectacular reception, greetings, and accolades."

"Where is Prophet Muhammad, peace be upon him, at this moment?"

"He is by the pond of Kauthar. Every person from his nation who successfully passes the accountability process is taken to him; he greets each person with a drink from the Kauthar. After drinking from the Kauthar, not only does a person forget the hardships and thirst of the Plane of Judgement, he also never feels thirst again. By the way, do you remember that drink from the Kauthar?"

"Of course, I do!"

After listening to Saleh, I had an intense desire to meet the Prophet. I said to Saleh:

"Shall we first go and present ourselves to the Prophet?"

The sentence had hardly left my lips when a loud voice stated:

"The accountability of the successful people from among the nation of the last Prophet has been completed. The accountability of the nation of Jesus Christ will commence now. Jesus, Messiah and son of Mary, May there be peace upon you, a Messenger from God and the final Prophet sent to the Israelites, present yourself to God."

I looked at Saleh for an explanation.

He said:

"Now Prophet Jesus [PBUH] will bear witness on his nation. He will present a summary of his teachings when the Almighty asks him to do so. This will be his testimony against the criminals of his nation, while at the same time, it will also serve as a means of salvation for those who held correct beliefs and performed pious deeds. Thereafter, the Almighty shall forgive mistakes of those from his nation whose beliefs were in conformity with his teachings; they will be declared successful following a cursory accountability."

"Did something similar happen to the Muslims as well?"

"Yes, the last Prophet was called upon first of all to be a witness. His testimony was considered as evidence against those who had rejected his message as well as those who had disobeyed it. If only you could have seen the scene when all such people wished for the earth to split open and hide them in. However, his testimony proved to be a source of salvation for people like Leila. In essence, the true reason for their reprieve was that their faith and deeds were, on the whole, in conformity with his testimony."

"This means that so far only those people from the nation of the last Prophet have attained redemption whose beliefs and deeds were in accordance with his teachings."

"Yes, the Almighty ignored their mistakes. The same would happen with the nations of other prophets as well. Those people, whose faith and deeds were largely in accordance with the teachings of their respective prophets, would be forgiven. After that, only criminals and disbelievers would be left behind in the Plane of Judgement, waiting for a decision."

"What will happen then?"

"After that, general accountability will commence."

"General accountability?" I asked.

"In the accountability of all nations, the first phase entails declaration of success of the pious people as well as the cursory accountability of people like Leila. After that, general accountability will commence in which decisions will only be based on a thorough investigation of deeds. Obviously, because of this the criminals will find themselves in trouble. However, many people with true faith will get salvation despite their sins, because of God's mercy; they will find that the right arm of the scale of justice bearing their good deeds and attitudes will become heavier due to his intervention. For them, the humiliation and hardship they experienced in the Plane of Judgement will become their penance and an excuse for their forgiveness. This is what I mean by general accountability.

However, some people who will be held back until the last moment before they are called for accountability. They will be those believers who carry a very heavy burden of sins. For them, this extraordinary lengthy wait may continue for thousands or even hundreds of thousands of years, during which they will have to endure the worst hardships, difficulties, and torments. Only after this may they have a chance for reprieve."

"What would be that chance?"

"That chance would be the manifestation of God's mercy. He would not award full punishment to them in accordance with the norms of his justice; instead, the penance in the Plane of Judgement would become a reprieve for their sins. Furthermore, he would allow his prophets and in particular, the last Prophet to intercede on their behalf by allowing them to request the start of their accountability."

"But to suffer so much hardship in the Plane of Judgement and then attain reprieve is not a good way to get it." I said in a remorseful tone.

Saleh replied:

"That is why the prophets had come to show people a better way, that is, to accept faith, perform righteous deeds, and seek forgiveness after any mistakes. It was the simplest and the easiest way to salvation. But, people in general did not pay heed to them and have thus suffered its consequences today."

I said in agreement:

"You are correct. This pardon would be attained after great hardship and disgrace. I could not withstand Leila's sorrow although she received reprieve in the beginning; what would be the state of those who would have to wait and endure hardships and difficulties of the Plane of Judgement till the end!"

"My friend, the circumstances you saw Leila in were comparatively much better. Now the environment of the Plane of Judgement has turned horrendously worse. The reason is that the gates of Hell have been opened fully. That has resulted in not only intense heat in the Plane of Judgement but also the view of Hell and the spectre of going in it is enough to make it worse manifold. The guilty are facing the wrath of God Almighty. People can see the gates of destruction and disgrace open in front of them.

All of it is so fearsome that it is beyond the endurance of human beings. Most importantly, no one knows what will happen to him. You cannot even begin to comprehend the fear, mental and physical anguish, and psychological torture that these people are now experiencing."

I thought to myself, was this the way people had chosen to gain reprieve in the Hereafter? Alas! If only people would have understood while being in the previous world that the only way to salvation was through faith and righteous deeds. The last Prophet preached this all his life. But, what could one do about the wrong notions of the people? They forgot the teachings of their Prophet and created a false world of their own, built solely on their desires and whims. They thought that even if they did not do anything, they would be saved due to the intercession of the Prophet.

But today, it had become abundantly clear that salvation would only be attained through true faith and righteous deeds. They will have to face punishment for every major sin that they did not repent for, in the shape of hardships in this plane, beneath the dreadful spectre of Hell.

Alas! If only the people had realised it in the previous world, their entire lives would have been spent seeking forgiveness.

I was lost in my thoughts when Saleh looked at me and said:

"I think before we go to the pond of Kauthar, we should see testimony of Prophet Jesus Christ PBUH, and then go to Prophet Muhammed PBUH!"

===============

We were back in the Plane of Judgement once again. However, this time we were standing on the right side of the Throne. The earth and skies were gloriously lit up with the brilliant luminescence of the Throne. For the successful people, this light was a source of jubilation and elation, whereas it was falling on the criminals as the wrath of Almighty. On all four sides of the Throne there were rows upon rows of angels standing, their hands folded together. The closest were the Bearers of the Throne, and after them, there were other angels positioned according to their status and position. On their lips were supplications, salutations, and words of gratitude and praise for the Lord. Prophet Jesus PBUH was now present in the Court of the Almighty. The angels had gathered all the Christians, from the first to the last, closer to the Throne. The Almighty spoke:

"Jesus, son of Mary, come forward."

Angels moved to make way for Prophet Jesus PBUH as he walked forward and stood close to the Throne. His hands were folded together, his head bowed. The Almighty said:

"Jesus, you delivered my message to your nation. How did they respond?"

"Master, I do not know. Only you have the knowledge of the unseen."

His reply was an acceptance of the fact that he was not aware of what his nation had done in the world after him. On hearing the reply of Prophet Jesus PBUH, pin-drop silence ensued in the Plane of Judgement.

After a few moments, there was an explosion in the sky. Everyone looked up. A sort of film started. In this film, the Christians were prostrating in front of statues of Mary and Prophet Jesus PBUH. One could see people taking out processions on the roads carrying the cross. In churches, Jesus and Mary were being worshipped. People were praying to Jesus to solve their problems. Songs were being sung in his praise. Priests could be seen making every effort through their speeches to prove that he was the son of God.

Seeing this, I thought to myself that Christians had given birth to the biggest case of polytheism in the history of humanity despite the fact that God had sent Prophet Jesus PBUH with the message of Oneness of God. During that period, the Jews had made it extremely difficult to follow the religious laws given by Prophet Moses PBUH because of their multiple juristic alterations. These people had converted the spiritual and loving relationship between a servant and his God into a superficial legal association devoid of all emotions and soul. They laid great emphasis on a few obvious and trivial obligations but ignored the commandments related to morality and a deeper relationship with God. It was in this environment that the most honourable Jesus Christ was sent to them. He severely criticised the shallowness and moral bankruptcy of the children of Israel. He once said while criticising the religious people of his time:

"What sorrow awaits you, scribes and Pharisees, hypocrites! For, you illegitimately grab the homes of widows; and prolong *your prayers, only for deception. Your punishment will be even more... What sorrow awaits you, scribes and Pharisees, hypocrites! For, you give a tenth of your mint, dill, and cumin (as obligatory charity on your harvest), but have neglected the more important matters of the Law: justice, mercy, and faithfulness. You should have practiced these things, without neglecting the others. You blind guides! You strain your drinks so you will not accidently swallow any gnats but you deliberately swallow whole elephants! What sorrow awaits you, scribes and Pharisees, hypocrites! For, you clean the outside of the cup and the plate, but within you are full of extortion and unrighteousness. You blind Pharisee! First, clean the inside of the cup and the plate, that the outside also may be clean. What sorrow awaits you, scribes and Pharisees, hypocrites! For, you are like whitewashed tombs, which outwardly appear beautiful, but within are full of dead people's bones and all uncleanness. So you, too, outwardly appear righteous to people, but inwardly you are full of insincerity and disregard of God's law."*

On hearing his criticism, the Jews became his sworn enemies, so much so that they became intent on his murder. However, God saved him from their deception and raised him unto Himself. Unfortunately, afterwards one of his staunch Jewish opponents by the name of Saint Paul reshaped all his teachings while claiming to be one of his followers. On one hand, he declared that adherence to the religious law was only obligatory for Jews and not for the rest. On the other hand, he exaggerated the status of Prophet Jesus PBUH and his mother to divine deities. Thus, gradually, Christianity became the biggest polytheistic religion of the world. Christians considered Jesus to be the son of God, and prayed to him for help in every difficulty, regarding him as someone capable of solving their problems. But, it was a fabrication and it became abundantly clear today.

As I thought about it, I heard wailing and crying of the Christians present in the Plane of Judgement. The Christians had clearly seen their ill actions, and their horrible end in the shape of Hell was visible right in front of them, with its mouth wide open. Suddenly, some of them began to shout:

"Our Lord, we only acted upon the teachings of Jesus. You sent him to us as a Messiah. He told us that he was your son and he was sent by you to save us."

A stern rebuke suddenly spread in the atmosphere and startled everyone into silence. The Almighty said to Jesus Christ:

"Jesus, did you tell these people to worship you and your mother instead of me?"

On the face of it, it seemed like a straightforward question, but as soon as Prophet Jesus PBUH heard it, he began to tremble. It appeared that his feet were struggling to carry the weight of his body. On seeing this, God said:

"Jesus, you are my beloved Prophet. My prophets have no fear in my presence. Answer my question at ease."

Two angels came forward and helped him onto a chair.

This scene was heart wrenching. Prophet Jesus PBUH was a very dear and beloved prophet of God, but regrettably, for no fault of his own, he was made the foremost personality in history to have been worshipped and placed in rivalry to God. People prayed to him, sang his praise and salutations, and worshipped him. But today, the state that he found himself in after just one question from the Almighty was enough to make those who considered him God shed tears of remorse. Today, everybody had found out that all were insignificant compared to God.

I thought in my heart that all such pious servants of God, who were given names and attributes by their followers that were only worthy of God, would come forward one by one and would deny ever having made such claims. Like Prophet Jesus, none of them will find the strength to dare stand in front of God. If only those people who put them on such high pedestals had known about the true greatness of God before the dawn of this day! If only they had not placed human beings in competition with God.

Meanwhile, as the effect of fear of God lessened a bit, Prophet Jesus PBUH stood up from his chair and said:

"Master, you are exalted and free of all flaws! How could I dare to say something that I had no right to say? If I had said such a thing then you would have known about it… I only told them what you had commanded me to say, that is, 'worship only one God, who is my Lord as well as your Lord.' I remained a witness upon them as long as I was amongst them. Then, after you had raised me, only you watched over them; and you are a witness to everything. If you punish them, they are your servants; and, if you choose to forgive them, you are the most mighty and wise."

On hearing this, God said:

"Today, only truth will be beneficial; it will benefit people who adopted it sincerely."

Prophet Jesus Christ was allowed to leave after this and angels were given their orders:

"All those in the nation of Jesus Christ whose knowledge and actions conform to his teachings, should be brought forward."

===============

Chapter 8: At the Kauthar

After having seen Prophet Jesus's testimony before God, we started towards the pond. I asked Saleh en-route:

"Prophet Jesus [PBUH] pleaded to God to forgive his people. He had submitted that only God was prevailing and wise, and only he could do so. Did his words not have any effect?"

"Did you not listen to the reply of the Almighty that today the truthful will benefit only from their truthfulness?"

"I heard that, and it appeared that his pleading had not been accepted."

"No, that is not the case. God had clarified his Law. Basic criterion for success or failure is to accept the teachings of the messenger as true, and then to affirm it further through actions. The meaning of God's statement is that he will deal mercifully with those who meet this basic criterion. This implies that because of his blessings, God would not hold such people accountable for those sins and shortcomings that they had not managed to redeem or repent for in their lives.

All prophets are similarly pleading for their nations discreetly or will do so when it is their turn. But at present, only this level of leniency is being granted as a consequence of their pleading. So far, only mistakes are being forgiven, not crimes. These are the mistakes that were deemed trivial at the time and thus forgiveness was not sought for them. They have become a source of humiliation today, similar to what your daughter Leila had to endure. Those who maintained a steady regime of faith, righteous deeds, repentance, and self-improvement have been safe from the very outset. Those who maintained a constant attitude of disobedience and committed major sins are now suffering the toughest hardships."

We reached a place where angels were hindering people from going further. Saleh held my hand and walked towards them. On seeing him, they moved out of his way. As we walked a little, I began to see a lake. On seeing it, Saleh said:

"This is the pond of Kauthar."

I said, "But, I can't see the last Prophet here."

"He is further ahead. We have entered from another side. I wanted you to have a detailed view. That is why I chose this way."

When I thought about what Saleh had said, I realised that it was not an ordinary pond. Somewhat surprised, I said:

"My friend, it is more of a lake, or perhaps a sea as I cannot even see its other shore."

"Yes, it is so. Can't you see so many people drinking water from it? If it had been an ordinary pond, it would have run dry rapidly."

He was correct. A large number of people were everywhere around the pond.

On account of the information in the sayings ascribed to the last Prophet, I had some idea even in the previous world that Kauthar would not be an ordinary pond but would be more like a sea. In fact, based upon his sayings, I used to think that it would probably be somewhere around the Red Sea that separated Arabia and Africa in the previous world. When I shared my thought with Saleh, he replied:

"To a large extent, it is true. Even though the planet Earth has become massive due to expansion, thereby changing location of landmarks, it is more or less the same place."

"Does this mean that the Plane of Judgement is in Arabia?"

"Yes. It is in Arabia."

I remained quiet, thinking about the time when Earth was still inhabited. People were busy in the affairs of the world. Alas! If only they had realised that the real life would begin after death. God had sent his prophets to remind people and make them understand in every possible way, but they did not pay any heed to them. Thereafter, God sent some prophets as messengers as well. Those messengers not only invited people to the right path, but went even a step further. They warned them that if they did not follow their teachings, rather than waiting until the end of the world, God would punish them in their lifetime, and only those who were on the right path would remain unscathed. Thus, the nations of Noah PBUH, A'ad, Thamud, Lot PBUH, Shoaib PBUH, Pharaoh and the Quraish of Mecca themselves suffered that fate.

The messengers sent to these nations warned them about the wrath of God, but when their message was ignored, they were punished in the world, much before the Day of Judgement. The nation of Noah PBUH and the followers of Pharaoh were drowned in water, A'ad were destroyed by a fierce storm, and the nations of Thamud and Shoaib PBUH were annihilated by a jolt. Similarly, the nation of Lot PBUH was flattened with a wind that rained stones, and the swords of the believers wiped out the residents of Mecca who rejected the call of the last Prophet. The Almighty saved the believers and awarded them rule of the earth. In particular, the incident of the last Prophet and the disbelievers of Mecca had happened in recent history and thus its record was also preserved in the Qur'an. The history is witness to how the companions of the last Prophet became masters of the world within a few decades. Hence, an example of eternal reward and punishment was established so that no one could deny it. Despite all that, people still did not prepare for this day.

Above all, in this area where the accountability is taking place today and what used to be the Middle East, the children of Abraham were the subject and example of this principle of reward and punishment for four thousand years. The dealings of God with the two branches of the children of Abraham, namely the Ishmaelites and the Israelites were based on a law that his blessings were showered upon them if they were obedient, and alternatively, if they were disobedient, they were punished as a nation. Historically, the children of Israel had to face major destructions twice because of their disobedience. Once, at the hands of the Babylonian king Nebuchadnezzar and the second time, by the Roman General Titus. Similarly, the Muslim nation had to suffer severe punishments twice for their crimes. They had to face destruction and humiliation of slavery firstly at the hands of the Tartars and then by the European nations.

Along with these punishments, whenever humans sought forgiveness and turned towards God, the doors of power and rewards were opened for them again. One of the examples of this process was when, after complete destruction at the hands of the Tartars, the Muslims took the message of Islam to them and in a short period of time they became a super power again. Yet sadly even after seeing these lucid examples of reward and punishment in the world, people did not take the absolute certainty of reward and punishment of the Day of Judgement seriously. Involuntarily, a sigh escaped my lips and I said:

"My Lord, you did not leave any stone unturned in making people understand, but man was a very obstinate creature. This is why he is facing this tough day today."

Saleh looked at me for a moment and then spoke:

"No! All were not so. Just look at the people around the pond of Kauthar, you can see so many people here."

I nodded in agreement but did not add anything. The reason was obvious. Saleh was looking at the people present at the pond and I was thinking about the people who were outside in the Plane of Judgement, my son Jamshaid included. I had returned to the Plane of Judgement to look for him, but after seeing Prophet Jesus's testimony, I had given up. Therefore, for the time being, I decided to leave his fate in the hands of God.

===============

We were moving ahead. On reaching a certain place, Saleh said to me:

"Come on; Let us go to the VVIP lounge of Kauthar."

I did not comment, but I had an idea about what he meant.

Saleh explained:

"There are two ranks amongst the people who have succeeded today. Some practiced the religion in a way that ensured compliance with all of its obligations and stipulations. They fulfilled their commitments towards God and human beings and obeyed his each and every command. They are the ones who will earn the reward of entering the Paradise.

Among them, were people who opted for the religion and sacrificed for it rather than just practicing it. They displayed patience and steadfastness in the face of extremely adverse circumstances and severest hardships. They excelled at all virtuous and righteous deeds. In all circumstances, they upheld the truth and happily faced the consequences for doing so. They dedicated themselves to supporting the religion of God, performing extra supplications, and serving his creatures. They are the people who will be amongst the VVIP's on this Day of Judgement. Their privileges, status, closeness to God, and respect will be far more than those of the other inhabitants of Paradise.

This is akin to the previous world where every society had commoners and then an elite class consisting of those placed in the high gentry. The same is happening today. Successful people of the world have been placed around the picturesque region of the pond of Kauthar, away from the hardships of the Plane of Judgement; they will get a choice abode in the Paradise as well. Obviously, it is a huge accomplishment.

But there is a class even higher than that. It is reserved for those blessed souls who are close to God; they are the highest placed from among the dwellers of Paradise. Their real status will only become apparent in the Paradise, but even at the Kauthar, separate lodgings have been provided for them. That is where we are going now."

He stopped for a moment and spoke whilst looking in my eyes:

"It is because you are not one of the common dwellers of Paradise, Abdullah. In fact, you are one of the leaders and worthy of a very high status."

I bowed my head in all humility.

===============

We entered a place of such immense beauty that words would fail to describe it. The snowy white, clear water of the lake was spread over its bed like moonlight. My eyes were getting a strange soothing satisfaction by just looking at its still and flat surface. The banks were made of glittering hollow pearls. My soles experienced an indescribable relief as I walked onto some very thick and soft carpets that were laid out by its shores. Comfortable regal chairs were placed on the carpets. Glasses made of gold and silver glittered like stars on tabletops that were more transparent than glass. A pleasant fragrance was emanating from the lake that made all pores of my body thoroughly scented.

I asked Saleh as I took a seat, "Where is this enchanting fragrance coming from?"

"The lake bed is made of a soil more fragrant than any scent in the previous world. You are noticing its effects."

Saleh filled a glass from the lake and, putting it in front of me, said:

"Enjoy!"

I took a sip. I had heard it being described in the previous world as milk, honey, etc. But it was a far more superior drink than any of them. I had taken it once before but the pleasure of drinking it in this environment was a totally different experience. There was an extremely strong and piercing sunlight outside in the Plane of Judgement, yet we were experiencing evening twilight over here. The breeze was pleasantly cool, refreshing, and steady. It seemed as if the sun was about to set. A dusky hue was spread over the clear sky. Different parts of the sky were draped in shades of deep red, orange and yellow. Their reflection on the surface of the clear waters of the lake was creating a façade of a fair-skinned maiden wearing a colourful headscarf. No doubt, it was an extremely lovely and enchanting scene.

I glanced around; it looked like a picnic spot. People were sitting or standing by the lake, alone, in groups, or with their families. They were talking and laughing. They looked very happy and at peace. The contentment and satisfaction on their faces conveyed the message that they had succeeded. They had left behind all possibilities of death, sorrow, illness, grief, and sufferings forever to reach the shores of an everlasting ocean of eternal and true happiness.

Today they had achieved a success that would never end, a happiness that would never diminish, and pleasures that would never lessen. They now had a life that would never cease and comforts that would never be taken back. They had achieved such a huge reward with such little effort! As they celebrated their success, their laughter could be heard far and wide. The smiles on their faces enlivened the atmosphere.

That reminded me of my family. Saleh looked at me and read my thoughts straight away: "While we are here, let me take you to your family; they have also been moved here."

===============

Leila saw me first. She was sitting by the pond along with the rest of my family, but perhaps her eyes were searching for me. She saw me from a distance, got up from the chair, and came running to embrace me. She just wept, unable to say anything. I patted her for a long time. Then I separated her from me to look at her face.

When I had seen her last in the Plane of Judgement, she was in bad shape. But now, my daughter was looking as beautiful as a fairy. Seeing her in this good condition, I involuntarily thanked the Almighty for his blessings due to which she was back with me again. I said to her:

"Leila, the sufferings and hardships are now over for good; you will only experience happiness and comfort from here onwards."

By now, the rest of the family had also reached us. My other daughters, Arifa and Aaliya, were looking as pretty as ever. My younger son Anwar was holding his mother's hand. I hugged all of them. Then I said:

"My children, I am proud of you! You preferred to wait for your Lord's promise instead of being dazzled by the worldly life. You did not infatuate yourselves with the benefits of a temporary world; rather, you chose this eternal life. This is the day of your eternal success. Let's celebrate this success with a drink from the Kauthar!"

We sat down on the chairs nearby. I said to Leila:

"Leila, I want to hear your story, but before that, Anwar, Aaliya, and Arifa tell me, did you have any difficulty in joining your Mama?"

All of them responded that they were quite safe right from the beginning of the Day of Judgement. Various angels had escorted them to the area in the shadow of the Throne.

Then Leila narrated her story:

"Papa, I have been through some very tough times. When I emerged from the grave after hearing the sound of the trumpet, it was chaos and horror everywhere. Everybody was running in the same direction. Nobody was wearing any clothes at that time but everyone was in such a state of fear, terror, and worry that no one looked at anyone else nor did they care about their own bareness. I tried to find all of you but could not locate anyone. Finally, I also started running in the same direction as everyone else.

I don't know for how long I kept running. Everyone seemed obsessed with reaching the same destination. People were terrified and worried but felt compelled to continue to run."

I interrupted her:

"It was the effect of the trumpet blown by Archangel Rafael that forced everyone to run towards the Plane of Judgement. No matter where people were in the world, they were all forced to head in that direction."

"You are right, Papa. Everyone was running in the same direction. I got blisters on my feet. They started to bleed. My body felt like breaking down with exhaustion but there was something deep inside me that did not let me stop. I was dying of thirst but water was nowhere to be found. It was extremely hot but there was no tree or shade anywhere. Papa, all along the way there was nothing but a huge flat plane. There were no mountains, rivers, seas, trees or even ditches; in short, there were no heights or depressions anywhere. I cannot tell you in words how terrible that journey was! If it had happened in the previous world, I would have literally fallen down and died of exhaustion. But over there, no one was lucky enough to have relief from falling or dyeing! Thus I was forced to continue running endlessly!"

"What happened next"? Anwar asked woefully.

"I don't know how long it took me but I finally reached the Plane of Judgement. However, another misery was waiting for us there. Horrifying angels were walking around everywhere. Just their sight was enough to petrify anyone! They did not say anything to me but they were mercilessly beating many others. Seeing that scene was enough to scare me to death."

"Where did you find Aasmah?" I asked.

"I met her somewhere in the Plane of Judgement in a terrible state. Papa, she was brought up in a highly privileged environment. After seeing her, I almost forgot my own miseries. We stayed together to keep our spirits high, but after she met you, her will and hope for deliverance faded completely."

Aaliya asked, "Where did you see her last?"

"When everybody was ordered to bow down, I prostrated right away. She was standing next to me but she was unable to take a bow. In the previous world, she always said that God did not need our worship or prayers, and even if there were a requirement for praying, God would forgive us, as he was merciful. She did not even fast as she thought it would ruin her beautiful skin."

"Where was she when you got up after the prostration?" Arifa asked.

"She was still there, right next to me, but when God ordered the angels to take away 999 people out every 1000, the angels dragged her away. Then I was presented in the Court of the Almighty for my accountability."

"What happened next?" Naimah asked.

"I was afraid that God was going to hand over my record of deeds in my left hand and then order the angels to drag me away. But my Lord is most compassionate and merciful; he was very kind to me. I was asked questions about faith and worship. I replied that I had faith in all the required beliefs in the previous world and I used to perform all the prescribed prayers and rituals. Thereafter, I was asked about major moral obligations, rights of relatives and other people around me. I managed to give acceptable answers to all those questions as well. I was afraid that I was going to be asked specific questions about bad deeds and sins I had committed. However, he did not ask me any further questions."

I commented, "Leila! If the Almighty had asked you that question, you would have been doomed. He does not ask questions whose answers are bound to be in the negative from a person he has decided to forgive. He only asks such questions from those whom he wants to punish. You were asked only those questions whose correct replies were already present in your Book of Deeds. Although bad deeds and sins were also recorded in that book, the Almighty ignored them."

"Oh I remember, at the end the Almighty said something to me. He said that you are the daughter of Abdullah; you should be with him. Then the Almighty ordered the angels to hand over the Book of Deeds into my right hand and to take me to my family. I am unable to express the joy I felt at that moment."

Saleh, who was sitting next to me, said:

"Your forgiveness was not because of your father. However, your status was elevated due to him. Now, you are sitting in the VVIP lounge by the Kauthar. Are you aware that you, your mother, and other siblings have been awarded this honour only because of your father? It is a special blessing from God that from amongst the successful family members, whoever has the highest stature, the rest of the family members will also be elevated to his or her level."

At this, Aaliya said: "Oh, that's why none of our own family members were allowed to come here. The angels only allowed us brothers, sisters, and our mother to come here. Some of our other family members are also around but they have not been allowed to come to this area."

Signs of distress appeared on Naimah's face as she listened to this; forced by her maternal instincts, she added, "Yes, all are here except Jamshaid."

Everybody became quiet. Anwar broke the silence by saying:

"Papa, I was saved by that article of your teacher Mr. Farhan, which you often quoted. I had made its message the cornerstone of my life."

Arifa asked, "Which article was that? Let's hear it too."

Anwar closed his eyes and said, "He wrote:

'The reformers of our era want to eliminate this natural desire for advancement from the people. However, God does not endorse it. He only wants to divert the course of this desire towards the Hereafter, and away from the present world. Instead of hoping to be a part of the elite and privileged sections of the worldly society, he wants people to strive to be amongst the people close to God and the elite of the Paradise. If you read the entire message of Qur'an, you will find that it does not want to nurture any other mindset in people apart from that. The personalities of the companions of the last Prophet, who were the first addressees of the Qur'an, had the same traits. The charity of Abu-Bakr and Umar, the generosity of Abdul Rehman and Uthman, and the simple life of Ali and Abu-Zar, May God be pleased with all of them, are manifestations of the same firm belief in the Hereafter. To understand the transformation that belief in Hereafter brings in one's life, study the following verse of the Qur'an:

> Whatever things you have been given are merely for the necessities and adornments of this worldly life. And whatever you will get from God is much better and will last forever. Why do you not think? Is the person to whom we have made a good promise, and which he will get, equal to the one whom we have given good things of this life only but who is going to face the punishment on the Day of Judgement? (Al-Qasas 60-61)

Just imagine about the life of the person who believes firmly in this one verse. When such a person earns his livelihood, he will never take the risk of disobeying God, the result of which is Hellfire. After he fulfils his needs, the best purpose of wealth for him would be to spend it on adornment and beautification of his eternal and much better life in the Hereafter. He will never jeopardise his Hereafter for the sake of any blessing in this world. Before he even thinks about building a home, he will first think about the home in the Hereafter; similarly, before planning to buy a car in this world, he will plan about his transport to the Hereafter. He will never risk losing those heavenly maidens whose moon-like faces, attractive beauty and eternal youth will never wither, for the sake of short-lived gratification of his eyes from the exposed and semi-exposed women of this world.

The needs and wishes of his family can never take him on a path that ends up at the brink of Hell. Rather, his love for his family will compel him to take them along on the road to Paradise. He will want to groom them, and spend time on them. He will tell them that to live is in fact to live for the Hereafter. The real success is to gain Paradise. This world is nothing but an illusion, a place where countless others were tested before us, and we are also being tested. It's just a matter of a few years after which, neither will we be here nor would these testing times be. If at all, it will be the blessings of God that will last. It will be his Paradise, and his never-ending rewards. It will be the pinnacles of esteem and appreciation that will last. The voices will have honour in them. The faces will have a glow on them. One's company will be that of righteous people. Friends will be all around. There will be palaces made of pearls and jewels, and vineyards of musk and ambrosia. They will be embellished with silk and silk brocade and adorned with rubies and corals. They will have streams of milk and honey; and waves of purified water. There will be trees made of silver and gold, and seas of water and wine. Angels will be paying their salutations, and appetising meals will be available to savour at any time.

Hence, it will be an eternal world of luxury and delight, of water and wine, and of castles and luxurious tents. It will be an eternal world of prestige and style, and pleasure and rewards. It will be a world of perpetual peace and relaxation, enjoyment and blessings. In such a world, there will be no sorrows, no worries, and no disappointments. It will be a world sans regrets, deprivations, and limitations. An unfortunate person is not someone who did not succeed in the finite world; indeed, unfortunate is the one who failed to be a winner in the eternal world!"

As Anwar recalled the last few words, his voice became heavy with emotions and eyes moist with tears. He was probably thinking of his brother Jamshaid. However, he did not realise that by narrating an abstract from my teacher's book, he had doubled my grief by reminding me of his fate.

I thought to myself, "It seems that one still has to experience some sorrows even in the Plane of Judgement. It will only be in the Paradise where one will be able to get rid of every sorrow and worry forever."

==============

Chapter 9: The Nation of Noah PBUH *and those who altered their Faith*

The dilemmas being faced by my teacher Farhan Ahmad and Jamshaid had plunged me into deep introspection. Saleh had a fair idea of the mental anguish I was going through. To divert my attention, he said:

"It has escaped your mind that we had actually come here to meet the last Prophet, peace be upon him. You stopped here on our way. In the meantime, he has himself asked for you."

"Has Papa not met the last Prophet yet, peace be upon him?" Anwar asked, quite surprised.

Saleh clarified:

"Every person who returns successful from the Plane of Judgement goes straight to the last Prophet first. The Prophet rewards him by giving him a glass of water from Kauthar with his own hands. His family members are also called on that occasion. Thereafter, they merrily proceed and take a spot of their choice on the bank of the pond or, as your father calls it, 'a lake'. However, your father was fond of roaming in the Plane of Judgement, thus prior to his meeting with the Prophet, and at his request, he was sent back to the Plane of Judgement. However, now the Prophet has himself asked for him."

"Is everything alright? Why has he been summoned"? Naimah inquired.

Saleh replied:

"As the accountability of different nations continues, now is the turn of the nation of Prophet Noah PBUH. But his nation has flatly denied that they had received any message of God from him."

"What a position! How can they say that they have not received any message of God? They were drowned right there in the world because they had denied the message of Prophet Noah. After that decision from God, how can they say that Prophet Noah PBUH did not pass any message to them and that too in the presence of God?" Arifa asked.

Leila added further to her earlier comment:

"And even if they have taken a stubborn stance and have chosen to lie, Qur'an had stated that the mouths of such people will be shut and their hands and feet will be asked to testify. How can they say such a thing?"

Saleh explained the situation further:

"The people who are making that claim are not people of Prophet Noah's nation who had incurred the punishment. They are the children of those who had embraced the faith as prophesized by him and then their siblings inhabited the world. Nevertheless, to a significant number of them no prophet was sent after Prophet Noah. They relied on guidance about the Oneness of God and Day of Judgement that was in essence a remnant of Prophet Noah's teachings, even though after the passage of such a long time, they may not have recognised it as such and they may have even distorted it to some extent. It is for this reason that they have denied having received any guidance from Prophet Noah."

I interjected to further clarify Saleh's reply:

"The fact is that majority of the humanity originated from Prophet Noah PBUH. A number of groups among them, particularly the descendants of his son 'Shem', who inhabited the central areas of Earth like Middle East and its adjoining regions, benefited from a continuous chain of prophets and messengers. Yet, there were many groups who did not directly benefit from a prophet after Prophet Noah. In particular, after Prophet Abraham PBUH, no prophets were sent to nations other than his descendants. These people are now considered as either descendants of Prophet Noah or belonging to his nation.

At the time of accountability, they were presented along with the nation of Prophet Noah. However, they did not directly know the teachings of Prophet Noah nor did they appreciate their relationship to him in a way other people like the People of the Book and the Muslims did. Therefore, they denied ever having received the message of Prophet Noah PBUH. Their refusal is not entirely unjustified either."

Saleh added, "Abdullah is correct. It is a fact that people from the nation of Prophet Muhammad delivered the message of God to such off springs of the nation of Prophet Noah. For this reason, all initial and final witnesses from the nation of the last Prophet are being called upon to bear witness, as in the previous world they had conveyed the truth to these people through their actions. Today these witnesses will testify that one way or the other, they had managed to convey the message of Oneness of God to these people; this message was the real inheritance of the teachings of Prophet Noah and was forgotten later on. Following the arrival of the last Prophet, this message was preserved till the Day of Judgement and his followers fulfilled their responsibility of passing it on to the children of Noah."

Naimah looked at me and asked, "Why were they not presented along with the nation of the last Prophet then?"

"They would have been if they had embraced Islam. However, they did not do so and continued to follow the disfigured religion of their ancestors. Since every nation is being presented for accountability along with its prophet, all such people have been brought forward as the nation of Prophet Noah. The reason is that their forefathers had embraced faith through Prophet Noah." I replied, and then summarised the discussion in these words:

"In short, Prophet Noah PBUH personally delivered the message of God to the early followers of his nation while the Muslims delivered it to the later generations being the upholders of the message of Oneness of God and Day of Judgement, and that was the main message of all prophets including Prophet Noah."

"Come on Abdullah, we are being called" Saleh said to me.

We got up and started moving towards our destination.

================

Once again, we were in the presence of the last Prophet of God, Prophet Muhammad, peace and blessings be upon him! He had the same radiance on his face as well as the same attractiveness and aura that I had observed when I saw him the first time. I felt as if I had known him since centuries, and his love continued to grow in my heart.

I was sitting at the rear of the gathering of his companions, looking at his glowing face as he talked to them. Then someone went close to him and said something in his ear.

Saleh whispered in my ear, "That is his servant Anas, and he is telling him about you."

At that moment, the Prophet raised his head to look at me and welcomed me with a heartening smile, confirming what Saleh had whispered in my ear. Then he smiled and said to the people sitting around him:

"The nation of one of the forefathers of humanity and Prophet of God, Noah has refused to accept his testimony by saying that he did not directly deliver any message to them. In fact, my followers had delivered the same message to them. All of you sitting here believe in all prophets of God, and the religion that I passed on to you is the same religion that was given to Prophet Noah. It is therefore, your responsibility to present yourself in the Court of the Almighty, and testify on behalf of Prophet Noah. You have to testify that the invitation to believe in one God and righteous deeds that Prophet Noah had extended to his followers, and which I also passed on to you, was delivered to his nation by you, without any omissions or additions, thereby fulfilling his and my mission."

He then asked his companion Abu-Bakr, sitting next to him, to rise. Abu-Bakr, May God be pleased with him, did so.

The Prophet said to the people around him:

"He is my friend Abu-Bakr. In addition to him, there are followers present here representing my nation from my time to just before the Day of Judgement. All of you should follow him to the Court of the Almighty and be witnesses to the truth that you bear."

The Prophet PBUH rose as he finished his sentence. After that, everyone also stood up. Abu-Bakr kissed his hand and moved on. Following his lead, everyone kissed the Prophet's hand. My turn was at the end. I also availed the sterling honour. Thereafter, all of us started towards the Plane of Judgement with Abu-Bakr, May God be pleased with him, in the lead.

===============

I was walking at the rear of the group along with the exalted personalities. Saleh was not with me. Before departing from the Prophet's gathering, he had told me that I would have to testify on my own, and that he would meet me when we return.

On the way, a thought came to my mind that I was not worthy of representing the nation of the last Prophet along with such honourable and exalted personalities. This feeling gradually overwhelmed me, to the extent that I decided to leave the group quietly. Who would notice? The Almighty would call someone else from my era in my place.

I started to walk slower with this in mind. Soon, the distance between the rest of the group and me became considerable. I decided to avail this opportunity. Just as I turned around to head back in the direction of Kauthar, I heard a voice behind me:

"Abdullah, what are you doing?"

I nervously turned around and saw Abu-Bakr, the Truthful standing behind me. I felt ashamed as if I had been caught stealing. My initial inclination was to make an excuse, but then I realised that this was not the previous world; God could reveal the truth to him at that very moment. Therefore, I told him the whole story, and in addition requested him to take someone else along rather than me.

Abu-Bakr, May God be please with him, started to laugh; then he said:

"God selected people for the testimony himself. He is the one who informed me through an angel about the reason for your intent to leave."

He gently held my hand and started to walk forward. On the way, he advised me:

"Listen, Abdullah! The Almighty himself has selected every person in this group. Do you know what the criterion is for this selection?"

I remained silent, and looked at him.

He answered the question himself:

"In the eyes of your Lord, the most eligible people to bear witness are those who rose above all prejudices, emotions and desires to make submission to the truth their prime concern, and then dedicated their lives to the Oneness of God and Hereafter.

In your era, the religious people may have managed to rise above their desires but most failed to overcome prejudice and emotions. Sectarian and communal priorities had enslaved their thoughts. They would accept only the ideas proposed by people from their own sect. They would call people only towards their sect. They lived their lives under strong influence of the perceived greatness of their leaders.

In contrast, you lived your life only under the influence and appreciation of the greatness of the Almighty. You accepted the truth no matter what the price was and applied it to your life, regardless of any prejudice. Oneness of God was your main concern; the prime objective of your life was to help people prepare for this encounter with their Lord. In addition, you did not confine your work just to your own nation; rather, you were involved in a long struggle to spread Qur'an's message of Oneness of God and the Hereafter amongst the non-Muslims. These are the reasons that have led to your selection today."

==============

Prophet Noah [PBUH], his hands held together in front of him, was standing to the right of the Divine Throne. All of us, under the leadership of Abu-Bakr, the Truthful, stood behind.

In front of us, as far as the eyes could see, was a sea of human beings. Every one of them appeared worried and looked ill. They were standing with their heads bowed. Their faces were dark with fear. In the surroundings, apart from a faint whisper, no voice could be heard. This was the nation of Prophet Noah, who in fact were people born to his children.

In a little while, a loud voice was heard:

"The witnesses of Noah be presented in the Court."

I expected that Abu-Bakr, May God be pleased with him, would move forward and say something. However, at this juncture, I saw that the last Prophet came forward and stood in front of the Throne.

A voice was heard, "Speak O' Muhammad! What do you want to say?"

The Prophet PBUH spoke in the presence of the One and only:

"My Lord, you gave me prophethood and revealed your Book upon me. In that Book, you informed me that Prophet Noah had also brought with him the same religion that you endowed me with, which was based on a belief in the Oneness of God. I bore witness upon the same righteous religion and passed it on to my nation. Now these people are present here in front of you to bear witness that they took this righteous religion from me and passed it on to the children of Noah without any addition or omission."

The Almighty said: "You have spoken the truth. Present your followers."

"On this, Abu-Bakr, the Truthful took a few steps forward and stood next to Prophet Noah PBUH. All of us also moved forward and stood behind him.

A voice was heard: "Who are you?"

Abu-Bakr, May God be pleased with him, introduced himself and then introduced each of us by stating our names and the time periods we lived in. He stated that we were all from the nation of Prophet Muhammad. He said that the final Prophet bore witness of the true religion upon us and told us that Prophet Noah had also brought the same religion with him. He further stated that we then took this religion of Prophets Noah PBUH and Muhammad PBUH to all the nations of the world. We also took this truth to those who were present in front of the Almighty, as the nation of Prophet Noah.

After this evidence, there was no excuse left for the nation of Prophet Noah. It was apparent that the religion of Prophet Noah was the same as that of Prophet Muhammad and that his followers had delivered this religion to the rest of the world. Now the accountability of the nation of Prophet Noah was to take place in the light of this evidence.

We had completed our task; hence, we embarked on our return journey.

================

Our group was moving along on the way to the pond of Kauthar. This time the leader of our small convoy was the final Prophet himself. Accompanied by angels, we were passing through the Plane of Judgement, heading towards Kauthar. I stayed at the rear of this group, afraid of embarrassing myself. Suddenly someone put a hand on my shoulder and said:

"And where were you trying to run away, my friend?"

I looked back and saw Saleh, who was smiling. I remained silent, feeling embarrassed. He spoke laughingly:

"Praise the Lord that the leader of the group was Abu-Bakr, the Truthful. If Umar was in his place, he would have given you at least a few lashes as punishment!"

I also started to laugh. After a pause, I said:

"In fact, it is not about Abu-Bakr or Umar, May God be pleased with them. The honourable Umar would have done the same. The reason is that the one who arranged it all is the same. That is my merciful God, who has concealed my sins throughout my life."

A worrying thought then came to my mind. I asked Saleh:

"By the way, how did you come to know about it? Does everyone know about it as well?"

"No, no... Abu-Bakr is very kind-hearted; he did not say a word. As for me, I know about it as God sent a message to him regarding it through me. Anyway, your statement is correct. Guess, what was the message that the Almighty asked me to take to Abu-Bakr?"

He answered his own question without waiting for my reply:

"Look after my servant. In his humility, he is about to neglect his responsibility."

I bowed my head with mixed feelings of embarrassment and gratitude.

After a few moments, I inquired from Saleh:

"How is the accountability process going on in the Plane of Judgement?"

"The evidence against nations of various prophets is being presented. All prophets and messengers are testifying that they had passed the message of God to their respective nations. After that, the sins of all those people whose deeds were largely in accordance with the teachings of the prophets are forgiven and their success is announced". Saleh replied.

I recalled everything. Saleh had told me earlier that after the initial period of accountability, general accountability would begin. I had a faint hope that perhaps at that stage a decision for the salvation of my son Jamshaid may be announced. However, obviously I could not do anything for him.

I inquired from Saleh:

"What is the state of people over there?"

"Don't ask! No one is able to comfort anyone. Furthermore, no one knows what is going to be his fate."

We were walking behind the entourage, talking, when suddenly we heard a loud noise. The reason for it was that a huge crowd of Muslims was heading towards the Prophet PBUH chanting his name. They were screaming, crying, and begging the Prophet to help them, saying that they were his followers. However, the angels were beating them with lashes to keep them away. They had become so fed up due to the hardships in the Plane of Judgement that despite being beaten up, they were still trying to move towards the Prophet. The Prophet appeared to them as the only ray of hope.

On seeing this, the Prophet, peace be upon him, called the leader of the angels. He asked him for the reason this treatment was being meted out to those people, despite the fact that they claimed to be his followers, ascribed their faith to him, and mentioned his name in their proclamation of faith.

The angel answered with utmost respect, "O Prophet of God, no doubt they take your name, but you are not aware of all sorts of innovations, alterations, and changes that these people had introduced in your religion after you had left the world."

On hearing this, an expression of extreme dislike appeared on the face of the Prophet and he said:

"May those people be distanced from me who distorted my religion after I had left!"

Saying this, the Prophet PBUH turned towards the pond of Kauthar and walked away, with the rest of the people in the convoy following suit.

I was also about to move forward but Saleh stopped me by saying:

"Wait and see what happens here."

I saw that the angels then started to attack these people heartlessly. In the meantime, more angels joined them from the left of the Plane of Judgement. They started to beat them mercilessly. Their strength was such that when they lashed out once with a whip, thousands of people were hit by it and were thrown yards away, crying and screaming. In a short while, the entire area close to the pond was cleared of such people. Beaten up and crying in pain, they, who had invented new beliefs and actions in the religion of Islam, left that place, moaning and groaning on their humiliation and ill-fate.

I was standing next to Saleh, watching the horrible scene. I thought to myself. They were the unfortunate people for whom guidance of Qur'an and practical example of the Sunnah of the Prophet were not sufficient. Therefore, they made additions and alterations to the religion and tried to deface it. They had a senseless logic for their misguided and sick deeds. When someone with insight tried to make them understand their fallacies, they became their mortal enemies. They were told that there was no room for inventing beliefs outside Qur'an and no deeds apart from the ones that were part of the Sunnah would be reliable in the Court of the Almighty, but they regarded such advice as absurd and remained engrossed in their misguided ways. Thus, they had suffered the consequences of their attitude today.

As I was thinking about it, Saleh said to me:

"Abdullah, I have not managed to grasp this habit of human beings. Why is it that after receiving such lucid guidance, nations of all the prophets heavily indulged in alterations and innovations?"

"You have asked a good question. I also deliberated a lot on this issue during my previous life. In my opinion, the real reason for this tendency was exaggeration and extremism. Human beings are very emotional by nature. They go to extremes in either direction. The followers of the prophets also suffered from it. Some people, because of their inclination towards materialism, ignored the teachings of the prophets while others went to the other extreme in their love for prophets and righteous people and enthusiasm for worship. It is these exaggerations and extremist behaviours that became the main reasons for innovations in religion."

Saleh nodded on hearing my reply and said, "The most glaring example of this extremist behaviour and exaggeration were the Christians. On one hand, they discarded the Law brought by Prophet Moses, and on the other, they invented a creed of self-denial and introduced such worships, practices, and innovations in the religion that it became extremely difficult for an ordinary person to live a normal life and yet maintain a religious identity. In addition to the innovations in deeds, extreme exaggeration in beliefs also became rampant amongst them. Despite being a nation with so many prophets, they managed to invent a wife and a son of God. But my friend, the truth is that you Muslims were not far behind them either!"

He spoke, especially emphasising the last part of his statement. I replied as a rejoinder:

"And today, both Christians and Muslims have had to suffer the consequences for the same."

As I said so, the scenes of events that I had just witnessed a few moments ago were alive in my mind.

================

Chapter 10: Accountability & Inmates of Hell

I had felt quite dejected after seeing the treatment meted out to those who had indulged in bringing about alterations and innovations in their religion. My misery had compounded as I had also found quite a few acquaintances amongst them.

Saleh took me back to the pond of Kauthar to soothe my nerves. I felt better after I had spent some time in that pleasant environment all by myself. Thereafter, Saleh brought me back to the Plane of Judgement.

On our way back, he informed me that testimony of the remaining messengers of God had been completed in our absence and the general accountability stage had commenced. This stage had also begun with the followers of the last Prophet. Most people of this group had already heard Almighty's verdict after having gone through the process.

"It means that I missed a very important part of the accountability process." I said.

"Yes you did, but don't worry. In the Paradise, you will be able to watch its audio-video recording whenever you wish to do so". He laughingly responded to my question.

"But that would be no match for watching it in real time!" I responded with a smile.

"Let me tell you something very interesting, though. When those followers of the last Prophet who had indulged in Shirk were taken to task, a large number denied that they ever participated in these heinous practices. Interestingly, they included people not only from the later eras but also those idol worshippers of Mecca who had directly benefited from the presence of the last Prophet."

"And what was the reason for their denial?" I asked.

"The reason was that everyone has realised that today nobody has any power except the Almighty. Initially, these idol worshippers tried to find and call their gods, goddesses, and idols. Obviously, nobody answered their prayers. Even the angels and pious human beings they used to call for help instead of God denied having anything to do with their actions. Hence, they had no option but to deny their doings. Obviously, it was of no use and they were sentenced to a lifetime in Hell."

"Who is going through the accountability process now?" I asked.

"Right now, it is the people from your era. It is for this reason that I have brought you here. As you can see, one by one, people are being presented before the Almighty for accountability. Two angels accompany each person. One walks behind him, escorting him to the Throne while the other walks along with him, carrying his Book of Deeds.

The angel who is behind is called 'Saiq' and the one who has the Book of Deeds is known as 'Shaheed'. Saiq is responsible for escorting a person from the Plane of Judgement to the Throne whereas Shaheed testifies about his deeds as written in the record. In fact, they are the same angels who were present with every human being in the previous life. The one on the right had the job of noting down good deeds whereas the one on the left documented the bad deeds. They were referred to as 'the honourable recorders' in the Qur'an."

"But over here, who gets the role of Saiq and who has the responsibility of the Shaheed?" I enquired.

"Only God knows it. He assigns their responsibilities just before an individual is to be presented before him."

When we reached there, we saw a civil servant who was in the dock.

The Almighty asked him:

"What did you accomplish in the world?"

Trembling, he replied, "Oh God, no doubt I committed some mistakes. However, afterwards I worshipped you a lot. I dedicated the rest of my life for your religion."

The angel standing by him said, following a cue by the Almighty, "He has told the truth, my Lord."

He was asked again:

"You were a civil servant. Did you indulge in bribery? Did you force people to offer you bribes? Did you illegitimately enforce the law too harshly so that people were forced to offer you bribes?"

He admitted, "Yes I did. But I repented afterwards."

The Almighty thundered:

"You repented? Did you?"

He could not utter a word in reply.

The angel moved forward and started to read out aloud from his Book of Deeds. According to the record, he had constructed a house with his ill-gotten money and had lived in that house all his life. He had invested the money to increase his net worth, and then used it to pay for the higher education of his children. He bought lots of ornaments and jewellery for his wife using the same illegitimate income. He continued to benefit from this wealth until his death. However, he did repent verbally and after retirement, he adopted the usual religious practice and appearance of a typical Muslim, such as keeping a beard, wearing a cap, praying regularly, etc.

As soon as the angel stopped speaking, the Almighty said:

"Put his Book of Deeds in the scale of justice."

The angel on the right, Shaheed, took out his good deeds and placed them in the scale. Then the angel called Saiq on the left side took out his bad deeds and placed them in the other arm of the scale. The civil servant watched all this, totally helpless and terrified.

As soon as the angels finished their task, the result was obvious. Left arm of the scale had completely out-weighed the right arm. What he had earned through bribery, injustice, and abuse of power completely overshadowed his good deeds.

He started to weep and begged for mercy.

Almighty's voice boomed:

"Did you ever feel pity for the people you abused and extorted the money from? See that all you had earned is of no use to you today. You are destined to Hell."

At that, the angel placed the Book of Deeds in his left hand.

The man started to lament even louder:

"I did not do anything for myself. Whatever I did was for the sake of my wife and children. For God's sake, let me go! Punish my family instead."

The angels replied:

"They will be dealt with on their turn. For now, move on to your cursed destination!"

The two angels dragged him away towards Hell, beating him heartlessly.

===============

Next person to appear before the Almighty was a senior police officer. The Almighty Lord did not even address him directly. He asked the angel standing next to him about the contents of his Book of Deeds. In response, the angel narrated all the crimes he had committed in his life. They included heinous crimes such as cruelty against public, murder of innocent people, patronage of gambling dens and brothels, adultery, drinking, corruption, and pleasure mongering etc. On the other hand, his good deeds were only those Eid prayers that he had attended half-heartedly to please his superiors.

The Almighty said to him, "Do you have anything to say in your defence?"

He replied, "My Lord! My conduct was a product of the environment I lived in. Bribery was prevalent all around. I did not want to indulge in it but was forced to do so due to the pressures of my superiors and the demands of society."

The Almighty thundered:

"So you were forced to resort to do what you did?"

He then summoned a junior police officer who had worked under him in the previous life. In a short while, a very good-looking man, dressed in fine clothes, appeared.

The Almighty addressed him:

"You also served in the police force with this person. Why did you not choose the path of oppression and corruption despite the prevailing atmosphere?"

He replied:

"My Lord, it was the fear of appearing before you today that kept me away from accepting bribes. I refused to do so despite pressure from my colleagues. Even though I spent my life in abject poverty, I did not compromise on justice for the sake of money."

"You are right! As a consequence, I have given a lot of weight to the small number of your good deeds and have awarded you with the life in the everlasting Paradise."

He then addressed the first police officer:

"The choice you had was not about whether to get rich by choosing corruption, oppression, and injustice, or to live a life of poverty. Rather, the choice was to live a life of righteousness and go to paradise, or indulge in oppression and go to Hell; you chose to go to Hell. Thus, Hell is your fate for the rest of your life!"

The police officer was not willing to give up so easily; he started to weep and said:

"My Lord, Satan misled me."

The Almighty thundered:

"No! In reality, you were yourself a devil! Even though, for me, you were even more helpless than an insignificant ant. You are a worthless man. Even when you oppressed other human beings, I was watching you. However, I gave you time to correct yourself. You did not avail of it! You were under the impression that you would not have to face me in this court. Now you can see that you were wrong."

As these words, full of wrath & fury were delivered, the sound of the roaring flames of Hell coming from left of the Plane of Judgement became progressively louder. The hearts of people present there were trembling with fear. People were petrified to death! Everyone seemed extremely tense. Their eyes had a blank look and the faces had darkened with misery. Their hearts beat so fast as if they would pop out of their chests. However, today, there was nowhere to run to, and no place to hide. As each wrongdoer received the verdict, other offenders felt increasingly worse.

There were all sorts of people waiting for their turn. They included emperors, extremely powerful leaders, wheeler-dealers, dictators, billionaires, famous celebrities, and power brokers. All of them were waiting helplessly for their fate to be decided, like slaves, perhaps more like a flock of sheep. Today there was no one who could save them.

Record of deeds of the police officer was put in the scale of justice; as expected, the left arm was significantly lower. The angel tried to hand him over his record in his left hand but he pulled it back. Obviously, he was nothing in strength as compared to the angel, who tied his hands at his back and then shoved the record in his left hand. Thereafter, both angels started thrashing him and dragged him away towards the roaring flames of Hell, where an even worse fate awaited him.

==============

The person brought in next was a fabulously rich man.

He was asked:

“You left behind mounds of wealth. Say, how did you earn it and how did you spend it?”

He submitted:

“My Lord, I earned my wealth through trade. Whatever I earned, I spent on the poor.”

The Lord signalled to the angel standing next to him. He started to narrate the details. The man earned billions. Initially he had a small business. He earned huge profits through adulteration and hoarding of essential goods like, sugar, flour etc. His business expanded rapidly due to these despicable practices. Later on, he expanded in to other businesses. However, this time he formed a cartel of criminal-minded Businessmen. The basic purpose of this cartel was to manipulate the market in order to inflate prices for various commodities. This cartel included influential people who used their political connections as well as bribery to fix favourable prices. As a result, the common man suffered while the profits of these Businessmen increased from millions to billions and then to trillions. In order to project a good image of himself in the society, he donated petty sums to charity from time to time and earned praise for it.

Once the angel had completed his statement, there was not much left to say. However, the Businessman was quite cunning. He started to shout and claimed that what had just been said was not true and that he was innocent. He claimed that he did everything according to the prevalent law and in response to the requirements of the marketplace. He alleged that the angel was lying and that there was no proof against him. He was wailing relentlessly.

The Almighty replied:

“So you need proof? That shall be provided!”

With these words, his ability to speak was taken away. Suddenly, his hands started talking. They narrated more or less the same statement as was put forward by the angel. A similar testimony was provided by his feet, and by the rest of his body. Finally, his heart started talking and brought forward hitherto unknown intentions that were not even recorded in the angel’s ledger.

After this account, there was nothing left to say. The only additional misery ordained on him was that the angels were ordered to heat up all his wealth and sear his body with it. That was in addition to the regular sufferings of the Hell. The angels dragged him away mercilessly towards his final abode.

================

One by one, people were being brought in and their cases were being decided. Some of them were too horrible to watch.

A person was brought in. It looked like he had tons of good deeds to his credit. Prayers, Pilgrimages to Mecca, Fasting, Nawafils, and all kind of supplications one could think of. However, once the angel started mentioning his relations with other human beings, it became obvious that there were people against whom he had used foul language, some he had deprived of their belongings, others he had wrongfully accused, and a few he had beaten up badly and so on.

All of his victims were called in. His good deeds were divided amongst them in proportion to the grievances caused to them. This went on until he ran out of good deeds. However, there were some more victims still in the queue. To compensate them, their bad deeds were transferred to his account. When it came down to weighing, left side of the scale weighed a lot more.

The man started to cry, but in vain. The angels mercilessly dragged him away to the Hell.

Watching some of those cases got me worried about my own fate. One of them was a scholar. Having been reminded of the blessings bestowed upon him, he was asked what he had done to express his gratefulness to God. He boasted about his scholastic achievements and preaching efforts. He was told that he was lying. He had done whatever he had only to be known as a great scholar. That reward had already been given to him in the world; he had become known as a renowned scholar.

The decision was obvious. Angels dragged him away face downwards towards Hell.

A martyr and a generous person met the same fate. When questioned, they boasted about their good deeds, but they were given the same verdict. All they had done was to earn fame and a name in the world, which they had already received. They did not do anything for God. Hence, today God did not have anything good to bless them with either. They were also sent to Hell.

Watching these scenes, I was trying to visualise those of my deeds that I had performed solely for God as well as those that I did to earn a place in the hearts of people in the world.

===============

During this process of judgement and accountability, some strange and hitherto unknown things were being brought to light. They included facts about conspiracies, assassination of famous personalities, events that took place at homes, in offices and at local or international level. The factors behind those events, the people involved, details of secret & closed doors meetings, how the things started and then reached their culmination came out as they had actually happened.

Everything had become clear as daylight today. Honourable were becoming dishonourable. Noble were coming out as ignoble. God witnessed each & every moment of the lives of people who lived their lives totally oblivious of him. Neither a word was uttered, nor did a thought or intent come to a mind without being noticed by Him. Every act, even smaller than the smallest particle, had been recorded. Today, the truth was being brought to surface for all to see in such a way that every person felt denuded.

I was witnessing these scenes and thinking about my own sins & shortcomings. I was afraid for my own fate. What would happen if my sins and misdeeds were revealed? Even without punishment, the awareness that everyone would come to know about my misdeeds would itself be the greatest and most humiliating punishment of the day.

Saleh had probably read my mind. Patting me on the back, he said:

"God will never humiliate his pious servants. His exalted benevolence will conceal their bad deeds. Nobody will come to know of their weaknesses, faltering or sins. Do not worry. You won't find anyone more benevolent and magnanimous than your Lord."

"I have no doubt about it. However, right now I am witnessing the grasp of the Almighty. The façade of nobility is also being torn away from the faces of evildoers prior to their departure to eternal torture". I muttered worriedly.

Saleh consoled me, "this treatment is being meted out to the criminals only. Before subjecting them to physical punishment, they are also being put through the mental torture of humiliation."

Meanwhile, another person was brought in. As soon as he approached the Almighty, he lamented, "O God! I was born in a very poor family. I spent my childhood in extreme poverty. I made some mistakes during my youth. Please forgive me!"

He asked an angel:

"Did I test him through poverty?"

The Angel replied respectfully:

"O God, he is right about poverty. However, what he calls "some mistakes" were actually crimes of the most heinous nature. He chose to be a bandit. To grab a little cash, a mobile phone and such other petty things, he not only injured a lot of human beings but also killed many".

"So this is what the truth is!" These words were uttered with such rage and ferocity that the future of the man became crystal-clear.

"O despicable creature! No doubt, I destined you to be born in a poor family. Yet I gave you a chance to progress by endowing you with a healthy body and lot of capabilities. If you had endeavoured the right way, I would have given you your share of livelihood that had already been destined for you. However, you got the very same share by looting and killing humans.

Now, you have to face the consequences of your misdeeds by taking over sins of all those people you had either killed or harmed. The verdict is that you will burn in eternal Hell and you shall live through that torture forever. You are cursed! You have to face endless pain."

As soon as the verdict was finalised, the angels pounced on him and, thrashing him mercilessly, dragged him to Hell.

===============

When I saw the next person who was presented for accountability, I felt miserable. It was no one else but Aasmah, Leila's friend. She was in a state even worse than what I had seen her in, the last time. She was presented to the Lord.

First question was asked:

"Did you pray five times a day?"

Aasmah stood, silent.

She was asked again:

"Were you paralysed? Did you not believe in God? Did you think you were God? Did you have no time for me? Or was it someone else besides me who had bestowed worldly blessings on you?"

Aasmah could not find any words to say in her defence.

An angel replied instead of her:

"Lord, she used to say: God does not need our prayers."

"She was correct. By now, she would have understood that I did not need her worship. She was the one who needed her prayers. Prayer is the key to Paradise. How can anyone enter Paradise without it?"

Thereafter, Aasmah was asked a few more questions. How did she spend her life? How did she spend her youth? How did she earn money and where did she spend it? How much knowledge did she acquire and how much of it she actually put in practice? Questions about obligatory charity, helping other people, Fasting, Hajj etc., and other questions were asked one by one. However, these questions only increased her misery and humiliation.

At last, Aasmah started to wail loudly.

She said:

"My Lord, I was oblivious to this day. I spent my entire life like an animal. I spent my days in pursuit of money, fashion, friendships, worldly relations, and enjoyment. I had forgotten about this Day of Judgement and your might. My Lord, please forgive me. Send me back to Earth once again. I will spend my whole life in praying and praising you. I will never disobey your commands! Please grant me one more chance."

"If I send you back once more, you will still do the same deeds as you did the first time. Even if I grant you one more chance, your behaviour will not change. I had conveyed my message to you but your eyes were closed. You had become blind. That is why you shall be thrown in the dark chasm of Hell. There is neither forgiveness, nor a second chance for you!"

Aasmah faced the same horrible fate as meted out to other criminals prior to her.

==============

Having witnessed Aasmah's fate, I became extremely disturbed. Subconsciously, I was afraid that if the same horrible punishment was awarded to my son Jamshaid, perhaps I would not be able to witness it.

I said to Saleh, "I do not have the strength to stay here anymore. Please take me away."

Saleh understood my condition. Without a word, he held my hand and started moving in a certain direction.

All along the way, we saw horrible scenes. There were people who were in the last stages of extreme suffering after being exposed to the severest hardships in the Plane of Judgement for innumerable centuries. People who had possessed all sorts of abilities in various fields were moving around in a pitiable condition. They included the wealthy, the powerful, the influential, the intelligent, the beautiful, and people who had authority in the world. They had everything in the world. What they did not have was faith and abundance of good deeds. They were the most deprived today.

The wealthy were the saddest. Those who were free of all worries in the world were in the worst shape here. Those who had been made to suffer for thousands of years were praying for death, hoping for mercy, seeking intercession or favour. They were wandering around in a miserable state and being randomly beaten up by the angels. Forlorn and completely exhausted with hunger and thirst, their condition was pitiable. The intensity of heat was taking its toll and they were prepared to do anything to gain respite, no matter how brief. They were even willing to sacrifice their children, wives and families, their entire wealth and previous possessions in return for an escape from their predicament.

However, it was not possible. The opportunity of being eligible to receive the gift of paradise in return for spending a little money or time in the way of God was now lost. They had spent their entire lives on their careers, children, and property. Alas, if only they had also spent a portion of their time in the service of God and in preparation for this day, they would not have been in such a dire state.

In the Plane of Judgement, names of people were being called regularly. When a person was called, two angels would quickly move in his direction and present him in front of the exalted Creator. It seemed that the angels had their targets in sight and from a crowd of millions; they could find the required person in no time. My eyes searched for Jamshaid subconsciously, but I could not locate him anywhere.

Saleh saw my predicament and said:

"I am not taking you to him deliberately. A verdict for Hell has already been announced for his wife, children and in-laws. No one knows what will be his fate. It would be best if you do not meet him till such time God decides something for him."

On hearing his opinion, I should have become gloomy and despondent. However, somehow, and for an unknown reason, a different feeling overtook me. I said to Saleh:

"Whatever be the decision of my God, it will be entirely acceptable to me. I may love my son a lot, but God loves him and all of his creatures thousands of time more than anyone else does. In fact, if the affection of all beings is taken collectively, my Creator loves his beings much more than that. Even if there is one per cent chance of being forgiven, he will be forgiven! On the other hand, if he is not worthy of forgiveness under any circumstances, then I have no sympathy for someone who is a criminal of such magnitude in the eyes of my Creator, even if he is my son."

On hearing this, Saleh smiled and said:

"You are so different, so very different!"

"No. I am neither different, nor better. In fact, my Creator is supreme. He has filled my heart with peace & tranquillity. I am not concerned about anything now."

"That's the correct way to think. Now you have taken a turn for better. You have again become Abdullah, a servant of God rather than being merely a father. I can tell you that even now there is a chance for Jamshaid to be forgiven. God Almighty is using hardships suffered in the Plane of Judgement as redemption of sins for many, and after taking into account their good deeds, he is forgiving them. It was a coincidence that you witnessed the accountability of the convicted. Even now, some people are being forgiven as according to the exalted standards of justice of God, no truly good deed is ignored."

I replied, "No doubt, God values all good deeds. Where are we heading now?"

"We are going to go towards the Hell. I would like you to meet the inmates of Hell."

"Do we have to be actually in the Hell to do that?"

"No. The condemned have now been moved in close proximity of Hell. On the left where you can see flat ground, a path progressively gets deeper and ultimately becomes a ditch. The seven doors leading to Hell are located in it. As you read in the Qur'an, there are seven categories of convicts. Each enters through one of the seven doors."

While Saleh was explaining these details, I saw a path that was sloping downwards in the flat field. We did not go down that path but started to walk on the higher ground adjacent to it. In a short while, the lower path narrowed and took the shape of a ditch. Since we were on high ground, we could see the scene down below clearly. Angels were positioned all along the path; they were bringing the convicts, beating and dragging them in the process.

A little farther on, there was a huge crowd on the narrow path and in the ditch. Ugly, wretched men and women were jam-packed there like sardines in a can. They were cruel, lewd sinners whose fate had already been announced; they were being held there like animals in a pen prior to being sent to Hell.

Every now and then flames of Hellfire rose and reached skywards. The impact of these flames had coloured the sky red. Noise of the fire burning with ferocity was shaking the hearts of these convicts. Every once a while a stray spark, as big as a palace, would fall in this ditch and would cause a huge commotion. In order to avoid this ball of fire, people would run trampling and jumping over others. The frequency of this increased whenever a major convict was brought towards this group. A ball of fire would welcome him, enhancing the anguish and suffering of the sinners.

Saleh pointed in a certain direction and said to me:

"Look there!"

When I looked in that direction, I could suddenly hear the voices coming from there clearly.

They were leaders and their followers arguing amongst themselves. The followers said to their leaders, "We opposed the truth at your behest. You promised to save us if we were to face any punishment in the Hereafter. Can you now take over some of our punishment from us or at least show us a way out of it? After all, you were all very intelligent and had a solution for every problem."

The leaders replied, "If we knew a way, we would have saved ourselves first. In addition, we did not say that you must follow us. We did not force you to do so. You followed ways suggested by us as it was in your interest. We will have to face the music together."

On hearing this, the followers said, "O God! These leaders led us astray. Therefore, make them suffer twice the punishment we receive". The leaders replied, "How would cursing us help you?"

Witnessing this, Saleh commented, "There will be double punishment for all of them as the followers became the leaders of those that came thereafter and thus lead them astray. Look over there! More of their followers are arriving."

When I looked in that direction, I saw that the commotion had increased. Fervent pushing and shoving had started in the crowd as more sinners were brought in to the already overcrowded space. The leaders lamented that the place was already packed and still more of the wretched and condemned were being brought in.

On receiving such an unwelcome reception, the new comers also lost their cool. Verbal abuses flew in the air; scuffles ensued soon. It was not possible for me to truly appreciate the condition of these miserable people just by watching them and listening to them in this suffocating environment of kicking, punching, pushing, shoving and shouting; one had to personally experience such misery to fathom its true extent. However, I was sure that these people must have been remembering their previous lives with utmost regret where, they had every opportunity to strive for paradise but sadly, they chose Hell. They earned eternal misery just for the sake of a few days of pleasure, benefits, desires, and prejudices.

Saleh said to me:

"These people have not even been sent to Hell yet. The punishment over there will be much more severe. They will have a yoke placed around their necks as a mark of slavery and disgrace. Their clothes will be inflammable, made from sulphur and coal tar that would catch fire from a distance. The fire would scald their faces and bodies. They will writhe in pain but no one will come to their help, nor will anybody have mercy on them. Their skin, once totally burnt, will be replaced by a new skin that will develop a severe itch. They will scratch themselves so strenuously that they will bleed from everywhere but the itch would neither go nor decrease in severity.

Whenever they are hungry, they will have thorn-covered bushes and fruit of bitter poisonous Zaqqum trees. For drinking, there will be pungent and smelly sediment of pus, boiling water and bubbling hot oil. It will burn the innards of their stomachs and will boil inside their bellies. The intensity of their thirst would be such that like a camel that is dying of thirst, they would be forced to drink whatever is available to them. These boiling liquids will burn and destroy their intestines, pushing them out of their bodies.

In Hell, angels will bludgeon them with mammoth hammers. Their bodies will be severely wounded. The blood and pus that will ooze from their wounds will be given to other convicts to drink. Thereafter, they will be tied by chains and will be thrown in a tight place. Death will approach them from every side yet they will not die. At that moment, the best news for them will be to die but they will not die. At short intervals, they will continue to suffer these tortures and punishments forever."

On hearing these horrendous details, I was shaken up. Saleh added more to his earlier discourse:

"The condemned, prior to being sent to Hell, will be brought here and made to sit on their knees around the corners of Hell. Thus, their first punishment would be to watch the entire process with their own eyes. Then, in groups, they will be rammed into the narrow and dark crevices in Hell and the process of punishment I have just described will commence."

"So, will all dwellers of Hell be subjected to the same treatment?" I asked.

"No. What I have narrated will be the fate of major sinners. Others will receive a somewhat lighter punishment. However, even that light treatment will be beyond endurance!"

Saleh then pointed in another direction. I noticed some hideous and ugly characters. Saleh gave their identities explaining to me as to who had denied the message of which messenger of God and opposed him. I particularly took a good look at Nimrod and Pharaoh as I had heard a lot about them. Along with them were Abu-Jehl, Abu-Lahab and other leaders of the tribe of Quraish. Their condition was so horrible that it was beyond words to describe. These so-called powerful leaders of their times were in a condition much worse than that of even the lowliest slaves. Their crime was that truth was revealed to them in its ultimate state but they did not accept it. They chose to be defiant against God and chose the path of being unjust and cruel against his creatures.

While I was lost in the scene, Saleh brought a very strange scene to my attention. A giant sized man was standing in the middle of this commotion. Flames were emanating from his body and he was enslaved in chains.

He was addressing the condemned in these words:

"See! What God promised you was true, and the promises I made to you were all lies. Do not curse me today! I am not responsible for any of your deeds. I am not at fault. I had no control over you. Whatever you did was of your own free will and accord. If you listened to me, how could that be my fault? Do not blame me; blame yourselves! Today, neither I can do anything for you, nor you can do anything for me."

I could guess from the contents of his speech as to who he was. To confirm it, I turned towards Saleh. He said:

"You have guessed correctly. He is Satan, the one who was the most disobedient towards God. Today, the harshest punishment will also be for him. However, other people will also receive punishment for their doings."

I was witnessing this scene from a vantage point, and was thanking God Almighty in my heart for having protected me from the deceptions and evils of Satan. Even though this disgraced character had tried to mislead me from the right path on a number of occasions in my life, God had always kept me under his protection. It was my routine to seek God's protection from the accursed Satan often. Thus, my God had kept my dignity intact. Yet, those who followed their carnal desires and befriended Satan had met the worst end.

At that moment, Saleh turned towards me and said, "Abdullah lets go. You are being called."

"Why?" I asked.

"Jamshaid is about to be presented for his accountability. Your testimony is required."

"My testimony?"

"Yes, your testimony."

"Will I be a witness for him or against him?"

"Listen! If God has decided to forgive him, he will ask you something whose answer will go in his favour. On the other hand, if he has decided to punish him for his sins, he will ask you something that will go against him. It is also possible that the Almighty decides to deal with him in an entirely different way. Only God knows the final outcome."

My nerves that had calmed down by now started to play up again. With a trembling heart and unsteady steps, I accompanied Saleh.

===============

Chapter 11: At Last...

Jamshaid had yet to be presented for his accountability. Two angels stood beside him close to the Throne while he waited for his turn. His face was numb with fear and stress. His appearance showed no signs of affluence of fifty or sixty years spent in the world, but the story of suffering of thousands of years in the Plane of Judgement was clearly etched on his face. I tried to strengthen my heart before going to meet him. As I got nearer, the angels beside him stopped me from getting any closer. However, they relented when Saleh intervened.

Jamshaid had seen me by then. He dashed forward and embraced me. Taking a good look at me, he said:

"Papa, I have cried so much that even the tears have dried up."

I could not say anything except patting him on the back.

He whispered, "Papa, maybe I wasn't that bad".

"But you associated with bad people, Son! Association with bad people never leads to good results. You married a girl whose only qualities were beauty and wealth. These attributes are no qualities in the eyes of the Lord. You distanced yourself from us and joined your father-in-laws' business even when you knew it was tainted with ill-gotten wealth. For the sake of your wife, children and wealth, you became an accómplice. These wrongdoings have brought you to the sad situation you are faced with today."

"You're absolutely correct, Papa. However, I did perform good deeds too. So, is there any hope?"

I kept quiet. My silence conveyed the answer to him.

He said in a dejected tone:

"I have got a fair idea, Papa. After seeing my wife, children and in-laws being condemned to Hell, I have realised that today, no one has any say or power. All authority belongs to the Almighty God, whose commands I ignored. If a person's deeds do not save him today, no power in the Universe will be able to help him. I have been wandering wretchedly in this Plane for thousands of years. I have seen innumerable people going to Hell. I have no hope. I have repeatedly sought forgiveness of the Almighty. However, I know that it is of no use today. Papa, maybe God will not forgive me. Nevertheless, I want you to forgive me. After all, you are my father!"

After saying that, Jamshaid started to weep bitterly. I tried my best not to cry, but my eyes started to rain tears on the predicament of my son.

In the meantime, Jamshaid's name was called. The angels separated him from me immediately and presented him in front of the Lord.

He stood, arms folded and head lowered, in front of the Lord of the entire Universe. There was pin-drop silence. He kept standing there however, no question was asked of him. I could not understand the reason for it.

The reason became apparent in a short while as Nạimah arrived along with a few angels. At the same time, Saleh gestured to me and I stepped forward to stand besides Naimah.

Naimah's face was numb with worry & stress. She wanted to ask me something but the grandeur of the Court of the Lord was such that she could not utter a word.

Jamshaid was asked:

"Do you know me? Who am I"?

The Lord's voice had such a neutral tone that I could not fathom whether it was the harbinger of a hurricane or a sign of the Lord's infinite mercy.

"You are my Lord. You are everyone's Lord. This is what my father had taught me", Jamshaid replied.

He was asked majestically:

"Who is your father"?

Jamshaid looked at me and said, "It is him".

My heart missed a beat at this sentence. I feared that there was no hope for Jamshaid. Besides teaching him about the Oneness of God, I had also explained quite a few other things in which his record was not up to mark. I had a feeling that I would be asked about all the things I had taught him, and that would be used to declare him as guilty since he had not followed what was told.

However, unexpectedly, the Almighty did not order me to appear as a witness. He asked a completely different question from Jamshaid:

"What did you just say to your father a few moments ago? Did you say, 'maybe God will not forgive me? However, I want you to forgive me. After all, you are my father'"?

The hope that had kindled in my heart a second ago died with that question. Jamshaid had also realised that he was now being taken to task for his deeds. His face darkened with fear. His limbs started to tremble. He had not suspected that the Almighty, who was apparently occupied in the accountability of other people, had also been listening to our conversation. He realised that not only had the Lord been listening to what was said, but in addition, he had also taken offence to it.

He said helplessly, "Yes, I did say that but you have misunderstood me".

"How do you know what I have understood from your words?" The Lord replied, however the neutrality in the tone of the voice was still there, as before.

"No, no... I do not know... I have no idea about what you understood from my words!" Jamshaid replied in a stuttering voice.

The Almighty addressed the next question to Naimah instead:

"My slave, he is your son. How did he treat you"?

Naimah replied, "My Lord! He treated me very well. He served me until the end. He provided tender loving care to me using his wealth and physical abilities. His wife used to deter him from looking after me but he paid no heed to her objections. He had devoted his life and money to my care".

Naimah was desperate to say more in Jamshaid's defence, but she was aware that to utter a word more than what was asked of her might put her own self in jeopardy. She was therefore forced to become quiet after saying these words.

The Lord looked at the angel standing next to her and asked, "Is this woman telling the truth"?

The angel looked at the scroll of Deeds and replied, "My Lord, she has spoken the truth".

What happened thereafter made my heart beat faster. It was ordered that Jamshaid's deeds be placed in the scale. First, the sins were placed in the scale to the left, which caused the left arm of the scale to become heavier. All three of us were distraught. Thereafter, his virtues and good deeds were placed one by one in the scale on the right. They were few, and weighed significantly less than the weight of the bad deeds in the left arm of the scale.

Only two good deeds were left to be placed in the scale now. The decision seemed obvious.

Naimah closed her eyes with mixed feelings of dejection and helplessness.

Jamshaid dropped down on the ground, helplessly holding his head in his hands.

Ever since I had arrived in the Plane of Judgement, I had not dared to look towards the Throne. However, at that moment, perhaps for a fraction of a second or even less than that, my eyes involuntarily turned upwards in the direction of the Almighty, the All-powerful Lord of the Universe. At that very moment, the same call emanated from my heart that used to be on my lips whenever I had to face a sudden unexpected trial or tribulation in the previous world:

'La Ilaha Illal-Lah... there is no God except for the one God'.

I then immediately lowered my gaze and my head in prostration.

The angel placed the first remaining good deed in the scale. It was Jamshaid's behaviour towards Naimah. Unexpectedly, the right arm of the scale started to move downwards as it became heavier. I shook Naimah's arm and said, "Naimah, open your eyes".

My voice reached Jamshaid's ears too. He opened his eyes and slowly stood on his feet. Hope started to gain ground in him as the scale of virtues became heavier.

However, all of a sudden it stopped. The left arm of the scale was still heavier than the right arm. The glimmer of hope that had arisen in our hearts suddenly started to dwindle.

The angel took the last virtue and said aloud, "This is the belief in the Oneness of God". As soon as it was placed in the scale, it became decidedly heavier than the left arm, the arm holding the scale of sins.

I involuntarily uttered, "Allah-o-Akbar walillah-hil-hamd - God is great and praise is only for him!"

The Almighty spoke in a soft voice:

"Jamshaid, your father had also taught you that my love for my people is seventy thousand times more than the love of parents for their children. In fact, you did not value me! That is the reason you had to face so much hardship in the Plane of Judgement. My justice is without prejudice; however my grace overshadows everything else".

The angel wrote down the decision for Jamshaid's salvation onto the scroll of deeds and placed it into his right hand.

Overwhelmed with emotion, a scream emanated from Jamshaid's throat. He had been blessed with the ticket to the Paradise. Not only had he been saved from the tribulations of this day, a day that had comprised of many thousands of years, he was also relieved of every pain forever, as of now. He ran towards us and embraced us. Naimah was overwhelmed with joy. Tears were running down Jamshaid's cheeks. With every element of my being, I was praising the most beneficent and the most merciful Lord who had forgiven Jamshaid.

==============

My entire family was present in the V.V.I.P lounge by the pond of Kauthar. My three daughters, Leila, Arifa, and Aaliya and two sons,

Anwar and Jamshaid were with Naimah and me. Jamshaid's arrival had completed our family reunion. The state of joy and the feelings of elation could not be expressed in words.

As I saw my family gathered together, I said to Saleh, who was sitting next to me, "What fun is Paradise without the whole family?"

Jamshaid, whose family and in-laws had all been doomed to Hell, replied instead of Saleh, "Yes! Who else would know it better than I would? You are very fortunate!"

This time Naimah replied to him, "This is because your Papa gave the upbringing of his children due importance and priority in his life. Only you proved to be the inept one; look at the rest of your brothers and sisters! They all did pretty well".

"You are right, Mama! But I was sure that Papa's intercession would save me. My father-in-law had a lot of faith in his Peer who had assured him that he would intercede for him on the Day of Judgement as long as he remained loyal to him. That gave me the idea that there is no one like my father. Therefore, his intercession would save me too".

I said, "You got it absolutely wrong, my Son! You know that the Peer was unable to save your father in-law. The truth of the matter is that neither the last Prophet nor the Qur'an ever advocated intercession as a way to salvation. The only reason the last Holy book was sent towards us was to clearly explain how to succeed in the Hereafter. It repeatedly stressed that the only means of salvation on the Day of Judgement are faith and good deeds. At the time of the revelation of Qur'an, Christians had the misconception that Christ's intercession would lead to their salvation, while the idol worshippers of Arabia believed that their idols would intercede on their behalf. That is why the Qur'an repeatedly clarified that intercession could not lead to salvation. Man would reap whatever he had sown".

"But intercession has been mentioned in the Qur'an, and also in the sayings ascribed to the last Prophet", said Jamshaid.

"Ok, tell me, is there any saying ascribed to the Holy Prophet [PBUH] or a verse of the Qur'an that advises us to rely on intercession as a means to salvation or to pray for it?" I asked.

Anwar, my younger son, replied instead of Jamshaid with full confidence, "No! It was not mentioned anywhere".

However, Jamshaid disagreed, "No, my friend! Did not we use to pray for intercession after listening to every call for prayer?"

I replied, "Actually, the people had themselves added to the saying ascribed to the Holy Prophet. All that the last Prophet [PBUH], had said was that if we were to pray for him to get the coveted place on the Day of Judgement, then it would be obligatory for him to intercede. He did not ask us to also pray for intercession and based on it, set side good deeds and carelessly indulge in sins".

Saleh said to me, "Abdullah, hold on, let me explain the concept of intercession in detail. The real criterion for success is adherence to true faith and righteous deeds. If someone is pardoned today despite weakness in the above, it is not due to anyone's intercession but because of God Almighty's infinite knowledge, authority, and benevolence. This point was explained in the Qur'an in the words that God would never forgive knowingly sharing partners with Him. Apart from that, he may forgive any sin and any person. In the previous world, he used to forgive minor sins in exchange for hardships as well as for good deeds. However, those people who chose a life of sin on a persistent basis without repenting had to pay the price for it today. Although, if such a person with some degree of true faith has paid a significant price for his sins today..."

"Just as Leila and I paid, through tribulations in the Plane of Judgement." Jamshaid interjected.

"Exactly", Saleh continued, "So, I was saying that when a pious person, after paying for his sins through sufferings in the Plane of Judgement, becomes eligible for pardon as per the Almighty's Law of Justice, the Almighty then uses the testimony of a few select pious people as an excuse for his salvation. This testimony is in reality a statement confirming the good deeds that the person had performed in the previous world. Your parents' testimony in your favour that led to your forgiveness is an example of such intercession, or the testimony that the last Prophet gave at the outset led to Leila's salvation. However, even in such cases you may notice that the presence of true faith and good deeds is obligatory; even in these cases, one still has to pay the penance. So, tell me, is it better to be pardoned after paying such a penance or is it better to gain salvation without suffering any punishment, by choosing a life of good virtues and regular repentance?"

This time Arifa answered, and in turn asked a question from Saleh, "It is obvious what is the better way, but what was really meant by the reference to the last Prophet's intercession"?

"If the Prophet's intercession had meant that people could get pardoned even if they had no good deeds to their credit, then the Qur'an would not have even mentioned anything about righteous deeds. Instead, all that would have been necessary would have been a simple statement by the Prophet in the Qur'an, advising people to believe in him in exchange for unquestionable intercession in the Hereafter", Saleh answered the question.

"This was in fact the faith of the Christians, and see how they have paid for it today", Naimah commented.

Saleh agreed with her, "We know that no such thing had been mentioned in Qur'an. On the contrary, all the emphasis was upon having true faith and doing righteous deeds to go to Paradise. As for the Hadith, whatever was mentioned in them about intercession would have been crystal clear and consistent, had people tried to understand them in the light of the Qur'an; the latter of course, was the ultimate source of guidance in such matters".

"And what is the truth"? Jamshaid asked.

"The truth is that today, all the sinners have received due punishment for their sins. Thereafter, the last Prophet's prayer resulted in the possibility for the salvation for the people. The first time it happened was when he prayed to the Almighty to initiate the accountability of the humanity. As a result, people were relieved from the agonising stay in the Plane of Judgement. The second instance when intercession took place was when he, along with the rest of the prophets, gave testimony about the teachings that they had passed on to their people. This testimony resulted in salvation for those whose actions, on the whole, were in accordance with these teachings."

"People like me!" Leila commented.

"Yes, people like you benefitted from that intercession. The third time the Prophet PBUH will intercede will be when the accountability of certain people will be adjourned. Their accountability will be delayed until the very end, and they will continue to suffer the consequences of their sins in the Plane of Judgement. He will pray for them repeatedly, however, he will only be allowed to say anything in their favour when the Almighty decides that the time for their accountability is appropriate, in accordance with his infinite knowledge and wisdom. Thus, following the request of the Prophet, their accountability will start that may lead to their salvation. All this will happen at the very end when these people will already have been heavily punished for their misdeeds, thereby becoming eligible for forgiveness, on account of their good deeds and belief in one God."

"I have a question", Anwar asked Saleh. "If everyone is being pardoned only after receiving full punishment, then it is being done as per the norms of justice. What is the role of our Lord's mercy and kindness in it"?

"This is a very good question," Saleh replied. "If the Almighty were to deal with these sinners only on the basis of his justice, then their appropriate punishment would be to go to Hell. The punishments in Hell are hundreds of thousands of times worse than the hardships of the Plane of Judgement. According to the rules of justice, all such people should have been sent to Hell. It is the manifestation of God's mercy that he will accept these tribulations as a substitute for the punishment in Hell. Hence, his attributes of compassion and justice have become manifest simultaneously."

As Saleh finished, Jamshaid exclaimed, "So, this is the fact of the matter! I had remained under this misconception that intercession meant that no matter how many sins we committed, the Prophet PBUH and other pious people would save us in the Hereafter".

"This line of thinking is against the very concept of God's justice. It was a misconception that arose because people did not read the Qur'an with due regard to its meanings.

Salvation can only be a consequence of good deeds and true faith. As for forgiveness, it is only granted because of God's beneficence.

All he does is that he makes the testimony or request of a noble person an excuse for declaring the forgiveness. The purpose of this exercise is to recognise and honour his beloved and noble servants. Salvation is granted only in accordance with the laws of the Almighty. Who knows this better than you that even if a person is not sent to Hell, he still has to pay penance for his sins in the shape of the extreme hardship and suffering in the Plane of Judgement?"

"Is there still a possibility of being forgiven even after one goes to Hell?" Alia asked.

Silence ensued until Saleh replied, "Does not the Qur'an state that the Almighty shall never forgive associating partners with him but other than that, he may forgive any sin and any person, if he wishes to do so"?

"Meaning thereby?" Anwar asked for further explanation.

"It means that there are certain sins that can take a person all the way to Hell. However, those who had even an iota of faith within them may still be pardoned eventually despite committing these sins. However, no one has the knowledge or ability to decide who these people are and when they will be pardoned.

My friend! Hell is not a place worth living in even for a moment. Nobody knows how long it will take before such people are eventually allowed to come out of it after having completed their punishment. This period may be so long that even billions and trillions of years may equal just a few seconds of it. It is better to not even think about it!"

"Oh my God!" Anwar cried out.

"What to talk of Hell, even spending a moment in the Plane of Judgement is unbearable", said Jamshaid, in the light of his experience.

Leila added, "These sins are such a huge calamity. If only we had understood this in the previous world!"

Saleh concluded the discussion by adding, "There have always been two great misfortunes of the mankind. Firstly, the principle theme of the Day of Judgement was accountability, but people changed it to intercession. Secondly, the pivotal position in the life of human beings was that of God, the most merciful Lord of the entire Universe. However, the human beings assigned this pivotal position to others".

Agreeing with Saleh, I commented, "You gave such an absolutely true statement, Saleh! I wish people had realised this in the previous world!"

I then addressed my children:

"My children! Life of the previous world is now a tale from the past. Now your destination is a never-ending kingdom in the Paradise. Get ready to enjoy its peace, comfort, ease, love, blessings, enjoyment, and gratification... all of them are yours. See! How beneficent and generous is our Lord. Let us praise him together and recite the words, 'Al-Hamdulillahi Rabbil-Aalamin - Praise be to God, the Lord of the Worlds'.

All of us joined in to recite these words, as a loud chant.

===============

After a while, Saleh said to me:

"Abdullah! The events in the Plane of Judgement are about to reach their culmination. If you are still interested, now is the time to go back".

"How far is the accountability process from its conclusion"? Naimah enquired.

"Most of the mankind was born in the later eras. They have all been through the process of accountability. Muslims, Christians, and others living in the same period, have gone through the general accountability process. Presently, Jews are going through it. In a nutshell, the destiny of the majority of the mankind has now been decided. The followers of other prophets were much less in numbers anyway, so it won't take long now." Saleh replied.

"Do you know what happened to my teacher, Farhan Ahmed?" I asked.

"No, I don't know, as I do not have anything to do with him directly. All I can tell you is that he is not here at the Kauthar. Only God knows about his outcome. I think it may be better if you get up and go to the

Plane of Judgement", Said Saleh.

"Ok! Let's go", I replied as I rose from my chair.

Naimah also got up along with the rest of the family, saying to me, "I am going to go and visit the families of our children. Only your children are allowed here with us in the VVIP lounge; however, their own kids cannot come here. They are waiting for them downstairs. I am going to go and meet them.

Oh yes, I also need to find a bride for my Jamshaid!"

All of us broke into laughter on her last pronouncement, except Jamshaid. I felt that he could not decide whether to laugh at her comment or show remorse on the misfortune of his previous wife.

===============

Chapter 12: Muslims & the Israelites

We were moving towards the Plane of Judgement. We saw Nuhoor and Shaistah on our way. Their sight kindled my sense of humour.

I said to Saleh, "Let's tease them a bit while we are on the way".

They were going towards the lake. Since we were at their back, they could not see us. I quietly got close to them from Shaistah's side and suddenly said to Shaistah in a loud voice:

"Hey, you! Come with us. We arrest you for strolling with an unrelated man".

Shaistah suddenly turned towards us, alarmed on hearing my loud and stern voice. Nuhoor however, did not show any concern. He looked at me confidently and said, "If that be so, you may arrest me as well. I am also an accomplice in the crime".

He presented his hands forward while saying so. Thereafter, he laughed and said, "However, you may have a problem, as there is neither a jail nor a place to execute the punishment over here".

"Even though there is no jail, you can still be punished. The punishment is that you have to marry the abducted. To live with the same woman all your life and that too in Paradise, is a severe punishment in itself!" I said.

Nuhoor roared with laughter. Shaistah had recovered from my earlier jibe by now; she smiled and commented, "You men are great believers in Oneness (of God). It's a wonder why your approach suddenly changes to sharing partners on this issue!"

With a mock expression of seriousness, Nuhoor replied, "Abdullah, you know that the punishment for assigning partners (to God) is Hell. Therefore, please don't make such polytheistic comments in Shaistah's presence in future; otherwise, you will be in trouble!"

Saleh intervened, "Be at peace, Shaistah. Abdullah is actually practicing oneness. He has only one wife".

"The credit for that, however, does not go to Abdullah. The custom of the society he lived in forced him to limit himself to only one wife. Let us leave this topic at that. Where is your wife, Abdullah?" Nuhoor asked.

I was not ready to get serious yet. I said teasingly:

"Unlike some others, I cannot afford the luxury of spare time to wander around with my wife".

"Yet you have the time to cast an evil eye on those who have the time to do so!" Nuhoor replied in the same teasing tone.

"We are not the ones to cast an evil eye. We are only pleased to see such sights."

"But you have cast an evil eye in my case!" Nuhoor replied and explained, "My Prophet Jeremiah PBUH has been called to offer his testimony. Since I was one of his close associates, my presence there is necessary". He had a look of seriousness as he completed the last sentence.

"Are you leaving?" Shaistah asked.

"Yes. You had better go to see your family. I will be busy in these affairs for some time, only because Abdullah has cast an evil eye on us!"

Having said so, he left with the angels who had come to take him.

"The prophets have already testified for their nations. What is Prophet Jeremiah's testimony all about?" I asked Saleh.

"It is time for the criminals who had wronged him to meet their fate. His testimony is in that regard." Saleh replied.

Then we also started to move towards the Plane of Judgement.

===============

All the Jews from Prophet Jeremiah's era were gathered in front of the Throne. His era was one of the most important periods of Jewish history. Jews, also called the Israelites, were the descendants of Prophet Abraham though his son Prophet Isaac (Ishaq) and his son, Prophet Jacob (Yaqub). Israel was Prophet Jacob's title. He had twelve sons. His descendants came to be known as the Israelites. Most prominent amongst them was Prophet Joseph (Yusuf). Prophet Jacob and his twelve sons had settled in Palestine. However, during the era of Prophet Joseph, all of them migrated to Egypt. They settled and stayed there for a few centuries; during that period, their numbers increased to hundreds of thousands.

At the time of Prophet Moses, Jews were slaves of the Pharaoh of Egypt. God saved them from the tyranny of Pharaoh through Prophet Moses, and gave them the status of his nation. For their guidance, the Almighty sent down the Scriptures and the Divine Law. However, after having lived as slaves for centuries cowardice, idol worship, and various moral ailments had become ingrained in them. Therefore, when the Almighty commanded them to wage a Holy War to take back the control of Palestine from the idol worshippers who lived there, they refused to do so. Palestine was eventually conquered many years later during the reign of Prophet Moses' successor Joshua (Yosha), the son of Nun, and the Israelites were then able to settle there.

Later on, during the times of Prophet Solomon (Suleman) and Prophet David (Dáud), the Israelites were blessed with a magnificent kingdom that was renowned in the whole world. Afterwards, they suffered another moral decline and various moral evils as well as idol worship became wide spread in the society. Their prophets tried their best to guide them back to the righteous path but to no avail. Consequently, slavery was ordained for them. The neighbouring nations attacked their kingdom repeatedly and weakened it considerably.

When Prophet Jeremiah PBUH was sent to the Israelites as a prophet, they were a vassal state of the Babylonian empire of Iraq, a superpower at that time, and its King, Nebuchadnezzar. The moral decline of Israelites at the time was at its lowest level. Idol worship was rampant. Adultery was common. Their behaviour towards fellow Jews was that of extremely cruel and oppression. The cursed practices of Usury and slavery were widespread.

However, in contrast to their moral decay, their political ambitions were very high. There was an on-going hate campaign against Nebuchadnezzar. The attention of their political and religious leadership was focused on liberating them from the political subservience. National reformation, character building, and strengthening their bond with their Lord were not topics of discussion at any level. There was a lot of emphasis on the visible rituals of religiosity but virtues like faith, moral values, and good deeds had no value.

Prophet Jeremiah started his work in this environment and raised the banner of faith in one God and high morals with full force and vigour. He criticised the approach of the political and religious leadership. He warned the nation about the consequences of its moral deficiencies, idol worship, and other criminal shortcomings. In addition, he emphatically warned them about the risks associated with their plans for mutiny against Nebuchadnezzar. He tried to dissuade them from taking any foolish or emotional steps against Nebuchadnezzar and warned them that if they did embark on that perilous path, Nebuchadnezzar would set upon them like the scourge of God.

However, his nation did not pay heed to him. Instead, they first hanged him upside down in a well, and imprisoned him thereafter. Afterwards, they revolted against Nebuchadnezzar. Consequently, Nebuchadnezzar attacked them with all his might. He killed six hundred thousand Jews and took away an equal amount with him as slaves. Jerusalem was raised to ground. When he left, the city looked like an abattoir. This incident was later referred to in the Qur'an, which declared the aggressors as the wrath of God against the Israelites, and a payback for all their mischief.

While I was lost in these thoughts, Saleh probably read my mind and said to me:

“Your own nation did exactly the same thing, did it not? They were at the rock bottom when it came to knowledge, education, true faith, and morals. Yet their so-called leaders continued to blame the super powers of the time and their political conspiracies for their problems. Instead of focusing on improving their faith and moral values, political power and dominance were their foremost concerns. Adulteration, corruption, excessive profiteering and exploitation, hypocrisy and polytheism plagued your nation.

Following the cessation of prophethood after the last Holy Prophet, it was their responsibility to deliver God’s message to the rest of the humanity. However, instead of reforming their nation and spreading the message of Islam to non-Muslims, they embarked on a path of hatred against them. They waged wars against them, like these Israelites here who waged a war against Nebuchadnezzar instead of reforming themselves. Unfortunately, like the Israelites, they also faced similar terrible consequences of their actions!”

As Saleh completed his sentence, there was an announcement, “Bring forth Jeremiah”.

In a short while, Prophet Jeremiah PBUH arrived, accompanied by a few angels. He stood in front of the Throne quietly without saying anything.

Saleh said to me, “The Almighty will present the case of his Messenger himself”.

As soon as Saleh uttered those words, a movie started to role in the sky in front of us and everyone looked up to watch it.

===============

It was a scene of absolute devastation. All around, one could see fires and their leaping flames. Thick clouds of smoke rose skywards from the burning houses and properties. Sobs, screams and suppressed wailing could be heard everywhere. The earth was awash with the blood of innocent and sinners alike. Human beings were being thrashed mercilessly without let or hindrance. Homes were being robbed.

Women were being molested on every nook and corner. Armed soldiers of Iraq's most powerful ruler Nebuchadnezzar were roaming freely in the streets of Jerusalem with only one thought on their minds, to destroy the Israelites' holiest city and annihilate its inhabitants.

In the midst of this mayhem and chaos, a group of soldiers on horseback accompanied by their commander were galloping in one direction. On reaching a Prison in a corner of the city, they dismounted. Their commander moved forward and asked the prisoners:

"Who is Jeremiah amongst you"?

He did not receive a reply. Instead, all heads turned towards a cage, where a prisoner was mercilessly tied with ropes. The Commander had found the man he was looking for. He looked towards the soldiers. They moved forward swiftly, opened the cage, and freed Prophet Jeremiah PBUH. He fell to the floor in an utterly exhausted state. The commander walked towards him and stood in front of him. He then asked courteously:

"Jeremiah, are you alright?"

The prisoner opened his eyes slowly but closed them again due to extreme exhaustion. The Commander looked at him pensively and said in a voice filled with pride:

"Jeremiah, your prediction has come true. Our King Nebuchadnezzar, the emperor of Iraq, has destroyed Jerusalem. Half of the population is dead and the other half is our slave; we will take them away along with us. The King has issued special orders that you are not to be harmed in anyway. You are an honourable man. You tried your best to warn your nation but they did not pay heed to you and now, they have been punished for their deeds."

Having said so, he turned around and issued a command to his soldiers, "Let Jeremiah go and kill the rest of the prisoners. Thereafter, quench your thirst with the blood of the men in the city, and satisfy your lust using the women. Plunder whatever you want and burn the rest".

The prisoners were murdered and soldiers spread in all directions to plunder. Prophet Jeremiah PBUH gathered all his energy and sat up against the wall of the cage. His city was burning right in front of his eyes. Every part of his body was aching but to witness the destruction of his nation was far more painful.

Thereafter, scenes from his era and his life were played in flashback. He was shown trying to beseech intellectuals and public, but nobody paid heed. His nation was slave to the supreme leader of Babylonians, the mighty king of Iraq, Nebuchadnezzar. Annual levy to Nebuchadnezzar was the only guarantee of their safety and lives.

The reason for this slavery was the moral bankruptcy that had spread through the very veins of the nation. Idolatrous practices were common amongst these guardians of monotheism. Fornication and gambling were routine happenings. Dishonesty and oppression of fellow Jews was their way of life. Making false claims by swearing upon God to sell their merchandise was prevalent. Mistreatment of neighbours was the norm. They lent money at usurious interest rates; and enslaved the whole families of those who could not repay. Religious scholars were busy fomenting national pride in the masses instead of reforming them. Ritual animal sacrifice was deemed the crux of the religion rather than true faith, high morals and abiding by the divine Law. Their rulers were tyrants and corrupt. Extravagance and luxury was their way of life instead of fairness.

However, the entire nation was unified on one issue; that they should liberate themselves from the enslavement of Nebuchadnezzar. The fact of the matter was that they had incurred the wrath of the Almighty God. Rather than explaining this bitter truth to the nation, their leaders indoctrinated them with false national pride and delusions of their glorious past during the times of Solomon and David. They were being challenged to take over leadership of the world while the fact was that they were afflicted with the worst religious and moral decline.

The screen then showed the scene when Jeremiah received the divine revelation to work for reformation of his people, and to guide them away from politics and towards the correct path. He was advised that once his nation managed to develop true faith, it would dominate the political sphere as well. He was ordered to forego any plans for marriage and devote himself to warn his people about the impending devastation.

However, when Jeremiah came forward with this message, almost everyone opposed him. The prophet of God beseeched all and sundry, including the religious and political leaders, but apart from a handful of people, no one heeded his call. His message was straightforward: instead of confrontation with Nebuchadnezzar, reform your faith and moral attributes!

The most dramatic scene on the screen was the one in which Prophet Jeremiah PBUH was shown attending the court of the Jewish king with a wooden yoke around his neck. It was a last effort on his part to make people understand that their current situation was similar to an animal with a wooden yoke around its neck. If the animal rebelled and tried to break free at this stage, an iron yoke would replace the wooden one. Nevertheless, the courtiers and intellectuals, paying no heed, declared him an agent of Nebuchadnezzar instead. The king moved ahead and personally cut the wooden yoke around his neck with his sword. With that, the Almighty made the decision that this yoke would now be replaced with iron shackles.

Thus, this Prophet of God was accused of being an agent of Nebuchadnezzar, hung upside down in a well as punishment and then tied up and imprisoned in a cage. Revolt against Nebuchadnezzar was announced. In reply, Nebuchadnezzar attacked and annihilated them as if he personified the wrath of God.

Thereafter, the opening scene was repeated on the screen in which Jerusalem was being rained with the fury of God. Prophet Jeremiah PBUH opened his eyes, looked around, and saw the denuded copses and utter destruction all around him. He then said in a loud voice:

"O people, I explained the situation to you threadbare. Yet you preferred to listen to the political jugglers and bigoted & ignorant religious leaders. You overlooked the ailments of your society. You lived your lives oblivious to the ills of the society around you and commandments of God; hence the punishment for your doings!"

Prophet Jeremiah PBUH then looked towards the sky and muttered, "The day for the perfect justice will come. It will surely come, but after a little while".

With that, the scene being projected ended. A raging, thunderous noise shook the environment. The Almighty's anger was at its peak. The treatment meted out to his prophet by the people of Israel was so heinous that the punishment inflicted to them through Nebuchadnezzar was absolutely insufficient. The time for the real punishment had now arrived.

The Almighty ordered that anyone involved in the mal-treatment of Prophet Jeremiah at any level or scale be brought forward.

First, a group consisting of the king, the peers and the clerics was produced, all of who were responsible for the tragedy. It included those involved in ordering and executing the actual punishment as well as those responsible for abetting his declaration as an agent of Nebuchadnezzar. All of them were sentenced to Hell.

Thereafter, the accountability of people of that era started on an individual basis. All those who had committed crimes against the prophet of God were dealt with in a manner befitting them, and the worst punishment was awarded to each of them.

This time, I stayed in the Plane much longer and watched many people being put through the accountability process. To be fair, I had seen it only a few times before, but it was evident to me now that the Almighty was carrying out a full and extremely comprehensive accountability. Deeds of every person were being reviewed in the light of his circumstances, environment, and personality whose development was in turn, influenced by upbringing, grooming, and various other factors. Even the most insignificant deed was recorded in the Book of Deeds. The intent, motivators, and actions were all being evaluated. The evidence included records kept by angels, testimony of other human beings as well as of inanimate objects in the environment; even the very organs of people were testifying. Final decision was reached in the light of all these testimonies. This exhaustive process ensured that nobody was wronged in the slightest. If there was even the minutest chance of forgiveness, it was provided. God's absolute justice and perfect beneficence were demonstrated in such a way that words failed to paint the right picture.

While I stood there, lost in the proceedings and environment, Saleh whispered:

"Naimah is frantically looking for you".

"Is everything alright"? I enquired.

"It's an interesting affair. You would better come along." Saleh responded.

After saying so, Saleh held my hand and in a moment, we were standing besides Naimah.

I was surprised to see the sight of a girl as pretty as a fairy, standing next to Naimah. I tried to recall who she was, but I could not. Naimah introduced her to me:

"This is Amoorah. She belongs to the nation of Prophet Noah PBUH. I met her over here. She desired to meet the last Holy Prophet or one of his eminent followers. I was not in a position to arrange a meeting with the Holy Prophet; however, I thought I would introduce her to you instead. After all, you are amongst his distinguished followers."

After that, Naimah started to give Amoorah more details about my life but in doing so, she started to shower me with excessive praise and tributes.

I interrupted Naimah and said to Amoorah:

"Naimah is my wife. So understandably, she exaggerates in praising me. However, she correctly pointed out that I could arrange for you to meet some of the eminent people from amongst the followers of the last Prophet, or even the Holy Prophet himself."

Naimah did not like my humility and uttered crossly, "If I am exaggerating, then please explain to us that why is this angel with you all the time? And what do you have to say about all the places he takes you to?"

In order to kill the argument I said:

"Ok, I give up! But, please provide more details about Amoorah".

Amoorah was amused by our conversation and said, "Human beings will never change; they haven't done so in a thousand years or even after being resurrected. You are quarrelling just like my parents used to do".

"I have met Amoorah's parents as well", Naimah said in a jovial mood. However, her next sentence solved the mystery of her excitement and the reason for calling me back from the Plane of Judgement:

"Amoorah's not married to anyone over here."

Saleh confirmed my suspicion as he whispered into my ear:

"Naimah called for you so that you could meet your future daughter-in-law."

Naimah was trying to find a suitable wife for Jamshaid. She had succeeded in her pursuit to the extent that she considered Amoorah to be a suitable candidate. Yet, I was not aware whether the bride and groom to be, had even met or approved this match. That aspect, however, did not seem to bother Naimah too much. In Naimah's view, her own approval seemed to the main prerequisite for this match.

I asked Amoorah, "Where is your husband, Amoorah"?

Amoorah answered shyly, "In the previous world, I died when I was only 15 years old. I used to be ill frequently since my early childhood. As compensation, the most merciful God decided to grant me entry to the Paradise without any accountability".

"And the rest of the decisions concerning you are being made by your future mother-in-law!" I mused.

Saleh probably heard my thoughts as a smile appeared on his face. Amoorah said:

"It was really nice to meet all of you. We shall stay in touch in the Paradise as well. I should leave now. My parents must be looking for me."

Naimah also turned to go along with her but I stopped her and said, "Hold on Naimah, I have something to discuss with you".

Naimah said to Amoorah, "Could you wait for me where we had met earlier, Amoorah? I will join you shortly".

I commented jokingly, "Naimah, take Amoorah's mobile number. Otherwise, how will you find her in the crowd?"

"What is a mobile?" Amoorah asked a bit surprised by my comment.

"A mobile is a devilish device. Once you get it, you won't be able to get away from Naimah", I replied.

Saleh intervened, "I don't think Amoorah will be able to get back to her destination on her own. I will accompany you, Amoorah".

==============

After Amoorah and Saleh had left, Naimah and I sat on a spot by the bank of the pond. I said to Naimah, "Are you aware of what you are doing?"

"Yes! I have selected a potential bride for Jamshaid."

"I am aware of that, but are you aware that your own like or dislike doesn't really matter?"

"Yes, I am aware, however, with his bitter experience of choosing Huma in the previous world, Jamshaid will not be able to object to my proposition. I have already spoken to Amoorah's parents regarding this matter and they are in agreement."

"This means that although you have already agreed to the match, the couple who are the main concerned parties are not even aware of this arrangement yet, nor has their consent been obtained. Naimah, this is not the old world. Over here, we are parents in a nominal sense only. Whatever the two of them desire will happen here. So, before you build your hopes too high, you would better seek their consent."

"What if they refuse?" Naimah muttered.

"Well, there are many other girls to choose from. Over here, there is no shortage of anything; there is abundance of everything. You should relieve yourself of any concerns in this matter."

Naimah became quiet; yet, I knew that her mind was still occupied with the thoughts of her future daughter-in-law.

I looked at her and said:

"Naimah, this is the first time we are alone over here. Why don't you set aside your maternal affection for a second and enjoy the beautiful atmosphere around us?"

I continued, "Naimah! Do you remember all the difficult times we faced together? I devoted my life to the cause of taking God's message to his beings. I dedicated my career, my youth, and every breath for this cause. As you can see now Naimah, the path I chose did not cause us any loss.

I used to tell you in the world that, whoever makes a deal with God never suffers a loss in the end. As you can see, we have been saved from losses of any and every kind. We have achieved such an outstanding success! We have won, Naimah! Indeed, we have won! From here onwards, life is forever death is no more; youth is forever old age is no more, and health is forever illness is no more! Now, there would only be abundance and no poverty, we would have eternal joys and no more sorrows!"

"I can't even remember any sorrows associated with the previous world", Naimah added.

I replied, "Indeed! Today, the residents of Paradise do not remember any sufferings of the world; neither do dwellers of Hell remember any of its comforts. That world was just like a thought, or like a dream, a story, or an illusion. Reality begins now; the real life has only just started".

"Abdullah, look at the view in front of us. See how the scene is changing." Naimah said.

I looked up and realised that the evening was nearing its end; Dusk was just around. I somehow felt that this change was an indication that something important was about to happen.

Suddenly, a voice from behind me said, "Yes, your suspicion is correct Abdullah".

It was Saleh's voice. He continued as he sat down next to me:

"This change is an indication that the process of accountability is about to end. Accountability of everyone has taken place".

"Tell me first, where did you disappear after taking Amoorah to her destination? You do not need to drink water nor do you require the use of the washroom," I asked jokingly.

"I was with Imsáeel", Saleh replied.

As Saleh finished his sentence, Imsáeel stepped forward from behind him and greeted me. He used to be the angel on my left hand side assigned to record my misdeeds.

I returned his greetings and smilingly said to Saleh:

"And what is the reason for the appearance of Imsáeel?"

"The accountability has reached its conclusion. Now, both of us will have to present you before the Almighty".

I started to feel apprehensive when I heard this. I asked anxiously:

"How come the accountability has ended so soon?"

"As I mentioned to you before, time passes very quickly over here while in the Plane of Judgement, its passage is very slow. Therefore, while you were here for what may have seemed like a short while to you, it was actually long enough for the accountability process to be concluded."

"What happened in the Plane of Judgement after I left?"

"After the accountability of most people was completed, only those people were left behind who had faith in their hearts but they had been held back due to the high volume of their sins. Following the request of the last Holy Prophet, those people were also held accountable. Finally, only the Shuhada and the prophets will be presented before the Almighty."

"Are Shuhada those people who were martyred in the way of God?" Naimah asked Saleh.

"No, Shuhada are not martyrs in the sense the word is used in your language, although the people who achieved martyrdom in the way of God have also been awarded tremendous rewards. However, these Shuhada are those illustrious people who were witnesses to the truth in their lives. In other words, they were the ones who dedicated their lives to give testimony about the veracity of God's religion to the rest of the world. They were the people who carried forward the message of the prophets to the subsequent generations."

"Will they also undergo Accountability"? I asked, as the mere thought of accountability was enough to cause anxiety to me.

"No, they won't. They will just be presented in the Court of the Almighty and then their deliverance will be announced. Having said so, I must say that the Almighty is the Lord of the Worlds and the sole master of everything. If he wants to call anyone for accountability, no one can stop him from doing so!"

I involuntary said:

"O' Lord! Forgive me and have mercy on me".

Saleh replied:

"I have only pointed out the authority of the Almighty. I am not suggesting that he will do so. In fact, the time has now arrived for people to enter either the Hell or the Paradise. As such, the residents of Paradise and inmates of Hell will all be gathered in the Plane of Judgement. In their presence, the success of the prophets and Shuhada will be declared.

Thereafter, people will be sent in groups to their final destinations. Eternal life will thus begin".

===============

Chapter 13: Journey towards the Eternal Destination

Once again, I was standing on the high point of Aaráf along with prophets and other Shuhada. The Plane of Judgement was clearly visible from this vantage point. As far as the eyes could see, people were divided into two groups in the vast plane. To the right, there were rows upon rows of people. They were the people of Paradise. They had glowing faces, smiles on the lips and a sparkle in the eyes. They were very well dressed. Their hearts were filled with joy and their souls were strongly indebted with gratitude. These were the people on the right hand side; what could one say about the good fortune of the people of the right side?

On the left side of the plane, a large crowd of people sat on their knees facing the Hell with their hands tied behind their backs. These were the people of the Hell. They awaited the final transfer to their eternal abode. Their faces were drawn out and their eyes looked lifeless; with foreheads drenched in sweat, their necks were bowed. Their complexions had darkened and their bodies were covered with dust & dirt. These were the people on the left hand side; what could one say about the utter misfortune of the people of the left side?

The Throne of the Almighty was right in front of us. What could one say of its grandeur and splendour? Rows upon rows of angels stood around it. In their midst, were eight extraordinary angels next to and around the Throne. They were the Bearers of the Throne. The angels were singing words of praise and glory. Behind the Throne, at a higher altitude, clear views of Paradise and Hell could be easily seen. Paradise was on the right side; the fragrance arising from it had spread throughout the right side of the plane and the songs emanating from it were having an enchanting effect on the hearts. One could clearly see the absolutely stunning greenery, serene valleys, and immaculate gardens of the Paradise from here; its palaces, lakes, and servants were also visible. These views of Paradise were enticing everyone. Those who had been awarded the Paradise were extremely pleased at their good fortune and were engrossed in relaxing chats with each other while they waited anxiously to be taken over to the Paradise.

On the other hand, the horribly fearsome view of Hell was visible on the left side of the Throne. The flames from the fire were rising repeatedly like the tongue of a serpent. The sight of different punishments waiting for their victims in Hell was making the hearts flutter with fear. Highly frightening and ugly angels with whips, chains, yolks, and hammers were waiting to welcome the people of Hell to unlimited punishments like odour, filth, fire, wild animals, venomous bugs, rotten fruits, thorn covered bushes, and food consisting of pus, blood, boiling water and oil slush.

The wretched state of people condemned to Hell was already miserable; it was further compounded on seeing the Hell with their own eyes. This view was enough to crush their hopes. They were watching the scene despairingly. Each one of them wished most earnestly to be awarded the death sentence. Alas! In Hell, there were all kinds of punishments but no death. Death would have been the greatest relief for the condemned. But then, Hell was a place for punishment, not relief.

A curtain separated the people assigned for Paradise and Hell. They could see and talk to each other through this curtain but could not cross it. The people of Paradise told the people of Hell that all promises that God had made to them had come entirely true. They then asked them if they had also found the Almighty's forewarnings about the Hell and its details to be true. In reply, they had no option but to bow their heads in acceptance and say, 'yes'.

The people of Hell were crying with thirst and hunger. When they saw the people of Paradise being served with all kinds of fruits, platters of meat and tasty drinks, they repeatedly asked them to pass on a small amount of this gift from the Almighty to them as well. However, they got the reply that the Almighty had forbidden these bounties for the people of Hell.

We were standing on high ground and witnessing this scene. I felt scared for some unknown reason, although the announcement of our fates was a mere formality. I was praying and pleading to God for his blessings and forgiveness. I was praying to the Almighty not to make me one of the people of Hell, and to grant me the company of the people of Paradise. Other people standing next to me were also praying for the same.

However, that was my own state of mind. Some other Shuhada, charged with emotions, moved forward and started to congratulate the people of Paradise. They were showering them with blessings and prayers. At this juncture, the prophets came forward and asked the incredulous leaders of their respective nations who had knowingly rejected the truth:

"Where is your rule today? Do you still take pride in the number of your followers? What happened to your arrogance?"

They then pointed towards the people of Paradise and said:

"Are they not the same poor people you considered as worthless? You believed that they did not deserve a share of the blessings of God, and neither would they ever receive it. See for yourselves! They have achieved such an exalted position today!"

Meanwhile, there was an announcement that the Books of Deeds be handed over to the prophets and Shuhada. Against my expectations, there was no accountability or cross-examination. Each one of us was in turn called forward to a place where all the people of Paradise and Hell could see us. Each person would move forward, escorted by his two angels, who would then take him to the Throne with utmost decorum. There, his accomplishments in the previous life were announced to everyone and success in the Hereafter formally declared.

Whenever a person from this exalted group was presented to the Throne, details of his struggles were narrated, like the times he lived in, the background of the people he addressed and their response to his invitation; in fact, everything surrounding his mission was narrated in detail. The audience listened with rapt attention and showered each person with generous praise. In the end, whenever a person's success and accomplishment was declared, the surroundings echoed with shouts of 'bravo' and 'glory be to God'. Dwellers of the Paradise expressed their joy by clapping, shouting, whistling and even, dancing.

When my name was announced, the people standing close by started to congratulate me. Along with Saleh and Imsáeel, I reached the edge; from where I was standing, everyone in the plane could see me. Imsáeel was carrying my Book of Deeds. Saleh was walking in front of me. When we reached there, I bowed my head and stood in silence. The Almighty said:

"Abdullah, the time to bow your head is over. Lift your head. People want to see you."

I lifted my head. Tears of gratitude flowed from my eyes with a triumphant smile on my face. With the permission of the Almighty, Saleh and Imsáeel started to narrate the details of my life.

I looked towards the plane and saw many familiar people waving to me; they included my family, friends, the righteous people who had supported me, the believers who had accepted my call and those men and women who had rectified their ways in response to my preaching about Oneness of God and the Hereafter. I also waved back.

However, my eyes were searching for Naimah. She was standing amongst our children. I could see tears of joy on her smiling face. When she realised that I was looking at her, she lowered her gaze shyly. Leila was standing next to her. She was most excited, standing on a chair and clapping passionately. Arifa, Aaliya, Anwar and Jamshaid were also stood on their seats and waving their hands vigorously.

I glanced to my left. It was an entirely different scene there. The people of Hell were engulfed in a never-ending darkness of various negative emotions, including shame, disgrace, regret, apprehension, humiliation, sorrow, disappointment, agony, hardships and self-blame. If the sky had the ability to lament, it would have recited an elegy on the misfortune of those who had failed on this Day of Judgement. If Earth had the ability to express itself, it too would have recited a tragic poem on the condition of the people of Hell. If words had a voice, even they would have decried their failure in portraying the utter misfortune of the people of Hell.

I felt the urge to somehow turn the wheel of time backwards, return to the old world, and show this scene to the people of the world. If that were possible, I would shout myself hoarse saying to them:

"O' all of you hard working people, competing with each other for the sake of worldly wealth and possessions; leave the rat race! If you have to compete, compete for success on this day. If you have to race against others, race to attain the Paradise. If you have to make schemes, scheme to save yourself from the Hell. You compete to leave others behind in material possessions like plots of land, shops, houses, status, carriers, cars, jewellery, and expensive dresses etc.

You rejoice at attaining worldly success and cry on losing it. If you want to rejoice, rejoice at the hope of attaining the Paradise, and if you have to cry, cry at the prospect of being sent to the Hell. Live for this day and die for this day... the day when life will begin, never to end again."

The flow of tears rolling down my face increased further. However, this time they were not tears of joy. They stemmed from the realisation that maybe if I had put in a little more effort, I could have got my message across to more people, and perhaps, many more could have been spared from Hell. I felt the pain of this remorse in my heart.

Alas! If I could get one more chance. Alas! If only the time bygone would somehow come back so that I could warn every person about this day even more compellingly!

An excruciating sigh escaped from my lips, rising from the depths of my heart.

I looked up towards the Throne with utter helplessness. As always, the exalted presence of the Almighty was cloaked in a veil of royalty. This elegant and graceful veil was like the unconcerned grace of a beauty, oblivious to its surroundings. The gaze of this insignificant servant got transfixed at the imagined feet of the Almighty behind an attire of his attributes. I had never returned unfulfilled from there. For this worthless beggar, his only asset was those feet. Whether the exalted emperor considered it of any significance or not, did not matter. This is all I had to offer; this is all I could hope for!

When the heart calmed down a bit, my eyes drifted towards the people of Hell again. I knew a few of them. Their number was quite large. Crouched and crowded, they sat slavishly with their shoulders rubbing together. They avoided my gaze and many of them had turned their backs towards me. As such, I could not see many of my acquaintances there.

However, their sight made me appreciate and realise the blessings of the God Almighty, which had saved me from meeting such a miserable fate. I felt that of all the infinite bounties of Paradise, perhaps the two greatest blessings were that one would be saved from the rigours of Hell and then would be sent to Paradise with such sterling honour.

===============

It was not long before all people present in Aaráf were processed. There were no more decisions to be announced. However, it looked like something else was still to happen. Everybody was standing at his place. A very stout and strong animal was brought in. There was a rope in its neck. Angels were dragging it towards the Throne.

Saleh whispered in my ear, “This is Death. It has been brought here so that it can be put to death.”

There was an announcement from the Throne, “The Death is being put to death today. As of now, neither the dwellers of Paradise nor the inmates of Hell will die”.

With this announcement, the angels laid the animal on the floor and slaughtered it. The residents of Paradise welcomed this through thunderous clapping while the inmates of Hell moaned and groaned. If they had any hope of escaping Hell, it had died with the demise of the death.

A command was issued from the Throne to take the inmates of Hell to their destiny in groups. The angels started moving swiftly. Panic erupted on the left side of the Throne. Amongst sighs and screams, angels would get hold of the criminals and the disobedient, and gathering them in a group, drive them towards the Hell. When each group reached the gates of the Hell, the guardian angels of Hell welcomed them. They then passed them into Hell through one of its seven gates, dependent upon the type of their sins.

Amidst all this, we would regularly hear the voice of the Almighty from the Throne, asking the Hell periodically, "Are you full yet?"

The Hell would reply in a raging voice, "My Lord! Are there any more people left? Please do send them".

On hearing this, wailing and pleading would get louder in the Plane of Judgement. Angels would swiftly move and grab the remaining criminals, dragging them towards their final abode. Hence, in a short time, all those condemned to Hell were sent to the final abode that they had been promised.

Thereafter, a command emanated from the Throne, "Take the people of Paradise to their destination".

When this announcement was made, there were still some people left on the left side of the Throne. I asked Saleh, "Who are these people? Why have they not been sent to Hell"?

Saleh answered, "They are the Hypocrites. They will be incarcerated in the lowest and the worst part of the Hell. They used to deceive God in their worldly lives. They will therefore be given the worst punishment. In fact, their punishment will begin with a deception".

"Deception? Please elaborate." I asked.

Saleh replied, "Well, they will get the impression that with the announcement of transferring the people of Paradise to Paradise, perhaps they have also been spared on account of their apparent faith. However, this is merely a misconception and it shall be rectified soon".

At that moment, a beautiful and captivating chorus reached my ears, singing the melody of praise for the Almighty, "All praise is for God, the Lord of the Worlds". This was the melodious voice of the

Bearers of the Throne and other angels singing the song of utter thankfulness for their Lord.

Saleh said, "This indicates that the Judgement Day has reached its conclusion".

Simultaneously, darkness started to set in the Plane. Apart from the light emanating from the Throne, there was no other source of light. I was not able to see anything at all. I asked Saleh worryingly:

"What is happening?"

"It is getting dark..." He replied briefly.

"I can see that, my friend! But what's the reason for it?" I asked.

"The reason for this is that only those who have the light of true faith in their hearts and righteous deeds to go with it will be able to cross this darkness and enter the Paradise."

He then passed over the record of my deeds into my hands. A unique light came out of it that allowed my eyes to see clearly in the darkness again.

Saleh added, "Everybody has been handed over his record of deeds. It is now the sole source of light for its bearer in this darkness. Everyone here except for the Hypocrites has this light".

"What will happen now?" I enquired.

"We will now go downwards. Each nation will go to the Paradise under the leadership of its prophet."

"Where is the way to the Paradise?" I questioned.

"It is very close to the Throne. Behind the Throne, on the right side, from where you could see the Paradise earlier is the way to it. However, the path passes over the deep pit of the Hell, where it is steeped in darkness. The brighter one's light is, the easier and quicker is this passage over the Hell."

"Oh, that means that there is still one more test to go!" I said.

"No, it is not a test. It only exemplifies the worldly life. During life, whoever travelled on the straight path to God with loyalty, obedience, conviction and steadiness, will be able to cross this path to paradise today with similar ease and speed. Regardless of whether they cross it quickly or slowly, all those who were given their Books of Deeds in their right hands will manage to cross over the deep pit of Hell and enter paradise. However, when the hypocrites try to cross over without the light of true faith and righteous deeds to guide them, they will fall off it into the lowest pit of Hell. There, they will be greeted with the worst punishments imaginable."

"Will my family accompany me on this journey?" I asked.

"No! Today, everyone has to go through this last journey alone." Saleh answered with certainty.

"Then what did you mean when you said that people would go to the Paradise in groups?" I raised a question.

"What I meant was that all the followers of a prophet will be taken to the gates of Paradise under the leadership of their prophet. However, they will enter Paradise one by one, in a manner appropriate to their individual deeds."

Saleh then asked me a question after a pause, "Do you desire to see yet another event"?

Before I could respond in affirmative, he moved forward swiftly, taking me along, until we reached a place where people possessed extremely bright radiance. This brightness covered them as they moved from behind, from front, from their left and right. They were saying loudly:

"O our Lord! Keep our Nur alight and forgive us. You have full control over everything. Verily nothing is beyond you".

I recognised them without asking Saleh. These were indeed the companions of the last Prophet, who was leading them. The Prophet PBUH himself was an epitome of Nur at its peak.

Following their lead, I also started to recite their words. I used to recite this prayer from the Qur'an often during my past life. However, the most appropriate time to recite it was indeed now.

We were walking in the same direction when Saleh said, "Watch what happens now".

As soon as Saleh uttered these words, I saw some people running towards the companions, many falling over in the process. They did not have any light with them. As soon as they came near, they started to plead to the companions to give them a little of their light. Some of the companions pointed to the rear towards the right side of the Plane of Judgement and said:

"We brought the light from there. You should also go back and get some".

On hearing this, all of those Hypocrites started to run back in that direction. However, as soon as they tried to turn right, they realised that there was a wall in the way. There were a few doors in the wall that were guarded by angels. They tried to enter through the doors but the angels started to beat them up to turn them away. They did not have any way to get the light.

They then ran back to the companions and pleaded again saying:

"Help us! We are also Muslims. We were by your side in the previous world. You know us well. Please do something to help us get some light"!

The companions replied, "Certainly you were with us but you put yourself in a malicious situation. You remained doubtful about this day till the end. Your real aim was only to attain benefits of the worldly life. You followed the way of Satan and he kept you in deception. Hence today, neither you nor any other rejecter of the truth can escape by giving any ransom or bribe".

On hearing this, the Hypocrites realised that their destiny would not be any different to all those who had rejected the truth.

It seemed dangerous to them to turn back. Therefore, they decided to try to find a way by moving forward in the darkness. Without any light to guide them, this attempt could have had only one consequence. One by one, screaming and wailing, they stumbled into the Hell below, where the angels of chastisement were waiting to give them a taste of their medicine.

We continued to move forward towards the Paradise, reciting the same prayer again:

"O our Lord, do not let our Nur extinguish! Save us from the fate of the Hypocrites, and forgive us. Indeed! You have power over everything."

================

Chapter 14: Entry in the Realm of Paradise

We had crossed the bridge going over the Hell's pit with considerable comfort and ease. I looked back having crossed it and saw a caravan of lights following us, reciting the same prayer loudly. The brighter the light, the easier it was for the bearer to cross over the pit. In front of us on the horizon, I could see the scene at the gates of the Paradise through door-like structures. The gatekeepers were welcoming the new arrivals by saying '*salam*' and praying for peace and blessings for them; the new arrivals were responding by reciting praise of the Lord.

I looked ahead and realised that we were very close to the Throne. The Throne was lit up like an epicentre of Nur, or a fountain of luminosity and Nur; its true description was impossible to capture in words. Having reached closer, our own lights paled in comparison to the brilliant resplendence of the Throne. Around the Throne were rows upon rows of angels who stood with hands folded obediently as they sang the enchanting praise of the Lord, "*Praise be to God, Lord of the Worlds*". As we reached closer, I saw that the angels had left a gap in their formation and people, using this gap, were going under the Throne in rows. As we got closer, we heard a voice:

"Welcome, my servants. Today you are entering the never-ending kingdom. Enter it forever in the protection of your Lord."

Having passed the angels, as we moved ahead, I looked at Saleh questioningly. He explained:

"The way to Paradise goes from underneath the Throne and then it turns right."

"But why do we have to go under the Throne? Why can we not turn right straight away?" I asked.

Saleh smiled and replied:

"You want to know everything before its time. Anyway, let me tell you the reason for it. Every human being will attain the final cleansing, or "Tazkiyah", after passing under the Throne."

"But we used to do Tazkiyah in the previous world."

"As you know, Tazkiyah was the purpose of every act of religion in the previous world. The main objective of religion was to purify the human soul. It was expected of a believer to keep his body clean and consume only clean and appropriate food. Through worship, he kept his soul purified, and by following the injunctions of the religion, he kept his society, economy, and morality clean and pure. Satanic suggestions, carnal desires, and animal instincts were unclean influences that a true believer in God endeavoured to avoid in order to keep his inner self cleansed. All of them were the attempts of the faithful at purifying themselves in the previous world. The Almighty has rewarded those efforts today by granting such people entry into his pure and clean Paradise. However, God will purify the believers himself before they enter his Paradise. Once this happens, their souls, bodies and morals will be washed of every impurity."

"What do you mean?"

"What I mean is that your physical body containing blood, unclean secretions, odours and other undesirable matter will now be filled with Nur. Thereafter, you will not emit unpleasant odour, pungent perspiration, or faeces. Your breath will exude fragrance. The only secretion exiting your body will be fragrant sweat. No secretions will excrete from your ears, nose, eyes, mouth, or any other orifice.

Likewise, all negative emotions such as jealousy, arrogance, spite, lust, hatred, prejudice etc. will disappear from your heart. Your thoughts, vision, body, and soul will all be purified."

I spoke ecstatically:

"Praise be to God! It will be real fun to live such a life!"

"In addition, your faculties and powers will increase extraordinarily. You will need neither sleep nor rest. You will not get tired or fatigued; nor will you ever get bored or weary. You will not suffer from depression or stress. You will eat and drink to your heart's content, without suffering any indigestion or the need to pass any excretions. You will have an enormous reservoir of strength. You will always remain healthy and young. Above all, you will become exceptionally good looking and handsome. This is only an account of some of the internal capabilities and gifts from the Almighty, the external blessings and awards are yet to be revealed."

"Will that be the case for everyone?"

"Indeed. However, the power, beauty, and ability will be directly proportional to one's deeds."

I exclaimed spontaneously:

"Praise be to God, Lord of the Worlds".

We had reached very close to the Throne while talking. Saleh said:

"Abdullah, I am going to leave you now. When you enter here, you will emerge at the entrance of Paradise. I will meet you there along with the gatekeeper of Paradise. Move forward confidently."

Saleh departed having said so.

I stood there pondering for a moment. Suddenly, a door opened in front of me. A voice said:

"O content soul; come back to your Lord, well pleased, well pleasing. And join my righteous servants, and enter my Paradise."

Encouraged by these words, I entered the door. The following Arabic words involuntarily came to my lips:

"Allahu Akbar Allahu Akbar, La Ilaha Illal-Lah., Wa llahu Akbar Allahu Akbar Walillahil Hamd" (God is great, God is great, there is no God but one; and God is great, God is great, and praise is for him alone).

As soon as I entered, I felt that I had come into a passageway. Here the floor, roof, and walls were all milky white. As soon as I entered, I started experiencing a very pleasant feeling. I sensed that the path was imperceptibly turning to the right. I had only gone a short distance when I was engulfed in a cloud of colour and Nur. A melange of rainbow colours started glittering around me. I kept moving forward in total peace and confidence. Suddenly a sheet of Nur went right through me. Along with that, every single pore of my entire being was immersed in a feeling of utter joy and ecstasy. I felt as if I was flying with the breeze. My body felt light and weightless. I felt as if my body had dissolved and I was left only in the form of my soul.

Enraptured, I moved forward. In a short while, the same milky white passage was in front of me. I kept on walking through it. I could feel a Sea change in my feelings. I felt that I had metamorphosed tremendously. I treaded along with an indescribable feeling of strength, power, peace, composure, and confidence.

As I walked in this state, I had to stop suddenly. I was at a juncture with eight different paths. There was an inscription on every path detailing as to which particular door of paradise it led to. As I was trying to read the inscription, I heard a voice:

"Enter through the door for Shuhada."

I noticed that the first door on the right was for the prophets; the door adjacent to it was for Siddiqeen and the one next to it was for the Shuhada. I entered that door.

It was also a passage that ended at a door. I exited through that door. Before I could look around, I saw Saleh standing in front of me. There was an angel standing next to him. Rather than Saleh, the angel stepped forward and welcomed me.

"Assalam-o-Alaikum, I welcome you to the community of ever-lasting Paradise. Saleh has given me your Book of Deeds. In this book, your name is given as Abdullah. However, there are so many awards and titles along with it that I cannot decide how to address you."

Saleh intervened and said:

"I think for the moment Lord Abdullah should suffice. It is because after Lord Abdullah's death, God sent me to welcome him by saying, "bring my servant Abdullah to me. He is a leader."

"Ok, Lord Abdullah! Welcome to the never-ending kingdom." The angel shook hands with me as he said these words.

"And what is the name of our host?" I enquired about the angel from Saleh.

"He is not the host. He is the gate keeper and his name is Rizwan."

Rizwan spoke laughingly, "You are the host here, Lord Abdullah. This is your dominion. Take a look around you."

I looked around and realised that I had entered a new world. The sky and the earth over here had changed dramatically. Comprising of a new Earth and a new Sky, this world most definitely was complete in every respect. However, I could not find the words to describe its beauty and absolute perfection. All my life, I had enjoyed an outstanding ability to explain situations using my exceptional command on language. Words served at my will and expressions were revealed to me almost supernaturally. God had given me the ability to easily explain even the most complex realities. However, at this moment I realised that any language of the previous world was incapable of explaining what was in front of me. My situation was similar to someone from the Stone Age suddenly finding himself in one of the modern cities of the Industrial Age. A person used to burning wood for lighting his cave would have been unable to find words to describe rainbow displays of laser and luminescent tube lights since there would be no expressions for those modern inventions in his vocabulary. I was experiencing a similar condition.

===============

Noticing my bewilderment, Saleh said:

"Lord Abdullah, there are many more things waiting to captivate you. It would be better to continue the journey towards your destination."

Rizwan pointed at a path and said:

"This way, Sir. Your residence is in that direction."

We moved ahead. A fabulously plush red carpet was spread in our path. We started walking on it. Angels lined both sides, waving silk handkerchiefs with bouquets in their hands. They greeted us with words of welcome as they showered flower petals and fragrances on us.

It was a long path. One reads or hears fairy tales of imaginary lands far away in the fairyland, when one is young. This path seemed to lead to such a fairyland. I was able to see the sky-high buildings of this fairyland from a distance. It was a scene composed of magnificent buildings and glorious palaces set on a background of lush-green mountains, with a base of still waters on the front and a canopy of a pearl-blue sky at the top, all of which looked like a scene straight out of a fairy tale.

I said to Rizwan, "Countless people are entering Paradise at the moment. That must be keeping you very busy. Do you have enough time to spare and accompany me?"

He laughed and said, "The time has stopped here. Understand it in this way; the time interval between two people entering the Paradise is quite long. Those who have been awarded lesser levels of Paradise may enter it centuries after the earlier inhabitants."

Looking worriedly towards Saleh, I asked, "What about Naimah"?

Rizwan answered my query instead:

"Lord Abdullah, you have entered the Paradise very early. Your wife and others will enter after some time. However, you have lots to do here until they arrive. You need to familiarise yourself with your Paradise, and also with the servants and staff that manage this world ruled only by you."

"Really? Who else is here?"

"Here are a few of your more prominent servants ..."

I noticed that behind the rows of the angels, there was a row of boys on either side. They seemed to be in their early teens. I realised that they were the Ghilmán. They were the boy-servants referred to in the Qur'an as 'pearls'. Indeed, they were like pearls, perhaps, even more sparkling, pure, and glistening. Having seen them, I realised why the Almighty had promised in the Qur'an to fully explain the true nature of all such heavenly phenomena only in the Hereafter. Human languages of the previous world had a very limited vocabulary of similes, metaphors, and terminologies. The facts that had become apparent today were of a nature suited best to viewing and experiencing, rather than describing in words. The case of the Ghilmán was also similar.

Like the angels, the Ghilmán welcomed me enthusiastically. However, as I approached them, they went on their knees and bowed their heads one after the other, as if a string of pearls was slowly unravelling at my feet.

When I saw that the column of Ghilmán was never ending, I said to Saleh:

"If these prominent servants are so many, how many of them are there in all? Secondly, what use will I have for so many servants?"

Rizwan, who was more knowledgeable about Paradise, replied instead of Saleh:

"You are the ruler of a dominion that stretches from Earth to the skies. The Almighty will assign numerous tasks to you to perform in this dominion. You will delegate them to these servants. Their responsibilities will range from your personal service to the bureaucracy and administration of your glorious dominion."

"It goes to prove that even Paradise is not a place to have complete rest and leisure. One will have to work even here!" I commented with a chuckle.

"Don't worry! The work over here will not be a chore rather it will be enjoyable. However, there will be no dearth of the sort of leisure and rest that people strived for in the previous world."

"But what will be the nature of work?"

"All I know is that you will rule without having to face the problems that accompanied authority in the previous world. Only God knows the real nature of the tasks expected of you. He will provide you details during the Grand Gathering at the Court."

As we walked further, Saleh said:

"Here come the Maidens of Paradise."

This reminded me of the poetic eulogy Saleh had showered them with when we were in the Plane of Judgement. At that time, I had thought that he was exaggerating. Now that I had seen them, I realised that his poem was, at best, an understatement. The reality was far better than what Saleh had vainly endeavoured to portray.

As we approached them, they welcomed us with a gesture quite different to that of the Ghilmán. Instead of going on their knees, they sat down on the floor with their legs folded underneath them, and bending over, bowed their heads.

I stopped and asked Saleh:

"What are they doing?"

Saleh chuckled, "They have laid their eyes and hearts in your way!"

Rizwan elaborated further, "In fact, the posture is to allow them to spread their hair on the floor, to provide comfort to your feet."

At his explanation, I saw that they had bent having jerked their heads back and forth in such a manner that their hair now laid spread across the path on both sides, like a soft silky carpet. I had seen such manifestation of beauty for the first time in my life. I smiled and moved forward gracefully, brimming with confidence. As soon as my feet touched their hair on this surreal path, a wave of rapture surged through my soul. I realised for the first time that although I was wearing the softest, velvety and finest princely clothes, my feet were bare.

Rizwan provided more information about the Maidens and Ghilmán:

"Don't think for a moment that their beauty is only skin deep, Lord Abdullah. They possess extraordinary strengths and capabilities. They have the ability to turn this world topsy-turvy at your command. Yet, it is only because of their deep love for you that they consider it a huge honour even to fill a goblet of wine for you. However, you do not have the slightest idea about the astonishing powers the Almighty has endowed them with."

I did not say anything. I felt extremely grateful to the One who had granted this helpless humble servant with such sterling honour as a reward for such meagre good deeds. Tears welled in my eyes and started to trickle down my face as I bowed in prostration. Words of praise for the Lord were on my tongue as I remained in this position for some time.

Suddenly, I heard a sound similar to the slight patter of raindrops. Saleh patted my back and said:

"Abdullah, get up and see the result of acceptance of your prostration!"

As I got up, an astonishing scene awaited me. The faces of the Maidens and Ghilmán were ecstatic. Their laps were full of the most beautiful glistening pearls. I looked at Saleh for an explanation. He replied:

"The Lord gave them a gift on your behalf. As tears shed from your eyes, the Lord conveyed his approval by sending down a rain of pearls. It is a gift for them on the auspicious occasion of your arrival, and will remain to be their most cherished possession."

We strolled forward. Eventually this welcoming queue came to an end at a huge door. Its two panels opened automatically even before we reached it. Rizwan turned back from there and I entered my residence, accompanied by Saleh. I used the word 'residence' since words like cottage, hut, home, house, building, bungalow, villa, mansion, castle, palace, and city etc. were inadequate to describe it. It was a vast land that extended as far as the eyes could see. It was a collection of towering palaces placed on lush green mountains with serene valleys extending in between. I could see charming gardens as well as glistening streams and rivers meandering through the green valleys. As I struggle to describe the scenery in words, I must caution that it is not possible to truly capture in words the beauty, majesty and the real nature of what lay in front of me.

As my eyes took in the vast surroundings, I asked Saleh:

"Which of these palaces is mine?"

He laughed and said, "None of them. They belong to your senior servants. Your residence is a long distance from here. If you wish, you can walk but it may be better to use your transport."

He gestured to move in a certain direction. I saw a magnificent, though relatively small, house close by. Although it appeared small compared to the other structures around but on the scale of the previous world it was like a huge palace. Interestingly, I would not have noticed it had Saleh not pointed it out to me, as it was made of crystal clear, see-through glass.

As Saleh moved forward, I followed assuming that there would be some sort of vehicle parked inside. However, he took me straight to a room in the middle of the house. I could see regal chairs in the room adorned with jewels and ornaments.

Saleh gestured to me to sit on one of them and said:

"This is your transport. It will take you to your destination. I will leave you now to go there on your own so you realise that you are the sole ruler of this place. You do not need any support, any servant, or any angel. Whatever you desire, will happen automatically. I will meet you at the other end, at your home."

Before I could say anything, Saleh left the room.

I was in a state of shock. In fact, I had been in a state of perpetual shock from the moment I had entered the Paradise. I felt dazed because of the pleasant shocks that I was continuously receiving every few moments.

I managed to collect my thoughts in a while. I thought about where I was and why I was there. I concentrated on what Saleh had just mentioned to me. I repeated Saleh's words in my mind. An extraordinary confidence developed in me as I realised the implications of what Saleh had said. I felt that my rule had begun in earnest right from that moment.

However, the question that warranted an answer was how to get my ride going. I thought in my heart that it did not matter if Saleh was not there anymore. My Lord was still with me, just like he had been with me throughout every second of my life.

I suddenly remembered the verse of Qur'an stating that by saying the words, 'Subhan-Allah' (All praise be to the Lord), one's every wish will be fulfilled in the Paradise. I whispered:

"Subhan-Allah"

The house began to rise in the air. I was ecstatic.

I said loudly, "In the name of God shall be its running course and its resting anchorage."

Those were the words of Prophet Noah as he sat in the ark at the time of the great flood. My ride started to move forward slowly in a certain direction.

I began to enjoy the stunning scenery below. The house was still drifting slowly when I realised that it was the time of dusk underneath. Soon there was darkness all around. Along with that, the glasshouse became lit with a pearly white fluorescence. Yet, I could not find the source of the light anywhere.

===============

My journey continued through the darkness. Outside, it was pitch dark as far as the eyes could see. But it did not instil any fear or concern. A deep layer of silence sat on top of the layer of darkness. The silence also did not invoke any fear or worry. Instead, like the darkness, this silence also instilled a strange feeling of serenity and tranquillity in me. I felt as if there were songs without sound embedded deep in this silence that were subtly trying to entice the heart, bypassing the ears. As if, there were melodies scattered in the surroundings without any audible music, seducing the heart into a mesmerising dance.

I could figure out only one reason for the darkness. It was probably there to make the light glowing like a lamp at a distance more prominent. That light was not of a star because, like the earth, the sky was also cloaked in darkness. The light was emanating from the peak of a lofty mountain. It looked so beautiful and pleasing in the darkness that it was impossible to pull my gaze away from it.

Then I thought that there was nothing else to see in the darkness anyway. I wished in my heart to see the panoramic view below with the help of this light. I said 'Subhan-Allah' and the darkness vanished. I could see the view below clearly now.

There was a vast green field spread out underneath as far as the eye could see. In the centre, was a mountain made of white marble. The mountain was not a part of any mountain range; rather, it was a solitary cliff standing on its own in the middle of the plane, as if someone had artificially hammered it in the ground. Its peak rose up into the sky and tapered off sharply like the tip of a spear. However, the mountain did not end at the tip; in fact, the tip served as the foundation of a glorious and magnificent palace, which had been built on top of the mountain. This scene seemed like a masterpiece of an artist's imagination rather than reality. The reason was that plane fields do not have such lofty peaks on them, lofty peaks do not have such finely chiselled ends, and huge palaces do not exist on top of such narrow pointed peaks in reality.

However, those were the limitations of the previous world. That world of trials and physical laws was no more. A new world had come into being now that revolved around my wishes and me. I realised that after passing through a journey spanning millions of years, the humans had finally entered an era of monotheism. The angels had taken over affairs of the world and turned all impossibilities into possibilities. They had created a world where darkness was devoid of any fear and silence was free of any dread. It was a world where darkness was only to highlight the light and silence was a medium of musical melodies.

===============

I wished for it to be dark again; the darkness soon prevailed. It reminded me of the dwellers of Hell. I wished to view their state. I said 'Subhan-Allah' again. Immediately, a screen appeared on my left. The first scene that appeared was highly gut wrenching.

It was a view of the central region of Hell. Horrendous and powerful angels were pulling out hideous looking people from the fire. They were shackled in heavy, barbed chains and tight collars around their necks. The flesh on their faces was severely burnt. Their attire was made of charcoal, thus the flames burnt the flesh even more. They were screaming in pain. They were crying and pleading to God to have another chance of going back to the previous world; they were saying that if that were to happen, they would never indulge in tyranny, rejection of the truth or injustice. However, it was futile to cry or scream now.

The inmates then started to scream and beg for water. The angels dragged them over to some streams. Steam was rising from the boiling water of those streams. The inmates were so thirsty that they were compelled to drink it. They would drink the boiling water, then scream, and pull away. However, after a short while, their intense thirst compelled them to go back to the same water once again, like a desperate, thirsty animal. Due to this, the skin of their faces had come off and their lower lips had drooped down.

I sought God's protection after witnessing these scenes and thanked him for saving me. Ignoring those scenes, I started to look at the eye-catching light emanating from my palace at the mountaintop. My vehicle was gradually moving towards it. I wished to view it before I reached there. As usual, I said, '*Subhan-Allah*' and instantly my room transformed into a cinema. However, the screen was not only in front of me but also all around me and above me. I could see scenes of the palace interior like a 3-D movie. I felt as if I was present inside the palace and was able to hear and see everything.

There was an atmosphere of celebration all around today. My palace was lit like a bright bowl of light on top of the tall mountain peak. It had lights without any light bulbs and its chandeliers were lit without candles or any other source. It resembled a bright island in an abyss of darkness due to the luminescence of that light emitting from every nook and corner of the palace. It looked more of a fountain of rainbow colours and Nur; through my eyes, it enchanted my senses every passing moment with a new delight. Who would have thought that mere light could be so delightfully enchanting? No eye would have ever witnessed it.

Periodically, melodious tunes would playfully touch the strings of my heart and then echo in the environment around me. Who would have thought that music could be so melodious? No ear would have ever heard it.

The world around me was not just filled with melody but was also enveloped in a light fragrance. Who would have thought that any fragrance could be so pleasing to the senses? No human could have ever imagined it.

The activity of servants as they went about doing their chores in the pathways of the huge palace gave the impression of pearls scattered around. Their faces were sparkling and attires beautiful. Their dialogues were delightful and mannerism attentive.

The destination of these servants seemed to be an expansive garden located in one of the corners of the palace. This garden presented the look of a bouquet of lush greenery. Flowers and trees were presented in a way so stunning that it would have easily surpassed any human standard of horticulture. Thousands of colours were spread across the garden; just the shades of green were so many that it was impossible to count.

Innumerable fruits adorned the tall trees. Each tree was distinguished by the unique coloured leafs dressing it. Thousands of species of plants with colourful blossoming flowers surrounded them. These elements were not placed randomly; the true beauty of amalgamation of colours and varieties was in the way the plants were placed and trees had been located. This garden was like the enchanting sonnet of a poet in which the strings of words were strung together in accordance with their poise, emphasis and ending to create a masterpiece.

Pathways made of precious stones like pearls, sapphire, ruby, and emeralds dazzlingly accentuated the stunning beauty of this garden. Between these spectacular pathways were running streams. Their beauty was enticing to the eyes while their resonance had a soothing effect on the ears. Some of them were of milk and some of pure fresh water; some had burgundy wine flowing in them and some were filled with honey. Each stream had a unique fragrance that mesmerised the passers-by. Along the streams, at short distances between the trees, were sitting areas comprising of regal seats and couches bejewelled with diamonds and emeralds, and furnished with luxurious rugs and comfortable cushions.

This beautifully laid garden with attractive footpaths, scenic streams, colourful flowers, lush leaves and delicious fruits on offer, as rewards for a visit, had no boundary walls to protect it. There was an unfathomable but pleasant sense of coolness inside. Every so often, a draft of breeze would fill the atmosphere with a new fragrance. One could easily see the views outside to a great distance from within the garden. The darkness outside was slowly engulfing everything; astonishingly, there was no sign of it inside the garden.

The lights from the tall buildings of a spectacular city were visible over a wide area. Flickering of these lights in the distance seemed like millions of glow-worms glimmering in the night. The milky light of stars far away twinkled in the dark sky making its appearance even more striking. One glowing light in the sky stood out particularly as it slowly moved towards the palace. I realised that it was the vehicle inside which I was viewing these scenes. It was all due to blessings of the Almighty that enabled me to see my vehicle from outside heading towards the palace even though I sat in it.

I saw Saleh sitting in the garden, and was bemused to see that he was already there, ahead of me. The place he sat in was probably the most beautiful part of the garden. The floor in there was like clear glass. It was so lucid that one could clearly see beneath it for miles. Under the glass floor, there was a dusky hue all around. A lush green prairie draped in colourful flowers was visible below along with the numerous brooks running through it. The twilight made this picturesque scene even more enchanting.

It was a beautiful evening when one looked under the floor, whereas above the floor all around was a fragrant and gleaming night. On one hand, there were rivers flowing beneath the floor; and on the other, there were fruit-laden branches of trees above, desperately waiting for a mere gesture of the hand to stoop and present their bounties to savour. Some servants were chargrilling bird and animal meat in a corner. The aroma in itself spoke for its amazing taste; in addition, it did not lead to satiety, therefore, one could eat as much as one desired. Nearby, clearer than crystal chalices and goblets were stacked in an exquisite manner, waiting for the function to start, so that they could quench the thirst and desires of their masters.

As I watched these scenes, I had a sense of Déjà vu; I then recalled that I had seen all of them in Barzakh. At the same time, I felt that the speed of my vehicle had slowed down. I signalled and the scene disappeared. I was about to reach my destination. From the higher altitude, the dazzling palace looked absolutely amazing. I desired to continue to enjoy the view from above. In order to do so, I hovered around it a couple of times. It then occurred to me that Saleh was waiting for me, so I decided to land. The vehicle or one could call it 'Sheesh Mahal' – 'a palace of mirrors', slowly landed in the area where Saleh was waiting for me.

Saleh greeted me with a loud chuckle as I got off the vehicle and said:

"I thought you mistook this palace for the Throne and started to do Tawáf around it. It is good that you didn't go around seven times!"

Saleh's interesting comment also made me laugh, as I moved forward to embrace him. Separating himself from me, he said:

"Would you like to view your palace or would you rather eat first?"

"I am captivated by the beauty of this place. I could never imagine that beauty could take such shape and form." I replied.

"Abdullah, whatever you see till the Grand Gathering at the Court is what the Qur'an had referred to as 'Nuzul', meaning just a welcoming present. What you will receive after the gathering will be something no one has ever seen, heard, or imagined."

"You are correct, Saleh. These things have been mentioned in the Qur'an and sayings ascribed to the last Prophet PBUH However, Paradise is different from the description in Qur'an. I mean it is way more beautiful than what was mentioned in the book."

Saleh replied, "The reason for that is that the picture of Paradise painted in the Qur'an was in the context of what Arabs at the time of its revelation considered to be the ultimate expressions of luxury and enjoyment. So, the things considered particularly luxurious by them were mentioned in the book. But it would be foolish to think that Paradise is limited only to those luxuries."

"I agree. It would have been difficult for the Arabs of that time to even imagine the luxuries that were invented in my era, called the Information Age. Therefore, Qur'an focused on the ideas of welfare and extravagance imaginable by a man living in the Agricultural Age. But my friend, the vehicle I just used surpassed even my wildest imagination."

"You will come across many things that will have the same effect. Anyway, what are your immediate plans?"

Ignoring his question, I started to look around at the beautiful surroundings. I wanted to absorb the details of everything around me through my eyes.

When Saleh noticed my distraction, he said jokingly:

"Perhaps you are looking for the Maidens? They came out to welcome you but now they have gone back to their homes. However, if you wish..."

Before Saleh could complete his sentence, I replied earnestly:

"In my time, there were two major ideological leaders of mankind. One was Karl Marx, who considered stomach and hunger as the most important reality and motivator in life; while the second was Freud who deemed..."

I left the sentence incomplete and paused for a moment.

Saleh chuckled loudly.

Smelling the strong aroma of roasted meat, I added, "And at this point in time, I intend to follow the lead of the great Karl Marx."

===============

In the world, lives of all humans were spent as slaves of time. The wheel of time moved forward passing through seconds and minutes, hours and days, and months and years. Changing seasons depicted the passage of time. However, in this new world, time was enslaved to human beings. The time as measured in seconds, hours, months, years, decades, centuries and millennia was no more. The days when time would pass one by were gone, like the days bygone.

The only remnants of time left behind were the various times of day and the seasons. Even those were under one's control. Different parts of this empire ruled by the human beings had different weathers and times of the day, and all at the same time. Therefore, there were places where the morning twilight was present throughout; in other parts, the silence of early afternoon could be experienced while the gentle warmth of late afternoon existed in some areas on a permanent basis. The horizon was coloured crimson by the dusky hue of twilight in some regions of this realm, while other areas close by were enveloped by the deep hush of late night. At any given time, one could view early twilight before dawn in one section and the light of the full moon in another; starry nights in one and the soothing shades of spring in the other, or if one wished, one could enjoy thousands of colours of the fall elsewhere.

The weather was always calm and pleasant at the abodes of people who lived in Paradise. However, in order to cater to their wishes, some places were in the grip of a freezing winter while others had the desert summer climate in them. Still, there were regions experiencing perpetual rainy season or only the colours of autumn or spring. In short, all times of day and seasons were readily available for the fulfilment of one's desires.

I was now the exclusive and sole ruler of an enormous dominion. My long-time associate Saleh continued to be my friend and companion in this new world. He was the one who informed me that this dominion was a part of a vast universal system. According to the division of this system, the residence of all people of Paradise was on the same Earth on which humans were tested for hundreds of thousands of years.

The people of Paradise were divided into two classes, the masses, and the elite. The former were those who had been awarded one or more planets or stars. Obviously, instead of being balls of fire, the stars had now turned into beautiful havens and pleasant valleys. Elite were the ruling class of Paradise. Foremost amongst them were the Shuhada and the Siddiqeen. They had been made lords over galaxies containing millions of stars. I was the lord of a similar galaxy. Above them were the prophets of God who ruled over countless groups of galaxies.

It remained a mystery however as to who shall be awarded which area to rule as well as the nature of tasks to be performed in it. Saleh informed me that all of that would be revealed on the day of the Grand Gathering at the Court. On that occasion, everyone would be formally awarded his or her dominion. For now, everyone was residing on Earth and according to Saleh, the gifts that people had received so far were only of the nature of welcoming presents. The real blessings and awards that no one had ever seen, heard, or imagined were to be formally presented on the occasion of the Grand Gathering at the Court. Until then, the protocol being awarded to people was according to their status.

This protocol manifested itself during the parties and gatherings of the people of Paradise. Those gatherings were mainly held in honour of other residents. Not everyone had yet entered Paradise. However, a lively society was already thriving there.

On the side of the Plane of Judgement, the Salaiheen were entering the Paradise one by one. But as the time had stopped here, the interval between two persons entering the Paradise was in thousands of years on this side. I suspected, and Saleh later confirmed, that the Grand Gathering would take place once everyone had entered the Paradise.

Such was the early life in Paradise. In the meantime, many people were celebrating and having get-togethers. Majority of these gatherings were hosted by the prophets in honour of the Salaiheen from their nations as well as from the nations of other prophets.

I met a number of people during those gatherings. I used to interact with very few people in the world, but now I noticed that I had become unusually social. I started to make new friends. We shared our life stories and experiences. It was not unexpected, yet I was quite surprised to discover that most of those who had succeeded at the very outset, hence the elite, were poor and underprivileged in the previous world. I particularly noticed that amongst those exalted dignitaries of the highest order, there was a common trait. All of them had faced severe hardships and heartaches, but they persevered, always depended on God and God alone, accepted their fates with fortitude, and remained grateful to the Almighty in the worst of circumstances.

One day, Saleh introduced me to my parents. My parents had died in an accident soon after my birth. However, as long as they were alive, they remained devoted servants of the Lord. I found out that they had also wished me to dedicate my life to guide people towards the way of the Almighty but the fatal accident did not allow them the opportunity to do so.

Nevertheless, our most compassionate God honoured their commitment. The providence of the Almighty created opportunities throughout my life that allowed this orphan boy to fulfil their wishes. I had this incredible realisation only after entering the Paradise that all I attained was because of my parents. In addition, due to their intention to commit me to this work, they also reaped a share of the reward off every righteous deed that I had committed in my life. Thus, my meeting with my parents also served to introduce me to a new aspect of the blessings of my Lord.

================

Chapter 15: When Life Begins

Gradually my acquaintances had started arriving in the Paradise. I used to meet them regularly at various gatherings. They included not only the associates who had helped me in my efforts to make the way of God a success but also those who had embraced my message and had led righteous lives, manifested through strong faith and high moral character. Meeting any one of them was akin to a new door to happiness and love opening in my life. However, the person I was longingly waiting for had not arrived yet. This wait could not be construed as a cause for discomfort or concern in any way; On the contrary, it was enjoyable in itself.

One day, although there were no days or nights in the previous sense of the word anymore, Saleh came to me and said:

"Lord Abdullah! I have some bad news for you."

I was surprised as to what bad news he would convey to me in Paradise. However, the tone was such that I had to ask:

"My friend, how can there be bad news in Paradise?"

"Lord Abdullah! The bad news is that your days of joyous living free are over. You had a lot of play while Naimah was away. Now, she is about to arrive in person to supervise you."

"Really?" I exclaimed as I embraced Saleh, overcome with emotions

"Would I lie to you?" Saleh replied. Then patting my head, he added, "You better let go of me. I am the bearer of the news of Naimah's arrival, not Naimah herself."

"You are not worthy of being Naimah in any case!" I responded, as I let go of him. I continued:

"But tell me, why are you delivering such wonderful news as if it is a threat? Anyway, if this is what you expect from Naimah, I am sure you are in for a huge disappointment. Let's change the topic a bit and discuss something important. I want to give Naimah an outstanding present on this occasion."

"What would you like to present?"

"A palatial mansion..."

"My friend, you have your own home and Naimah will have her own. There is no family system here like the previous world where one had to provide a house and the wife had to stay back to look after the kids. So, what's the point in starting a new home?"

"I know that every resident of Paradise will have his or her own home and dominion. Yet I wish to build a house of my liking for Naimah in my dominion, and give it to Naimah as a gift."

"Do you not know that God has called those who indulge in extravagance brothers of Satan?" Saleh was in a mood to tease me.

"Satan is not allowed in Paradise; however, some of his disciples are definitely present here, trying to create a rift between husband and wife". I said with feigned irritation.

"Ok, Ok... forgive me! Tell me exactly what you want the house to be?"

I provided him with complete details.

When I was finished, he said:

"Ok, let's go and inspect the Palace you have just ordered to be built."

I asked in a surprised tone:

"What do you mean? Has it already been built?"

Saleh replied, “Do you think you are in the previous world where you would have to first purchase land, then get architectural drawings approved, thereafter find a contractor to build it over a number of months? Lord Abdullah! This is your dominion. The power of God is with you. You said, and it was done! This is the Law over here.”

===============

We were riding the crest of a vast sea. Saleh and I were aboard something that resembled a ship. I chose this mode of transport on Saleh's advice. According to him, the journey to one’s destination in the Paradise was as pleasurable as reaching the destination itself. He was correct in what he had said. In my previous life, I had never liked travelling by sea. But the journey today was unique. The so-called ship was more of a floating palace. We were both standing on its deck. There was a slight breeze, the weather was pleasant, and we were steadily moving forward towards our destination.

Our destination was a hilly island that had been constructed in the shape of a palace for Naimah. The palace was just like the one that I had described to Saleh.

I had asked Saleh for a huge island in the middle of the sea, with lush green hills, serpentine rivers, tranquil lakes, and rhythmic waterfalls. I wanted it to have hilly paths by the shore, huge green meadows and in the middle of all of them, a mansion. I wanted the floor of that mansion to be made of diamonds, sparkling and clear as a glass; so lucidly clear that one would be able to see flowing water in the ponds underneath it as well as the multi-coloured fish swimming around in it.

I wanted the walls of the house to be made of see-through pure silver so clear that one could view the scene outside through them. I wished for it to have high and mighty ceilings made of gold and studded with pearls, jewels, and precious stones. I wanted it to be built many stories high; so high that it would overlook the surrounding hills. I desired that its floors should be built in such a manner that every floor would depict a unique aspect of the surrounding nature as well as its own construction.

After coming here, what I saw was even more beautiful than what I had wished for or expected. The likely reason could be that my vocabulary was incapable of describing the blessings available to me in Paradise. I had described only a general sketch or idea but the radiant blend of colours, appearance, light, decoration, and other things found in the actual built structure was way beyond my imagination and description. Saleh had understood what I had wished in principle and then had the palace built, but it was an architectural masterpiece more magnificent than one could imagine. It was so massive that in order to see it all one required a lot of time. I said to Saleh:

"I am satisfied. Let's go now. When Naimah comes, we will then..."

"But I am here already." My sentence was interrupted by a melodious voice that was music to my ears.

I turned around and was stunned to see Naimah. Yes, she was Naimah, and yet she did not look quite like her. When I saw Naimah on the Day of Judgement, she looked young and very pretty. But to describe the woman standing in front of me, words like beauty, elegance, youth, freshness, attraction etc., would utterly fail. I was still in the state of trance when I heard Saleh's voice:

"Let me introduce you two. He is Lord Abdullah, and she is Naimah. And I know that both of you are very pleased to meet each other!"

"Why did you not tell me that Naimah would be here?" I asked Saleh, a little crossly.

Naimah spoke in Saleh's defence:

"I had asked Saleh not to tell you. I wanted to give you a surprise."

"Abdullah also wanted to give you a surprise. Did you see what an extraordinary home he has had built for you?" Saleh asked.

"Yes, I have seen it. I still cannot believe my eyes."

"And I cannot believe my eyes as well". I said, looking closely at Naimah. Then I said to Saleh:

"You don't have a wife to go to... What would you take to leave us alone?"

He replied laughingly:

"I was always with you in the previous world, and I wish to remain with you even now."

"But my friend, there I could not see you."

He replied in a mischievous tone:

"It is possible for me to be here but become invisible even now."

He then vanished instantaneously; then we heard his voice:

"Is it okay now?"

"No! It is not acceptable at all", Naimah replied right away. Saleh appeared again. Naimah took a sigh of relief and said:

"I want you to promise that whenever you come to us, you would be visible like humans and when you go, you will depart like humans too."

"Alright, alright..." He replied, nodding his head in affirmative. However, I could still see a mischievous look in his eye. He added very innocently:

"The problem is that I am not human, so how can rules for humans apply to me?"

This time, I replied smilingly:

"Think about it! I know your boss too! One complaint from me and he may make you a human!"

He replied with feigned sadness:

"My friend, you do not have to threaten me. I promise I will take your permission when I come to see you, and I will take your leave with your approval. In fact, if you wish, I can leave now."

He turned round after saying so, took a couple of steps to leave, turned back again, and said to Naimah:

"However, my leaving would not make any difference. As, your children are here now and they have decided to get you two married once again, under their own supervision! Only after that would they allow you to move into Abdullah's home."

"Saleh is absolutely right"! Said Leila, as she bolted like an arrow, straight to me. Anwar, Jamshaid, Aaliya, and Arifa followed behind closely.

My happiness was enhanced many folds on seeing all of them. I hugged them. When we were through with greetings, Naimah said in an agitated tone:

"What is this childish idea about getting us married again?"

Aaliya replied:

"Mama, none of us could attend your wedding in the previous world. Therefore, it is the combined desire of all brothers and us sisters to get you two married again in a befitting manner. We will give you away as a bride ourselves and until then, Papa would not be allowed to see you."

Anwar intervened, "I think it is a bit harsh. Let them see each other but they would not be allowed to meet without a chaperone."

"Thank you very much for your consideration! Tell me, when do you intend to have the wedding ceremony"? I asked helplessly.

"That will take place once the preparations are complete", Arifa replied, in a serious tone.

"And what preparations do you require?" I asked.

"I will provide the details" Leila replied. Then she added:

"This place is fine for the venue. All we require are the clothes, jewellery etc."

"And I also need good clothes... like Papa's outfit. After seeing his clothes my own don't appeal to me anymore!" Jamshaid also added his share to the demands.

"Ok, once all these preparations have been made, would it be ok to get married?" I asked.

"Indeed!" Everyone replied together.

"Come on then, let's go. I shall take you to the biggest shopping area of the Paradise. Usually, you would not be allowed to enter it but on this occasion, you can buy all you want at my expense!"

All of them gave out a hurrah of joy. We then headed off for shopping.

===============

That place also looked like a scene from the Arabian Nights. I had been there many times with Saleh but whenever I visited, I had found all kinds of new things to see. It seemed beyond what one would have called a shopping Mall or bazaar in the previous world. It was an area spread over hundreds of miles, glowing with the splendour of vibrant colours and radiance. It was always night-time here. There were so many items of food, clothing, and use that counting them was impossible; only the number of items and their varieties reached millions.

There were angels appointed everywhere. People would select something displayed at a shop and ask the angels to record it; it would then be delivered straight to their residence. Angels could easily check any individual's record and find out all they needed to know about him.

The "shopping Mall" had two sections; one for the ordinary residents of Paradise and the other reserved only for the elite. The former could visit the elite section but they could not buy anything as only the elite residents had that privilege.

My family was visiting the shopping Mall for the first time. I took them to the unreserved part first. They were ecstatic merely on seeing it. After that, they started to buy whatever they wished. However, Naimah remained with me all that time. After they were finished shopping, I took them out for a meal to the upper section of that place. From here, one could view the beautiful lights glowing for miles. Above us was the star-filled sky. Unlike the previous world, where the city lights used to cause the light of the stars to fade away, over here both glowed simultaneously without affecting each other.

The milky starlight and aroma of food in the cool breeze had made the atmosphere idyllic. Like in the shopping area, melodious tunes were playing in the background here as well. There were so many types of foods making it difficult to decide what to eat. Whatever one ate was so delicious that it was difficult to stop eating. It was a great blessing of the Almighty that satiety was not an issue; we could eat to our heart's content.

On our way back, I intentionally took them to the 'reserved-for-elite' part of the shopping paradise. They were awe-struck on seeing it.

"Is this also a part of the shopping Mall?" Asked Jamshaid.

"It is, indeed!" I replied.

Before I could complete my sentence, they had dispersed for shopping again. Only Naimah remained with me. I asked:

"Don't you want to buy something over here? You didn't buy anything in the previous shopping area either."

Naimah smiled and said:

"Your company is the most precious thing for me. I will not find this priceless gift anywhere other than in staying close to you."

The glow on Naimah's face enhanced even more as she said so.

We sat down and marvelled at this unimaginably beautiful place. The shopping centre spread across a wide area, contained all kinds of shops. The shops catered for clothing, fashion accessories, footwear, decoration, gifts and God knows what else! It took a few hours to go through each individual shop. The grandest shopping Malls of the previous world paled in comparison.

However, the real attraction was not the shops; it was the captivating atmosphere that prevailed all around us. The scene was set by the shops lit with sparkling lights and stocked with eye-catching items, perfumed air, moist breeze, mellow music, beautiful fountains, thousands of displays of lights and colours, all sorts of designs, scenic views and the most beautiful people walking around; amalgamation of all of them was creating an impressive ambience. It overwhelmed all senses, including the aesthetic senses. For others, it was a place to shop, but for me it was a most befitting way to satisfy my aesthetic sense for beauty and art.

However, for now Naimah's company had overshadowed everything else. Our moments together were short as Leila returned, and said:

"Papa, how would that crown made of diamonds look on me?"

"It would look gorgeous", I replied.

"But the angels said that I cannot buy it!"

"Really"?

I had barely managed to say that when the rest of them also returned empty handed.

Anwar said, "Let's go Papa; there aren't very many nice things to buy here."

"In other words, the grapes are sour!" Naimah commented laughingly.

I said, "No, these grapes are not that sour! Come along with me".

I took them to one of the angels and said:

"My name is Abdullah. This is my family. Please provide them with whatever they desire."

The angel smiled and said, "Lord Abdullah! I apologise that you had to undergo the inconvenience of coming here in person. They can have whatever they want."

On hearing this, their faces lit up with happiness and they left for shopping again.

===============

Grand Gathering at the Court was about to begin. Dwellers of Paradise and the elite amongst them, the courtiers, the prophets and Siddiqeen, the Shuhada and Salaiheen were present and were busy taking up their designated seats. The Almighty had arranged for a special feast before the main event. It was the grandest gathering held so far in the Paradise where the successful people from the time of Prophet Adam PBUH till the Day of Judgement had gathered. The Almighty had assigned the role of hosts to five distinguished prophets namely Prophet Noah, Prophet Abraham, Prophet Moses, Prophet Jesus and Prophet Muhammad, May peace be upon them all!

This gathering was held at the base of a lofty mountain. It was a vast and wide plane, spread out in the shape of a gigantic garden. Wide stretches of prairies and lush green meadows were visible as far as the eyes could see and were a source of comfort for them. A number of rivers meandered through the plane.

The arrangements for the gathering were an amalgamation of the Arabic traditions and the grandeur and splendour of non-Arab cultures. As such, the seats were like thrones fit for kings, built with diamonds and pearls. The earth was covered for miles with thick carpets and rugs.

Thousands of Ghilmán were walking around carrying wine filled jugs. Whenever the guests wished to have any kind, they just looked at it and the next moment, Ghilmán would be present next to them to fill their goblets with the desired drink. The wine was in fact a clear drink that was delicious, comforting, and tasty in every sense of the word without having the usual ill effects of alcohol like bad smell, headache, and intoxication. Cooked meats of various birds and animals were being presented for consumption in silver and gold platters. The trees were laden with fruit; whenever one wished to have any, the branch would bend down to allow the fruit to be picked.

Dressed in stunning attires, gorgeous women and handsome men were present everywhere. They had a glow on their faces and a shine in their eyes as they went around spreading happiness and laughter. It reminded me of parties in the previous world where women used to be covered in excessive make-up, showing off their beauty and femininity, disregarding the limits set by God. Men, rather than avoiding such displays, would feast their eyes on such occasions. That made the task of women who dressed modestly and men who guarded their eyes all the more difficult due to societal rejection of their noble efforts.

Now all struggles are over, I thought. This gathering was full of the most beautiful women whose attire and jewellery was exceptional and enough to dazzle any onlooker. However, the Almighty had made the hearts so pure that no indecent thought or lustful desire crossed one's mind. Every man and woman was living in a state of physical beauty and spiritual purification. Now there was neither a need to cover one's beauty nor any necessity to guard one's eyes. How trivial was that struggle and how enormous was this reward!

My family, friends, and associates were with me. Our kids were delighted after having arranged our wedding ceremony. We had also availed the opportunity to tie Jamshaid and Amoorah into wedlock as well, with their consent. Amoorah was now a part of our family. Life continued, brimming with happiness and bliss.

However, I continued to have a longing in my heart sometimes. It was so because all my loved ones were with me but for my teacher, Mr. Farhan Ahmed. I had a faint hope that may be I would meet him during the Grand Gathering.

After the banquet, people began to be seated in their designated seats. Muqqaribeen were seated closest to the Arsh. They were the people closest to God during their lives in the world; they included the prophets, Siddiqeen, Shuhada, and a large number of Salaiheen. The rest of the residents of Paradise were seated behind them.

The main attraction of today's gathering was that the people of Paradise were to receive their greatest blessing for the first time; they were going to have the honour of seeing the Almighty God. The last Prophet had said in the previous world that just like people waited to see the full moon, they would wait to see their beloved God in Paradise. Thus, people were extremely excited and keen to do so. In addition, the people were to be formally awarded their titles and honours today; that is why everyone was eagerly waiting for the proceedings to start.

All those present were now seated. Every tongue was singing praise of the Lord, every heart was proclaiming his Oneness and greatness, and every eye was moist with tears of gratitude. People kept repeatedly saying that the mercy of God that had guided them otherwise, they had no chance of entering the Paradise.

The proceedings started with angels reciting praise of the Lord. Thereafter, Prophet David came forward and sang a beautiful hymn in his melodious voice in praise of God. It was a mesmerising rendition.

The Bearers of the Throne thereafter announced that the Lord of the Universe would now address his servants. After a short while, the Almighty God started to speak in an extremely gentle and loving tone.

The Almighty commended his servants for their hard work, struggle, and fortitude, which helped them to attain this stature. He asked the people if they were happy with the reward they were given for their struggle.

Everyone replied in one voice:

"Yes, our reward was beyond our expectations. We received what was bestowed upon no other creation previously. Why would we not be content and happy with you?"

The Almighty replied that he would now give something much more valuable than everything else he had already bestowed earlier. He was granting everyone his blessings. On hearing this, the atmosphere resonated with loud slogans of 'Allahu Akbar' or 'God is great'.

Distribution of titles and awards started next. It was a long process. However, since all kinds of blessings were being conferred continuously, the audience waited patiently and in comfort. Like other people, my family was also seated with me in the front row.

As I witnessed those happenings, I thought to myself that humanity had managed to earn such a huge reward for such little effort in the previous world. It then occurred to me that conversely, the majority of human beings had failed in this test. I then began to think about my teacher Mr. Farhan again. I could not see him even today, although I thought that I would find him somewhere. I thought about asking Saleh. He was not present there, but then he appeared suddenly and stood next to me.

I said to him, "I thought I would be able to meet my teacher at some point today but I could not find him. Do you have any information about him?"

"No! I have not been able to find him anywhere in the Paradise. I think you should also stop thinking about him. It seems that the Almighty has made his decision regarding him. No power in the world can change his verdict. The justice of God always prevails."

"And what about his mercy?"

"Abdullah, you know very well that God's mercy and justice are based on principles. Nobody's desire can change his Law."

"But the Paradise is a world of possibilities; anything is possible here!"

Saleh replied, agitated:

"My friend, why are you arguing with me? The decision has been made. Why don't you speak to the Lord yourself? He often grants your wishes. I am only here to take you to the Arsh. Come along and request the Lord to roll back the wheel of time!"

I was not sure if Saleh was taunting me or was actually offering serious advice. However, I was not ready to follow his counsel foolishly. But he was right about taking me to the Arsh. Soon, my name was announced. I, seated comfortably up until now, got up with a trembling heart. Walking slowly, I presented myself to the being under whose grand favours every pore of my existence was buried.

As I reached closer, I bowed in prostration on the ground.

After a while, I heard a voice:

"Get up, Abdullah!"

I got up slowly and with lowered gaze, hands held together, stood in rapt attention.

The Almighty asked me very kindly and tenderly:

"Abdullah, what have you brought for me today?"

I had come here to receive, not to give hence the question was unexpected. However, I offered what I had:

"My Lord, all the good deeds I performed were in fact due to your support and blessings. I cannot offer what you had given to me. As for my own self, I have nothing to offer to your most exalted being except a lot of remorse and unlimited humility."

The Almighty answered:

"It's good that you have brought remorse and humility for me. I do not have these two attributes. I would accept them from you. Now tell me, what do you want me to grant you?"

I submitted:

"I have got all I wished for as well as all that you have granted most generously. My capacity to ask is so small that after all that I have been endowed with, it is beyond me to ask for anything else now. However, whatever goodness and alms you grant, I shall be in need of them."

The Almighty signalled to one of the Bearers of the Throne. He started to announce my rewards and titles. I knew that I was amongst the elite of this new world but what I was being granted here today was way beyond my wildest expectations, standing, or worth. As the angel continued to announce the awards, my head bowed with shame for I realised that if the Lord of the worlds was so magnanimous towards a sinner like me, how generous would he be towards the righteous!

When the angel stopped, the Almighty said:

"Abdullah, everyone sins, but I do not consider those people as sinners who duly repent and seek forgiveness. As for you, you spent all your life telling people about me and their meeting with me on the Day of Judgement. I have you as a loyal servant in my books."

After a short silence, the Almighty said:

"I am aware of what you were saying to Saleh earlier. I am also aware of what you were thinking about while you were receiving your Book of Deeds on the Day of Judgement. Were you not thinking that if only you could get one more chance, if somehow the time passed by could come back, you could warn people about this day even more vigorously?

Abdullah! I am aware of your passion and I am also aware of your expectations from me. You were correct in your understanding that I have power over all things. You were also right that I can do wonders and I am the greatest. I also know that all you can do is to convey your request by bowing down in my feet. You are important to me and so is your request, however..."

There was a pause. I thought with a trembling heart that nothing was hidden from my Lord; neither a word uttered nor a thought concealed in the heart. Involuntarily, I said:

"Verily, my Lord you are perfect."

"I knew that you would eloquently express your heart's desire in these words. Listen! It is not a part of my scheme to send people back to the world. Therefore, neither you nor anyone else can go back to the world. However, time is my slave! If I wish, I can turn the wheel of time back."

Then he signalled to an angel.

The angel came forwards towards me, carrying a stack of papers made from silver.

I saw that on the first page, the following words were written in gold:

"When Life Begins"

The Almighty said:

"Abdullah, this is your account. A part of whatever happened to you in this new world has been saved in this chronicle. For your sake, your story is being sent back in time to the previous world. I shall arrange for its distribution amongst the human beings. I will ensure that it reaches the hearts of all my humble servants. They will pass this chronicle of yours to their loved ones... They will pass it on to all those who they wish to save from the humiliation of the Hereafter, to help them reach the final destination of Paradise.

May be a lucky soul will alter his conduct after reading your account. May be someone's life will change, having read this account. May be it will lead to changing someone's destiny.

I want to give people another chance at your request... before the ultimate loss... before the ultimate demise."

I involuntarily uttered, "Allahu Akbar" and immediately went down in prostration on the floor.

==============

"Allahu Akbar, Allahu Akbar" - 'God is great, God is great' were the words of the call to the prayer from the mosque that startled and woke up Abdullah. He immediately said, "Allahu Akbar!"

He looked around with vacant eyes. He could not fathom where he was at that moment. He remembered that he was standing in front of the Almighty God. He thought hard. He realised that he was still in front of the Almighty; he was sitting in front of the Kaaba in The Sacred Mosque. It was the time for morning prayers and people were walking around.

Abdullah asked himself, "Was it all a dream?"

He replied to himself, "But all of that was real; The Day of Judgement, the gathering in the Paradise and my appearance in front of the Almighty... If all of that was real, what is this? And if this is the reality, then what was that truer-than-life experience? Was that a dream or is this a dream?"

Abdullah continued to mumble to himself:

"What if I wake up one day and realise that what I had experienced in the world was just a dream and the reality was in fact the life of the Hereafter?"

A Nur-like light was descending onto the courtyard of The Sacred Mosque. The atmosphere was lit with milky white lights. The sky was still dark but this place had more activity than seen elsewhere during the day. This was the Haram of Mecca. It was the Kaaba of the Faithful, the centre for those who loved God. The servants of God, both men and women, had gathered here from all corners of the world. They had come here from all nations of the world and had various ethnic origins. All were busy in reciting the praise of the Lord, the Almighty God.

It was Abdullah's last night in the sacred Haram. However, this last night had now become the most precious night of his life. By now, he had managed to come out of the state of bewilderment he was in earlier. He looked at the Haram and then all around him. Outside, tall buildings surrounded the Haram. This gave birth to a new emotion in him. He started to cry. He prayed most earnestly to the Almighty God:

"My Lord, the apocalypse is almost here. Barefooted goat shepherds are making tall buildings; the prophecy of your beloved last

Prophet has now been fulfilled. Now I have to convey your message to your servants. I must shake them from their slumber. I must apprise them about the catastrophe of the Day of Judgement before it arrives. I have to warn people oblivious to the impending danger.

Love of the world now dominates concerns for the Hereafter in the hearts of people. People are oblivious to the day when they will have to face you, my Lord! The rulers are tyrants and the commoners are ignorant. The rich are intoxicated with their wealth while the poor are content with their current state. Traders are steeped in profiteering, hoarding, and deception. Politicians are manifestly dishonest. The servants shirk from their work. Men have dedicated their lives to amassing wealth while women only seem to care about their beautification and showing themselves off."

Tears were running down Abdullah's face. He was beseeching the Lord with a prayer, whose acceptance was probably ordained by now:

"My Lord, today people are leading lives full of oppression and worldliness, oblivious to your presence. The religious people are fanning sectarianism in the name of religion or are entangled in politics. No one is there to remind people of the imminent meeting with you.

Please accept me as your humble servant to undertake this endeavour. Grant me the faculties that would enable me to paint the true picture of meeting with you and the life of the Hereafter. My Lord! Enable me to depict a life-like scene of that great event to your servants described by you in the Qur'an and warned of by your beloved last Prophet. The humanity is not aware that the time for action granted to it is almost over. Please accept me as the one who will warn your other servants.

My Lord! Guide the entire humanity towards you. And if you have decided to finish off everything, then make it easy for me to guide as many people towards Paradise as possible. To lead them to you... before the Trumpet is blown... before the time to act has passed."

==============

Abdullah completed the last Tawáf around the Kaaba in an unusual state of mind. To go around the Kaaba was a special event by itself. The last round had made it even more special. In addition, what he had experienced last night had made the Kaaba appear to him in a completely new light. For him, it now embodied the Throne.

Being human, after all, he was extremely tired after consecutive Tawáfs. He sat on the floor and kept staring at the Kaaba for a while. He then got up with mixed feelings of disappointment and optimism and with a heavy heart, he started what is always the most difficult thing to do for the lovers of God... to leave The Sacred Mosque before departing from Mecca!

Morning light was fully apparent now. Abdullah headed out in such a manner that he stopped every so often and looked back at the Kaaba. He then strengthened himself, and saying, 'Allahu Akbar', started moving forward again. However, involuntarily he looked time and again over his shoulders to sneak a final view of the Kaaba. Once, in doing so, he bumped in to someone.

Abdullah looked ahead and saw an elderly man with a white beard standing in front. He realised that he had bumped into the man who appeared to be his compatriot from his appearance. Abdullah's enthusiasm suddenly turned to embarrassment.

He said in an apologetic tone:

"Forgive me, Sir! It is my fault. I was not looking ahead."

"No problem." The man replied affectionately. He then added:

"I was also at fault to some extent. I was also not looking ahead. In fact, I was trying to find my family. We came here to do Umrah and got separated due to the crowd."

"Had you not agreed beforehand on a meeting point in case you got lost?" Abdullah asked. He explained further:

"It is important to do so in the Haram, otherwise it becomes very difficult to find the lost ones."

"Well, we agreed to meet near the gate called the 'Báb-al-Fatáh' as it is less crowded. However, I have been standing here for quite some time but they have not arrived yet." The man replied in a concerned tone.

"In that case, your problem is solved!" Abdullah replied smilingly. He added:

"You see, this is not your meeting point. You are waiting at the wrong gate. I will take you to your destination."

The man looked around briefly, embarrassed, and then replied as he started to walk along with Abdullah in the right direction:

"Actually, we only reached here last night. It is our first visit. As such, we are not fully familiar with the various landmarks. My daughter and granddaughter separated from me during Umrah. I had provided them with the directions but forgot them myself! Thank God, you bumped into me otherwise I would have been waiting there for a long time."

"There is a purpose in every act of God, Almighty", Abdullah replied. His tone suddenly became very affectionate when he said the word, 'God'.

"Oh, there is my daughter!" The man exclaimed cheerfully pointing in a certain direction, ignoring Abdullah's comment. He headed quickly in that direction.

Abdullah looked in that direction and saw the elderly man heading towards a middle-aged woman. Abdullah could not decide whether to follow suit or to go back his own way; he had finished the task at hand anyway. He felt that it would probably be more polite to take his leave before heading back, so he followed the man.

When he reached close, he heard him giving an explanation for the mishap to his daughter. When he saw Abdullah, he said:

"This young man showed me the way."

"Thank you very much for your help, Son", the woman said elegantly, although her face clearly betrayed signs of the toils of the journey, Umrah and the latest incident. She added:

"We had been waiting here for Daddy for quite some time."

The word 'we' drew Abdullah's attention towards a girl standing next to the woman. He looked at the girl for a moment and then involuntarily lowered his gaze. However, that moment was enough to cause an upheaval in Abdullah's heart.

This upheaval was not due to the girl's extraordinarily attractive features and complexion. There would have been few men with as untainted and untouched personality as Abdullah. In any case, the mental state he was in, inside the Haram would have usually caused most people not to note anyone, let alone be attracted towards the opposite sex. Such a state of mind would usually keep one focused sharply on Kaaba and the Lord of Kaaba.

Since this particular morning, Abdullah's belief in the Lord of Kaaba had grown many folds. The honour of being present in the Court of Almighty in a dream had left Abdullah in a state of Trance. It was quite difficult to remember other details of that dream in such a mental state.

However, the pleasant face of the girl helped him recall every little detail of the dream. Every scene and every incident of it was now fresh in his memory... so firmly cast as if it was written in a book that he could comfortably read page by page. And now the most prominent page of that book was open in front of him in the form of Naimah, who seemed to be made of light and Nur, from head to toe.

==============

The pause in the conversation was getting progressively longer, however Abdullah was oblivious to it, standing there with his head bowed. He was trying to convince himself what he had just seen was only his imagination:

"May be it is only my imagination. May be it has something to do with my age or the phase of life I am passing through... or maybe it is Satan's handiwork to distract me and waste all my hard work as I leave the sacred Haram. Satan can ruin the efforts of the most righteous of people visiting The Sacred Mosque in a second. The wish to take one look, or the urge to feel just one touch, on any pretext... to succumb to one's animal instincts, to satisfy one's lust for just a second... can destroy hard work of a life time in a second!

Yes, this moment has appeared in my life as a trial. Satan wants me to think that this girl is the culmination of my dreams, and therefore, let him enter my heart. I will not let him succeed. Never! I will never allow him to do that."

Abdullah decided that he would leave this place immediately. But before he could take leave, the long silence was broken by a tired but extremely melodious voice:

"Grandpa, we have been up all night. Let's go to the hotel now."

Her words made the matters even worse. Her voice sounded very familiar. He felt dizzy. The elderly man, oblivious to his state, said, "Okay. Let me say good bye to this kind man."

Before he could say anything more, his daughter asked Abdullah:

"Son, before you go, please tell us your name."

"I am Abdullah", Abdullah barely managed to say the words.

The man felt that it was appropriate considering cultural norms, to introduce himself:

"It is good Amnah that you asked his name. Let me introduce myself to you, Son. My name is Ismael. She is my daughter Amnah."

He paused for a second, looked towards his granddaughter, and said in love-laced tone:

"And the most tired of us is my granddaughter. Her name is Naimah."

It was Abdullah's strongest desire to hear an unfamiliar name so that he could convince himself a wee bit, but the word 'Naimah' rang in his ears as the last nail in the coffin. This time, no force in the world could stop Abdullah from looking at her.

He saw that it was indeed Naimah standing in front of him. She was the girl he was seeing for the first time in his life with open eyes, and also the one that he had seen last night in his dream.

Abdullah started to feel dizzy. He thought, "If that was a dream, then what kind of a reality is this? And, if this is the reality, then that dream...?"

All this was too much for Abdullah's nerves to handle. He felt even dizzier. He looked at Naimah once more, and then lost control of himself, falling down unconscious in a heap on the floor.

===============

THE END

===============

In the End, a few Words

Dear Reader,

If you have finished reading this Novel, I hope that like most other readers, it would have introduced you to a new world. You may now be interested and waiting for the sequel. God willing, it will be in your hands soon. However, of paramount importance is my sincere wish and prayer that this work also becomes your bridge to a new introduction of Qur'an, the last book of God.

Whatever I have written in this Novel is in accordance with the contents of Qur'an and Hadith, or is an explanation of those statements and pointers. God is the sole master of the Day of Recompense. Real success is Paradise. Ultimate failure is Hell. Earnings of this life are trivial and a façade. Eternal success of man lies only in accepting and following Qur'an's message of Faith in God and righteous deeds. This, in nutshell, is the summary of Qur'an and the messages of all prophets of God.

I am certain that after having read the Novel, when you read the Qur'an along with the translation and with the intent to understand, the meanings of its statements would start to become obvious to you. Qur'an would thus become an introduction to a familiar rather than an unseen world. If you succeed in receiving the message of Qur'an in this sense, I would consider it my greatest success.

I sincerely hope and pray that after reading this Novel, you read the entire Qur'an with translation at least once; and it would be the best reward for both of us if the teachings of Qur'an become a way life for you.

Yours truly,

Abu Yahya

Some Important Points - An Explanation

The Feedback received on the novel mainly comprised of praise and commendation. The volume of comments received was huge and the appreciation conveyed, highly generous. Such praise evokes in me only one thought - that only our Lord, the Almighty God, is truly worthy of all praise and excellence. The reason is that any beauty and goodness found in this world is in fact a manifestation of God's attributes of magnificence and excellence. The only significance of us, his creatures, is that he uses us for any purpose he desires. To accomplish his schemes, he can use a tiny mosquito or even a smaller being if he so wishes.

This statement is not an expression of humility but a declaration of truth. No doubt, the existence of creatures has no significance when compared to the excellence, magnificence, splendour, and majesty of the Almighty God. In any case, I remain grateful and indebted to my Lord for choosing me, a humble servant, to provide a service through writing this novel. I also request the readers to remember me in their prayers.

Overall, the feedback was highly favourable. However, some readers and friends offered suggestions for improvement. A few also asked questions and sought explanations. Occasionally, there were objections as well. I have made a few changes in the light of the useful suggestions I received. I thank those who took the time to forward them. I have also made a few changes on my own initiative as all works of this nature continue to be improved with time.

I have addressed the most important issues, questions, and objections as follows:

The First time Human Beings were created

The most common query was about creation and life of human beings for the first time, that is, before they were born again in this world. Oft repeated comment about what I had written was that people felt that their hearts were inclined towards the idea. However, was it based on any concept in the Qur'an?

In response, I submit that the basis of what I wrote is undoubtedly found in the Qur'an. The Qur'an has stated in chapter Al-'A`rāf (7:172) that humans were born once, before the life in this present world began. The verse clearly mentions that at one point in time all human beings were present together. The occasion is commonly known as the Covenant of Alast

Similarly, the idea that the human beings willingly agreed to be subjected to a worldly test is also explained in the Qur'an. The chapter titled Al-'Ahzab (33:72) clearly states that when this burden was offered to other creations, all of them declined to take it. It was only the human beings who came forward and accepted this test.

Both concepts as stated above, i.e. the presence of all human beings together in a previous life and their decision to undertake this test of their own free will are the basis of my extrapolation that each human being also chose the specific level of the test he or she wished to undergo. That is, each person chose one of the three tests: a test based on guidance found in one's innate nature, a test based on being the direct addressee of a prophet or a test based on being amongst the followers and nation of a prophet after that prophet had passed away.

It is obvious that the tests of people in this world are not the same. We also know that a Deity who repeatedly states that he does not inflict even the slightest injustice on his servants is conducting this test. How is it then possible that the absolutely just God would subject his servants to a test whose possible outcome includes the horrible fate of being sent to Hell, without informing them beforehand of the details of the test and seeking their consent to it? It is based on these facts that I have presented this particular point of view in the novel.

The Status of Hoors - The Maidens of Paradise

There were questions and objections regarding the Maidens of Paradise. The objections came from various dimensions. None of them was new for me. Some people may not be aware that it is one of the main objections against the Qur'an and Islam raised by Orientalists and people inspired by modern Western thought. In Christian ideology, the Hereafter is a spiritual concept. In such a spiritual world, the presence of women (maidens) is considered highly objectionable. According to this particular line of thinking, presence of romance and sexuality in Paradise is considered inconceivable in a truly divine religion. These critics feel that such talk by an apparently spiritual person puts the very character of that person in question.

In addition, the modern western thought considers women equal to men in all aspects of life. Even from this aspect, the concept of Maidens reserved only for men is difficult to accept for anyone brought up under the influence of modern education.

I have responded to this objection against Islam for years. It has progressed from being academic in nature to a high level of mockery and disdain; the following satirical verse that paints the picture of Paradise is a good example of the level of contempt held against this concept:

"Beastly Mullahs are running after the terrified Maidens..."

Obviously, due to such remarks even some less informed Muslims despise mention of the Maidens of Paradise. Some of our brothers in the religious circles are also at fault as the style and manner of their description of Maidens often evokes ridicule and criticism. It is nevertheless a fact that at least Qur'an does not describe the Maidens in a manner that would prompt such a reaction. However, is the Qur'an devoid of the concept of Maidens? Anyone who has read the book with deliberation knows that such is not the case. The Qur'an has clearly mentioned the Maidens of Paradise. If the Almighty has mentioned this concept so clearly, I have absolutely no problem in presenting it to people with full confidence. In fact, an in depth study of sociology and psychology tells us that such references in the Qur'an are a clear proof that it is a divine book revealed by our all-knowing and wise Lord.

The main point of wisdom to appreciate regarding this issue has been elaborated in a conversation between two of the central characters of the novel. In short, the basic reasoning behind this is that in this world, based on their roles, Islam has assigned the husband a level higher than his wife, in terms of husband-wife relationship. It is also a fact that practically speaking, because of their physique and social circumstances, women are usually dependant on men socially as well as for their physical protection. This will not be the case in Paradise. Women in the Paradise will be men's wives but they will be equal to them in every aspect and not dependant on them in any way. However, men will remain dependant on women for those physical needs for which they are dependent on them in this world as well.

This dependency on women that the men will have in the Paradise is the answer to the objections raised by the Western thought. The equality of men and women that the people of the West champion in this world will be fully present in the Hereafter, however, that will lead to an issue of inequality of rights for men, and not the women. That inequality has been addressed through Maidens. Therefore, the objection that the reference to the Maidens is unjust does not bear merit after this explanation.

It should also be kept in mind that a study of psychology of men and women reveals that they are quite different psychologically. It is a basic psychological need of women to be prominent and centre of attraction. Women will still have a higher status in the Paradise because unlike the Maidens, they will have become worthy of the Paradise due to their good deeds. Obviously, their status and beauty will be higher than that of the Maidens. For this reason, Maidens will not be able to take away the central role and status of women of Paradise.

However, the issues related to men are a bit different from women. I tried to explain this difference in the words that men are a necessity for women (in this world) whereas women are more than a necessity for men; they are in fact, a big blessing and a gift for them. I would like to humbly avoid elaborating this further in words. However, it is indeed true that the extent to which the Western civilisation has elaborated this fact by unduly using women in advertisements and media, perhaps no one else has done so in the entire history of the humanity.

The truth is that the main reason for describing the Maidens in detail was to target our younger generation, living in an environment of vulgarity, nudity and other similar evils. The people who criticise the Qur'an should first try to stop the rampant exploitation of women on the electronic media and the Internet, both of which have excessively abused the female figure and form. If that is considered acceptable on the basis of freedom of action and liberty, then what is the excuse for criticising the Qur'an? In fact, in my opinion these criticisms indirectly endorse the stance of the Qur'an. By using women for this purpose, they have clearly demonstrated one of the main psychological weaknesses and needs of men and have revealed how men are different from women in this respect. To demand absolute equality in this issue is unnatural.

The answer to the criticisms by Orientalists also lies in the human psychology. The objection from the Christian school of thought, to remind the readers, is that the mention of Maidens in the spiritual environment of the Paradise is inappropriate. This raises the question that if spirituality can be lost so easily, then why criticise the poor Maidens. Even the presence of women in the Paradise would lead to the loss of this so-called spirituality. They should either ask women to leave the paradise as well or force them to also live there as celibates.

Qur'an does not believe in such spirituality. Neither is the concept of spirituality as stated by Qur'an affected by the presence of beauty and aesthetic charm. In fact, we believe that God has created all things beautiful. It takes us closer to our Lord. It makes us more grateful to him. The only limitation is to avail it within the set bounds. I am amazed at the concept of spirituality in Islam every time I read a prayer narrated from the last Prophet PBUH in the books of Bukhari and Muslim; it is a prayer to be said before intimate contact between a married couple ("O God, protectus from the Devil and protect whatever you give to us from the Devil ").

The truth is that Islam has revolutionised the concept of spirituality. Spirituality in Islam does not represent rejection of the worldly blessings, aesthetic charms, and pleasures. Islam does not promote celibacy or abstinence from conjugal relations, either in this world or in the Hereafter. In Islam, spirituality is to remember one's Lord in the midst of everything. This is how we are supposed to behave in this world and it is also the concept of the Paradise that we learn from Qur'an. According to this concept, the servants of the Lord will live in the Paradise in his attendance and will thank him abundantly every time they will avail his blessings.

On account of the above reasons, it is my considered opinion that the Maidens of Paradise stand for what is clearly obvious from the statements of the Qur'an. That is, in addition to other blessings and gifts, the Maidens will be married to the dwellers of Paradise as reward (Qur'an 44:54, 52:20). The Qur'an has especially described their beauty and charm in many places (56:22-23, 55:69-72). The study of the statements of the Qur'an indicates that they would not be the ordinary women of Paradise. Rather, they would be those women who would be conferred upon the male inhabitants of the Paradise as gifts. It also indicates, among other things, that their marriage to these men would be the first such occasion in their lives (55:74).

Criticism on Romance and Humour

Some readers criticised humour and some romantic aspects of the novel. As far as I can understand, the objections were not to these two aspects per se, as they are essential components of human life and are difficult to criticise on a rational basis. They are the indispensable facets of human life without which one cannot remain human. They are found indispensably in this world and would be present in a more sophisticated form in the Paradise. Perhaps the objection was to their association with the main character of the novel.

I would like to put forward a few points in response. Firstly, my main purpose was to keep the size of the book small so that it is easy to read in this age of low readership of books. For this reason, I kept the number of characters limited. Therefore, various dialogues involving jokes, romance, and other similar delicate ideas had to be expressed through the same characters in the novel. The only other way was either to remove such aesthetic ideas from the Paradise or to create more characters. The Paradise would have been a boring place in case of former and the novel would have significantly increased in size in case of the latter option.

Some people have the notion that a person of high calibre who manages to achieve the exalted status of being close to the Almighty should not have such aesthetic sentiments. All I can say in response to this idea is that it may be their conception but it bears no relationship with reality. I have gone through very interesting experiences in my personal life pertaining to this very idea.

I am a modest student of Islam without any claim to a position of high standing; the following example is being narrated only to explain the point.

One of my dear friends and students saw me buying vegetables in the market. He remarked that it felt odd to him that I would also have to perform these meagre chores.

Another gentleman once mentioned some exalted scholars and said that it was difficult for him to visualise that they had to go to the toilet like ordinary people or that they also conceived children like ordinary folks.

Obviously, all of the foregoing notions may be our presumptions but they are not based on facts. Similarly, another reason for the hesitation to accept these facts is the Christian concept discussed earlier, which considers the Paradise a completely spiritual place, with little room for any materialistic, bodily or aesthetic human sensations. Such thinking inspires a vision of Paradise where all one does is chant a mantra of God's name.

Obviously, this image of Paradise bears no relationship to Islam; in fact, one of the main aims of Islam is to clear such misunderstandings. It is for this reason that I also added a shopping Mall in the description of Paradise. Such ideas have also been mentioned in the sayings ascribed to the last Prophet, and the reason for doing so is to clarify that life in the Paradise would be of a very high quality; however, that life would not be devoid of the excitements of this life. In fact, those excitements would be available on a much grander scale.

To summarise, after going to the Paradise, man's negative emotions would be washed away from him but his basic nature and character would not change. Man would not become an angel in the Paradise; in fact, his humanity will remain fully intact.

Glossary

Please note that the meanings and explanations of the terms related to Hereafter given in this section represent the interpretation of Abu Yahya. They are related to an unseen world; only the Almighty knows their reality and form.

1. **Abu-Bakr:** A close companion of Prophet Muhammad PBUH.
2. **Abu-Lahab:** One of the main opponents of Prophet Muhammad PBUH.
3. **Aaráf:** A high place/point in the Plane of Judgement.
4. **Allahu Akbar:** God is great.
5. **Ansar:** The helpers. The citizens of Yathrib who welcomed and helped Prophet Muhammad PBUH and his companions after they emigrated from Mecca.
6. **Archangel Gabriel:** Jibra'il-e-Amin; In Abrahamic religions, an angel who typically serves as a messenger to humans from God.
7. **Arsh:** The Throne of God, Empyrean.
8. **Báb-al-Fatáh:** One of the gates in The Sacred Mosque in Mecca, Saudi Arabia.
9. **Barzakh:** The temporary state of human beings after their deaths and before they wake up on the Day of Judgement.
10. **Bukhari:** One of the major books of Hadith, narrations ascribed to Prophet Muhammad PBUH.

11. Burqa: An enveloping outer garment worn by Muslim women in some parts of the world to cover their bodies, when in public.
12. Ghilmán: The boy servants of Paradise.
13. Hadith: Sayings ascribed to the last Holy Prophet Muhammad PBUH
14. Hajj: The obligatory pilgrimage to Mecca that must be performed by every able-bodied Muslim who can afford to do so.
15. Hashr: Day of Judgement.
16. Hoors: The Maidens of Paradise.
17. Jinn: Or Genies, are supernatural creatures mentioned in the Qur'an that occupy a parallel world to that of the humans.
18. Kaaba: A cuboid shaped building in The Sacred Mosque in Mecca, the Holiest site in Islam.
19. Kauthar: A pond or a river for the dwellers of Paradise.
20. Maidan-e-Hashr: Plane of Judgement, where people would be judged for their deeds.
21. Moulvi: An Imam of a mosque, also sometimes used informally for teachers who teach Qur'an to children in Arabic.
22. Muhajireen: Literally, the Emigrants. These were the companions of Prophet Muhammad PBUH who emigrated along with him from Mecca to seek refuge in the town of Yathrib. The town later became known as Madinah, and its welcoming citizens came to be known as the Ansar (helpers).
23. Muqqaribeen: People close to God; the prophets, Siddiqeen, Shuhada, and Salaiheen.
24. (Sahih) Muslim: One of the major books of Hadith, narrations ascribed to Prophet Muhammad PBUH
25. Nawafil: Extra or supererogatory prayers.
26. Nuzul: Welcoming servings for the people of Paradise.
27. Nur: Pure light.
28. PBUH: Peace be upon him – a prayer mentioned by Muslims along with the names of the prophets of God, especially the last Prophet.

29. Qiblah: The direction which a Muslim should face when praying; it is fixed as the direction of Kaaba in Mecca.
30. Saiq: The angel who will escort and present a person for accountability in front of God, on the Day of Judgement.
31. Salaiheen: The righteous and pious people.
32. Shaheed: The angel who will carry a person's Book of Deeds and testify about it, on the Day of Judgement.
33. Shirk: Assigning partners to God; polytheism.
34. Shuhada: Witnesses to the truth. They are the people who give testimony about the veracity of God's religion to the rest of the world even at the cost of their own life.
35. Siddiqeen: The Truthful. They are people who supported the prophets during their lifetimes.
36. Sidra-tul-Muntaha: A Tree that marks the end of the seventh Heaven beyond which, no creation can go.
37. Subhan-Allah: Glorified (and exalted) be God.
38. Sunnah: The second source of Islam after the Qur'an.
39. Tazkiyah: Purification.
40. The Sacred Mosque: Masjid Al-Haram in Mecca, the most sacred mosque in Islam, which houses the Kaaba.
41. Tawáf: Ritual circumambulation around the Kaaba in Mecca during pilgrimage of Hajj or Umrah.
42. Umrah: The optional pilgrimage to Mecca.
43. Zaqqum: A tree that grows in the Hell according to the Qur'an.

=============